Flight of the Swan

Flight of the Swan

ROSARIO FERRÉ

Farrar, Straus and Giroux

NEW YORK

Farrar, Straus and Giroux
19 Union Square West, New York 10003

Library of Congress Cataloging-in-Publication Data
Ferré, Rosario.
    Flight of the swan / Rosario Ferré.
      p. cm.
    ISBN 0-374-15648-4 (hardcover : alk. paper)
    1. Russians—Puerto Rico—Fiction.   2. Political refugees—Fiction.
  3. Ballet companies—Fiction.   4. Women domestics—Fiction.
  5. Puerto Rico—Fiction.   6. Ballerinas—Fiction.   I. Title.

PS3556.E7256 F57 2001
813'.54—dc21

                                               00-066283

Designed by Jonathan D. Lippincott

TO THE MEMORY OF ANNA PAVLOVA

The swan was a symbol of the beauty of our times, still trying to soar with the instinct for life as it was about to perish under the hooves of war. My beloved came from St. Petersburg and was the product of that baroque city, glimmering softly during its endless white nights. Onstage at the Maryinsky Theater countless feet scissored and stabbed the air in unison, hands flashed, heads nodded simultaneously to a musical chord. The windows of the pastel-colored palaces were reflected rhythmically on the waters of the Neva as our arms arched gracefully over our heads, and we flew in the stage lights like wingless angels.

Then we landed on this strife-torn island and the swan melted under the scorching sun.

—from the *Memoirs of Masha Mastova*

Flight of the Swan

Very few people know that Madame, the famous Russian ballerina, visited our island from April to September 1917. But my husband, Juan Anduce, and I remembered the time vividly. A few weeks ago, on April 23, 1932, Madame lay dying in an obscure hotel in Amsterdam, asking for her swan costume. "Play the last measure softly," she whispered to the friends who stood around her, the newspaper headlines quoted. No sooner did she pass away, as she lay still warm in her coffin, than her husband, Victor Dandré, was speeding toward London in search of the marriage license which would assure him of his inheritance: magnificent Ivy House, the mansion surrounded by English gardens and a lake full of swans that once belonged to the painter William Turner and which Madame had purchased with her savings. But I knew he'd never find it. I had destroyed the license, a yellowed parchment written in Cyrillic characters, years before. When I read the article I was overwhelmed with recollections.

I have lived for fifteen years on this island, almost half as long as I lived in Russia. I still love the color red, as all Russians do—*russ*, after all, means red, something few people realize be-

cause it's so obvious—but my Russian heart is beginning to feel
stifled. Incredibly enough, I am growing tired of this island's
splendid sun and I miss winter. I would give anything to hear
its silence, the stillness that precedes the blizzard, oblivion's
snowflakes sifting quietly over my graying head.

When my husband, Juan, was still alive, I had very little time
to brood about these things because we had the ballet school
and needed to keep our students whirling like tops in the studio we built together in San Juan. It was on the second floor of
an old house, with several wrought-iron balconies that opened
onto the shady Plaza de Armas.

The academy was Madame's gift to us when she left the island. The training is difficult and very demanding, but its benefits are countless. It not only gives young men and women the
opportunity to find jobs as dancers; it also gives them self-
respect and a sense of who they are. This was Madame's original wish, and I have done my utmost to put it into effect.

Juan died of a punctured appendix a few months ago and
now I live alone. Fortunately, I still have my studio. But when I
close the door after the day's last student has left, I plunge into
despair. Time erases everything and at the end we are left with
nothing. I refuse to become a ghost, a woman without a country, without love and without memories, clutching at my own
shadow.

I was thirty-nine years old when I made the decision to leave
Madame's company when she traveled to South America. I
stayed behind on this island, where I married Juan Anduce, the
cobbler hired to repair the dancers' slippers when our ballet
company was stranded here during the Great War. For three
months we were virtual prisoners; it was a nightmare for all of

us. The company's ballerinas wore out dozens of slippers each week and it was impossible to have new ones delivered during our tour because of the German submarines. So Madame had to improvise. That's when Juan Anduce, my future husband, turned up, his green eyes gleaming with the island's lushness and a mischievous smile on his face.

I had met Madame a number of years earlier, in St. Petersburg. I was young and naive, and one day I went to her apartment on Kolomenskaya Street and asked if she would take me on as a private student. Madame had only recently graduated from the Maryinsky Imperial Ballet School and gave classes at home to a small group of girls to supplement her income. It was from this group that she eventually picked the dancers that formed her company, later taking them on short tours on the Continent when war was about to break out in Russia. I joined the flock of young women and accompanied Madame from Russia to the Baltic when I was nineteen. From there we toured many European countries, until one day we sailed to the United States. Many of our relatives in Russia perished during those years, when the White and Red Armies were grappling in mortal combat along a frontier thousands of miles long. Madame saved us from disaster.

Like the rest of the girls in our company, I could have kissed the ground my mistress walked on, dragged myself over a bed of hot coals or needles of ice just to be near her. Those were anguished years, during which we, her followers, spent many sleepless nights worrying about the future. But Madame seemed to glide serenely over the troubled waters of her age: the Russian Revolution, the deaths of millions of her countrymen, even the suffering of this small island which she visited for a short time and to which she could have been indifferent, yet wasn't. It was hard not to revere her if you ever saw her dance; her Odile in *Swan Lake* and her Aurora in *Sleeping Beauty* were perfect. But our group held her in special esteem, because she always kept her promises.

Madame and I have known each other from way back. I'm the daughter of a Russian peasant from Minsk who used to beat me with a poplar branch every time he got drunk. I survived thanks to a traveling merchant who went by the house one afternoon and saw him beat me. He punched Mastovsky on the chin and took me to live with his own family in St. Petersburg. He had a brother named Dassily who was a ballet master. He came by the house one day and suggested I take classes with him. Of course I was thrilled to do so. A few years went by and I was perfectly happy, but when I turned sixteen, the merchant raped me and began to beat me. Eventually I went to Madame's apartment and knocked on her door. It was 1897 and Madame had just opened a small ballet school at home, and she took in private pupils. I had a strong, slender body, like the peasants of Belarus usually do. Madame took me in as a maid, and later decided to continue my training in dance.

Like so many of the young dancers who joined Madame's school, I was a fanatical admirer of the ballerina's art. Since I didn't have the training, I wasn't a good enough dancer to be a soloist, so I danced in the chorus. I was tall and lanky then, not fat and sluggish like I am now, wearing muumuus all the time to conceal my size. Because of my rawboned strength, I always danced at the tail end of the line of girls, always near the wings so I could dart off the stage to help Madame change into one of her costumes, or to help the stagehands out. I admit I was never attractive. I looked a bit like a stork, with a long nose and quick-darting eyes which Madame said were always suspiciously assessing my surroundings.

During our free time I washed and ironed Madame's clothes, made her bed, helped dress her, and brushed and tidied up her hair with the silver swan brush and comb one of her admirers had given her, which were always kept in their own leather case. Little by little I became my mistress's confidante.

I knew more about Madame than anyone else in the company: who her biological father was, for example, and why Madame would get so upset if anyone mentioned Matvey Federov, the reserve officer who had married her mother, Lyubovna Fedorovna, and who was killed in the war when Madame was only two years old. I knew all of her secrets: how Madame managed to enter the Imperial Ballet School in St. Petersburg, why she married Victor Dandré, a con man and a scoundrel, and why she had stayed with him for so many years.

This knowledge gave me power, and the other dancers respected me for it. I was Madame's right hand, the keeper of her flame. The desire for something we do not have is what makes us struggle to better ourselves, as our priest in Minsk used to say.

Madame admired and respected me for little things—for my patience and fortitude when there was something that had to be done which no one wanted to do, like mend her costumes, rinse her underwear, or scrub the toilets and pick up pubic hairs from the bathroom floor; for my frugality and generosity; even for my country bumpkin ignorance, which made me less dangerous than her sophisticated dancers from St. Petersburg and London, but also more reliable. I knew I represented the best of Russia for Madame: the *muzhik*'s soul.

One day Madame and I made a pact: "I'll take care of you and you take care of me," she said. I naturally agreed. Anyone who knows something about love knows it's the lover, rather than the beloved, who is the stronger, and my love for Madame made me as solid as a rock.

Madame embarked on her first South American tour with her company, of which I was part, on February 10, 1917. Victor Dandré, Madame's husband and manager, had persuaded her to take this trip while we were still performing in New York. During our tour of the United States we visited 140 cities in seven months. And yet we were hardly tired, fueled by the excitement and the adrenaline of success. None of us would have guessed the anguish that lay ahead of us.

There was an economic boom in Argentina because of the war, and Mr. Dandré was sure a pot of gold awaited us at the southernmost tip of the continent. He was as eager to reach it as a bear that smells honey. The United States had just entered the war on the side of the Allies, and German submarines now made the Atlantic crossing almost impossible so we couldn't return to Europe, no matter how homesick we felt. Very few ships managed to get through; most ended up at the bottom of the ocean. No one knew how long the war would last, and we couldn't just sit around waiting for it to end, Mr. Dandré told us. So he pointed out Cuba to us on the map and made plans for the company to ship out, making this island our first stop en route to South America.

Madame had anticipated the tour with grand illusions. She was a pacifist like the great Vaslav Nijinsky, who was also crossing the Atlantic by steamer on a tour headed for South America. Madame wasn't at all keen on the United States entering the conflict. She had gone to Germany several times and had danced for the kaiser just before the war broke out; she saw what the German troops were like up close, and the carnage they were capable of. In fact, that was one of the reasons she decided to make the tour of South America, because several nations there—including Argentina and Brazil—remained neutral and wanted no part in the bloody European conflict.

On the other hand, Spanish music and Spanish ballets in her repertoire were always some of Madame's favorites: *Paquita*, for example, or *Don Quijote*, during which she could flash the fire of her flint-dark eyes at the audience and hide a mischievous smile behind her sequined fan. That was Madame for you. She could become whatever she wanted when she danced—which was very handy when she mimed passionate loves.

Mr. Dandré set up a deal with Adolfo Bracale, the Italian impresario who had staked out the Caribbean as his private territory, bringing all sorts of artists here who wanted to make themselves known. Enrico Caruso, Hipólito Lázaro, Amelita Galli-Curchi, Sarah Bernhardt all sailed down the Caribbean at some point or another, looking for the goose with the golden egg and more often than not ending up omelets themselves because of Bracale's wheelings and dealings. He was famous for keeping more than half the money the agents put up, with the promise that he would send it later on to the performers; and then he never did. But he had an eye for genius, and many of the artists he brought to the area, often just beginning to bloom, went on to become international sensations. Madame, of course, was one of them. But she was never taken advantage of because of Mr. Dandré. Mr. Dandré was tough, and he oversaw all of her affairs.

At that time Cuba was at the crossroads of the Americas. Travel by boat was imperative if you wanted to reach South America, and there was neither rail nor road between New York and Buenos Aires. Businessmen sailed down the Caribbean on their way to their various destinations—Curaçao, Caracas, Panama—inevitably stopping at La Habana where ships took on coal. Karajaieff, Algeranoff, and other Russian friends of Madame who had fled the revolution and had already found refuge in New York knew Bracale, and cautioned her that he was secretly related to the Mafia, although no one was able to prove it. But as usual, Madame trusted Mr. Dandré blindly and agreed to go along with his plan. She told Lyubovna Federovna and me to pack her clothes and toiletries: her silk georgette nightgowns; her L'Heure Bleue and Narcisse Noir perfume bottles; the silver swan hand mirror, brush, and comb; and in less than a week we were ready to leave.

New York was a heady experience. Madame danced every night to enormous crowds at the Hippodrome, throwing all her previous scruples about Imperial Russian ballerinas appearing before rowdy vaudeville audiences to the winds. People needed to be happy and to forget about the Marne and Verdun, about the horrors of trench warfare and poison gas. Three months later, the United States would begin to ship soldiers to the front, and its youth would become cannon fodder. But no one could foresee the impending tragedy.

We sailed to Cuba full of expectations, sure that the presentations of *Giselle* and *Coppélia* at Teatro Nacional would be a huge success. Cuba was in the news then as the second greatest

sugar-producing country in the world, and La Habana's bourgeoisie was said to be enormously rich. We needed desperately
to send money home to our families. That winter in St. Petersburg was one of the worst in history: millions of people were
starving and dying of the cold. Letters—when they got to us—
told how people were burning fences and lampposts, and using
the furniture in their homes as kindling. The money we sent
was taken by friends to the Belgian or Swiss borders so that a
few of our relatives, after endless struggles, were able to escape
and cross over.

Madame, on the other hand, had heard that the Cuban capital was very chic. She ordered a completely new wardrobe
made in New York for her dancers, as well as new scenery.
Madame was a professional artist; once she signed a contract,
she delivered the best performance she was capable of, no matter what sacrifice it meant. The hold of the S.S. *Courbelo* carried
dozens of decorated flats, twenty hat boxes full of wide-
brimmed pamelas wrapped in clouds of gauze and adorned
with silk blossoms, and 194 trunks holding three thousand lace
and velvet costumes glimmering with sequins. "She's the czar's
ballerina," the customs inspectors in New York would say, nod-
ding to each other knowingly, convinced the costumes all belonged to Madame herself. Little did they know what the real
story was! Madame had actually been a Bolshevik sympathizer
in her youth, and she probably would have stayed in Russia if it
hadn't been for Mr. Dandré. She was in London after a tour of
the Baltic cities when Mr. Dandré, who was a member of the
Duma (the Russian elective legislative assembly, or lower house
of parliament) and served in several municipal commissions
which allocated city funds, was caught stealing the czar's rubles.
He was thrown unceremoniously in jail. Madame bailed him
out, but he could never go back to Russia.

After the first performance, when Cuba's upper crust turned out in full force to see Madame dance, La Habana's impressive Teatro Nacional remained discouragingly empty. Political turmoil was rampant on the island, and people were afraid to go out after dark; the city's streets were deserted, except for President García Menocal's hoodlums firing random shots from racing black Packards in the middle of the night. The threatening atmosphere reminded us of St. Petersburg during the recent uprisings. At night we could hardly sleep.

Madame, as usual, had spent a fortune before we shipped out of New York—a good part of her earnings during her successful tour of the United States—but not on herself. She would do anything to help her dancers feel confident on stage, and a magnificent costume was a good start. Her extravagance put the rest of us on a tight budget: we weren't living from hand to mouth as we would be later in Puerto Rico, but Mr. Dandré counted every penny we spent.

Our tour was financed in advance by Max Rabinoff, a millionaire impresario from New York who was a friend of Bracale's, and at this point his losses exceeded $150,000. In New York, headlines appeared in the press accusing Madame of dancing away fifty thousand dollars, which was really spent on our costumes and stage decors bound for Cuba. Apparently Mr. Rabinoff was in the middle of a divorce, and the money he lent Dandré had belonged to his wife, who had inherited it from her family. She filed suit in court, but the Cuban fiasco made it impossible for Dandré to return any of it. That's when we received the first of several anonymous threats, telling us that if we didn't pay up, our lives would be in danger.

Madame, on hearing this, was incensed and wanted to return to New York. She was sure she could contact another millionaire there who would finance the rest of the trip to South

America. But Bracale was adamant. He refused to pay for the company's fares north, or to count on the dubious promise that they would find a patron to subsidize their way to Rio de Janeiro. The best thing the company could do was to reach Puerto Rico and make some money there. He cobbled together a fresh itinerary for us, and after waiting an anguished week for our names to be put at the top of the passenger list on one of the local steamers that sailed from Santiago de Cuba, where the company gave one last performance, we finally boarded the S.S. *Courbelo*, bound for San Juan, on April 4, 1917.

The first day on board Dandré looked solemn and morose. He was dressed all in black, as if to underscore the seriousness of our situation. That morning he brought us all together and came sternly to the point: business in Cuba was a fiasco, and he simply was not in a position to risk another disastrous season. Either the dancers would have to accept a temporary solution—a 25 percent reduction in salary, which meant we would be making three dollars a day—or the tour would have to be abandoned. To some, this was onerous. Smallens, the English orchestra director, for example, spent three dollars a day on beer alone, but most of us were used to living on air, and we even paid our own expenses just to be able to dance on the same stage as Madame.

We had never heard of Puerto Rico before, but as it was on the way to Panama and Peru, where Dandré had scheduled numerous performances for us during the coming months, we gladly boarded the ship. Dandré pointed out that the island was the smallest of the Greater Antilles and that it was a possession of the United States. "Under the American flag there's bound to be progress," he said, dusting off his bowler hat before putting it back on as we walked up the ship's gangplank. "The island was until recently under military rule. There will be order and discipline and we will be paid in dollars," he added, looking satisfied with himself and plucking at his mustache, as he did whenever he didn't want anyone to contradict him.

None of the dancers cared for Mr. Dandré very much, and we felt sorry for Madame, who, in spite of being a star, couldn't live without him. He took care of her as if she were a child, and lavished attention on her. When we were on the S.S. *Courbelo*, for example, the captain improvised a pool made of canvas and pumped it full of seawater, so Madame could cool off from the heat. She spent hours diving and swimming in it, but when

Dandré begged her to come out, calling "Nanushka! Nanushka! Please, it's time for dinner," she would laugh and shriek, and send Poppy, her terrier, scrambling out of the water to jump all over him, so he would get dripping wet.

Mr. Dandré was very organized and solved all the logistical problems of our tours. He planned the itineraries and made the reservations, contacted the impresarios and thrashed out the contracts with them, figuring out the expenses of the trips as well as the possible profits and losses. But money often seemed to evaporate mysteriously in his hands, and then we'd find ourselves at the mercy of people like Bracale, who would send his thugs to threaten us or to supervise our performances. On one occasion, when we were playing at the Metropolitan Opera House just before we left on the trip for South America, a group of men wearing wool masks broke into the back office, blew up the safe, and made off with twenty thousand dollars, three quarters of it from Madame's back wages. After that, Madame took special care of her personal valuables, especially her jewels, which she carried everywhere with her in a small alligator case.

Dandré was always laughing and looking at the bright side of things. But he had a lecherous disposition and was constantly trying to pinch the girls' fannies or burst into our dressing rooms unexpectedly when we were changing our costumes. "Whenever Mr. Dandré is away," the girls used to tease Madame—and he traveled often because of the complicated quartermaster duties he performed for the company (or so Madame said, with a shamefaced smile)—"we all rejoice. You belong only to us then, Madame, to your sacred nymphs."

I felt the difference more than anyone. When Dandré wasn't around, Madame paid much more attention to me. She didn't have to drop everything at six in the afternoon to run him a bath, darn his socks, or see about his dinner that evening. "Time for Masha the ugly, time for Masha the awkward," I'd whisper to her under my breath; and then I'd do a little jig for her sake, to celebrate our privacy. In her hotel room I'd beg her to teach me how to weave my arms like a willow in the wind or to fly like a butterfly instead of like a moth.

No matter how hard Dandré tried to whittle down classical ballet to a mere way of making money, to crass bourgeois showmanship, it was much more than that to us. As Madame preached many times, giving us a little speech before class, dancing was a spiritual experience. In ancient times man's devotion to the gods, his happiness and bereavement, were all expressed through movement. The body was the harp of the spirit, the medium through which we achieved union with the divine.

When Madame approved of the way a dancer performed a difficult sequence of steps, she would stand before the stage lights during rehearsal and cry *"Harasho!"* while clapping ecstatically. But she wasn't always so generous. Sometimes she could be terribly cruel with girls who took a long time to learn the choreography for a new ballet. She would show them how to do a sequence of steps once, and if the student didn't remember all the details the first time around, she would explode. *"You have expression like cook! Are you artist or not?"* she'd call out from the sidelines. And if someone gained a pound or two—something easy to do in these islands, where the best food is fried by the roadside in smoking black cauldrons by turbaned black women, she would immediately call out to us: *"Vaches! How can you pretend to be dancers when you look like chateaubriands!"*

Dancers with weak ankles or legs had a hard time in our troupe. Madame was merciless with them, ridiculing and shaming them. Don't be misled, Madame only *looked* frail. Her exceptionally arched insteps, her slender ankles, her delicately drawn neck made her seem as fragile as a porcelain doll, but her muscles were tempered in steel. She wasn't like a swan at all; she was a hare, a racing machine. She never got tired; she could dance fifteen hours a day without stopping, sleep for six hours, and keep going the next day. She earned the right to every minute of the spotlight in every performance she was in, by sheer stamina. She was like a force of nature, and she rejected everything that was weak.

Madame was a jealous guardian of her leading roles, and with good reason. In classical ballet, as in every walk of life, there are opportunists lurking behind every painted flat, and mediocre dancers often take advantage of the excellence of others. For this reason, when she went onstage, if her partner got too close to her during a supporting turn, or if he stepped on the hem of her costume, she pretended nothing was amiss. She danced around the scoundrel with a radiant smile, and as soon as the curtain went down, she'd turn around and give him a sound slap across the face.

In any case, Madame had every right to be so demanding with other dancers, because she was just as exacting with herself. She could rehearse a combination of steps, which took ten seconds to perform, for hours; repeat a battement tendu, a bourrée, or an arabesque so many times the dancers began to feel the ground give way under their feet. The few times I watched her do the devilishly difficult fouettés, her leg an iron pivot on which her whole body turned while it churned like a butter pole, the other leg a whip of bone and flesh lifting and falling forty times in perfect rhythm, I was so amazed I was sure the holy Pantocrator was hovering over the stage, miraculously sustaining Madame inside the iris of His eye.

Once, just before a performance, Madame was watching the audience through a tiny peephole in the velvet curtains, leaning forward and already costumed to appear on the scene, when she said to me: "Look at them, Masha, how self-satisfied and complacent they are, after a rich dinner and an expensive bottle of Châteauneuf-du-Pape. Their bodies have taken over and their spirits are unable to rise. We'll try to help them with our dancing, but we can't promise them anything." The moment the curtain went up and she appeared onstage, it was her winged power countering their heaviness, her élan vital pitted against their dead weight. Madame's profile was serene and chiseled in snow; her walk unfaltering, like a panther's. By contrast, I was ugly and awkward, my face was full of pimples, and my arms were gawky; I was always tripping over myself and clumsily dropping things. But I couldn't let her see how much I loved her. When you revered Madame she exploited you all the more—and then discarded you like a dried corn husk.

Madame exerted a mysterious attraction on those around her. An aura emanated from her that pulled young girls to her like moths. One had to be careful not to get too close, or one could fall into the fire. When I was a child in Minsk I saw the Imperial Ballet give a presentation in the garden of a castle—my stepmother took me there because she worked in the kitchen. It was the first time I ever saw a ballerina, and they looked like fairies, dancing among the flowers. Madame was my fairy godmother.

When Madame lost patience with the girls, calling them muttons or *vaches*, Mr. Dandré immediately came running, supposedly to defend them. But he was really after something else: he wanted the girls to become dependent on *him*, so later he could do as he wanted. On one occasion, a month before the company arrived in Puerto Rico, we were staying at the Ansonia Hotel in New York when tragedy struck. A young dancer named María Volkonsky, who had recently arrived from Russia, was feeling very lonely. As a result of her anxiety María had begun to eat fattening foods and had gained ten pounds. Dandré realized it, and he immediately took advantage of the situation. He began to coddle her; he supervised her meals and was with her constantly, trying to win her confidence so that she would let him in her room when he tapped on her door at night. María felt terrible because, apart from me, she was the dancer who most revered Madame. Yet the more she admired her, the more Madame despised her because she was fat. Finally, Madame refused to let her perform. She made María teach the understudy her roles, and this made the girl even more unhappy. María became so distracted one night that she threw herself from her hotel window, which opened onto one of New York's dreary back alleys. It took the company weeks to overcome its grief and to be able to dance again.

One day Nadja Bulova, Madame's understudy, was feeling ill and Madame sent for me to rehearse the pas de deux of *Les Sylphides* with her. She bourréed next to me during Chopin's lyric arpeggios, and suddenly she leaned forward during an arabesque and her hand brushed my breast. It could have been unwittingly, but I felt a shudder of delight rush through me. Madame always made it a point not to touch any of us or let us touch her; it was part of her discipline when she gave classes. She usually carried a slender baton in her hand and would introduce it under an arm or a leg when it needed lifting, or tap us lightly in the back if our posture was deficient. To touch her on the shoulder or attract her attention plucking at her dress would have been considered a sacrilege. Her inaccessibility was part of her mystique, and we accepted the taboo without questioning it. For some reason, on the day of our rehearsal she broke her own rule.

The caress surprised me and an alarm went off in my head like a shooting star. Maybe I was wrong all along and Madame could love me! But I didn't say anything. I told myself I had to be careful, or I could end up like María Volkonsky.

For Mr. Dandré ballet was a business venture like any other. He never closed a deal with an impresario without first demanding half the money on the table as an advance. Even with Bracale we were never at his mercy, because Dandré demanded a good amount for our performances. Madame, on the other hand, never danced simply for the money. She wanted to give everyone the opportunity to enjoy the beauty of ballet, even those who had no money.

We were living in troubled times. More than ten million people had died in Europe and twice that many were wounded. Sixty million men served in the various armies, and now, with the United States having recently joined the conflict, there would be even more devastation. Europe was being torn apart, but compassion and love were still possible; that was Madame's message. *The Dying Swan*, the solo piece that made her famous all over the world, was a prayer for peace. Our beloved St. Petersburg was the swan, torn by strife and civil war, its churches smoldering to heaven, its golden domes now sheltering atheists who murdered priests as they tended to the devout.

Madame's relationship with Dandré was, after twelve years of living together, understandably more filial than anything else. Desire had long since run its course between them. I was sure of that, because I put clean sheets on their separate beds every morning. Dandré understood Madame and was content to serve her because he was making a good profit. He was like a huge punching bag, absorbing her explosions and always bouncing back when the crisis she had provoked was over. Dandré was one-dimensional, what you saw was what you got. Which was more than you could say of Madame.

Madame would say to her followers: "If you want to be an artist you must remain free." And at other times: "When you dance, you must dance for someone. Art is always a reaching out, an effort to meld with the beloved." How to interpret these blatant contradictions? During our tours, the girls often met rich, good-looking gentlemen who became infatuated with them and came knocking at their dressing-room doors. (Not me—I never considered leaving Madame for a minute; she was my sun and moon; my North Star.) If the gentlemen offered them diamonds or pearls it was fine; but if they came asking for the girls' hands in marriage, Madame would lock herself up in her room and begin to smash cups and saucers against the wall. Most of the girls didn't have the courage to cause her so much pain, and they would break off their engagements. One day she asked us to kneel before the holy icon of the Virgin of Vladimir and made us take a vow: "A career and love are impossible to reconcile. That's why, when you dance, you must never give yourself to anyone," she told us, as she lit a ruby-red votive candle in front of the Virgin with a long taper. And we kissed the holy icon and gave her our promise.

Had Madame ever fallen in love? Did she know what such a promise meant? I had heard rumors that in her youth she had loved someone passionately, but that she had had to give him up. In fact, she remained faithful to her oath until we arrived in Puerto Rico. Here she underwent a metamorphosis.

Most of the girls in the company had had unhappy love affairs, and they found consolation in Madame's celibate example. She was pure as snow, unsullied by the mud of sex and betrayal. I, for one, was always on the lookout to fend off marauders, who were usually not too far away. The girls and I were constantly pampering her. We would brush her hair, rub Pond's cold cream on her face, massage her feet. Once a woman has experienced the softness of another woman's caresses, the delicate fingertips like silk buds on her skin—even if it's an *amitié en rose*—how can she ever go back to loving a man? It was difficult to understand at the time.

It was true that during our tours around the world Madame paid her dancers miserly salaries—our wages were a pittance, more crumbs than pay—but we didn't mind. We knew *why* we were dancing and what we were dancing *for*. It didn't have to be mentioned; it was taken for granted, like the tide that pours from the Black Sea into the Dardanelles every day at dawn.

Madame's dancers lived like birds, totally at the mercy of God's will. We had to pay for our own hotel accommodations, our food, our taxis, even our toe shoes. The English and the French girls (there were both) wrote home constantly, asking their parents to send them money to survive. We Russians, of course, had no one to write to since our country had gone up in flames. Madame would become incensed when she was criticized for these things by her enemies. "The families should pay *me*, because now they can say their children were my pupils, and this will assure their prestige in the world," she'd maintain. But none of it mattered to us. We would have danced for nothing if we could have remained by Madame's side.

The S.S. *Courbelo* was really a cattle boat headed for Panama which was detoured to Puerto Rico for repairs, and as soon as it began to roll from side to side, the mournful bellowing of the animals below deck began to echo through the ship. We spent a miserable night and everybody was depressed, but there was no getting away from the steers or from the stench of their manure, which seeped through the cracks in the hold. No one slept. Seeing that the journey to Puerto Rico was a short one and that we would only spend one night at sea, we hung our hammocks up on deck, and spent the night under a sky full of stars.

As we approached the island the next morning, Madame came up on deck and stood near me. She put an arm around my shoulders and snuggled against me, then made the sign of the cross on my forehead. "Good morning, Masha! Have you had a glass of fresh milk yet? At least there's plenty of it on board!" she said with a little laugh. That's what I always liked about Madame. No matter how bad things were, she always saw the silver lining.

I smiled back at her and admitted I had had a cup of *café con leche* in the galley a few minutes before. "The coffee is very good. I hear the Catholic pope only drinks Puerto Rican coffee in Rome," I said to tease her, knowing how passionate she was about her Orthodox faith. I leaned on the rail and looked at the approaching coastline, a bare line of vegetation floating between two immense canvases of blue—navy-dark water beneath, a pale azure sky above—with not a cloud in sight. At this latitude sunlight was even stronger than in Havana; it fell on the waves like liquid bronze, bathing our arms and faces. I was in good spirits. "What sun!" I cried, spreading my arms wide. "I wonder what our dancing will be like here, with a sun like this to warm us!" Madame kissed me on the cheek. I embraced her and didn't say a word. Her kiss made everything I had endured worthwhile.

As we neared the fortified city of San Juan, the light became even stronger, refracted by the looming medieval walls and ramparts. Madame turned her face toward the sun's rays and closed her eyes. I imagined she was thinking of St. Petersburg, remembering its relentless drizzle, the sharp golden steeple of the Admiralty piercing the slate-colored sky. "If only I could absorb this sunlight and take it with me when I leave!" Madame said. "Maybe that way I could get rid of the periodic depressions that visit me, when I feel lost in the St. Petersburg mist."

When the cattle boat docked at the busy port, Madame and Dandré disembarked together, ahead of everyone else. I watched them from the ship, leaning on the banister. Dandré was carrying Madame's alligator *nécessaire* with her jewelry—her diamond necklace, her earrings and bracelets, and the czar's Fabergé egg with the tiny diamond fish inside—his gift to her when she graduated from the Imperial Ballet School. Madame carried Poppy, her black-and-white American bull terrier, in her arms. Custine, the ballet master, and Smallens, the orchestra director, walked along smartly behind them, each holding a birdcage. Madame had been presented with two beautiful silver-gray nightingales in Santiago de Cuba before she left, and naturally she had brought them along. ("Look, Masha, darling, nightingales on these islands have whiskers, little black hairs on their beaks!" she pointed out to me gaily when she saw them.) Madame never traveled without her pets, and she wasn't going to leave such wonderful gifts behind.

On the wharf a magnificent, four-door Pierce-Arrow was waiting with a uniformed chauffeur at the wheel. Madame was astonished; she wasn't expecting anyone to pick her up. She asked who had sent the vehicle and the uniformed chauffeur bowed, whispered something in her ear, and then conferred with Dandré. Dandré signaled that it was fine, and they all got into the car and set off, riding rapidly up the cobblestones of Calle Tanca.

The rest of the troupe—Lyubovna Fedorovna, Madame's mother and lady-in-waiting; the electrician; the seamstress; the beautician with her hatbox full of wigs; and myself helping to carry the luggage—all trundled heavily up the hill on foot toward the Malatrassi Hotel, a narrow, four-story building which stood on Plaza de Armas, the town square. It was a second-class establishment next to the Alcaldía, the mayor's house. Because of La Habana's fiasco we couldn't stay at a first-class hotel in San Juan. Everybody seethed, of course, and they all blamed Dandré. But although there were groans and complaints all around, nobody considered even for a minute going back to New York.

Madame was always followed around on her ballet tours by a group of admirers who called themselves the Swooning Swans. In Australia, two young girls followed her train for thousands of kilometers, admiring her from a distance until they reached Sydney and then, too shy to introduce themselves, turned right around and went back to where they came from. There was a time when her followers, myself included, could have killed for a strip of Madame's tulle skirt, for a ribbon from one of her silk slippers. We fought like cats over each little memento. When she danced the mad scene in *Giselle*, for example, and actually wrenched a handful of hair from her head, the girls searched around the stage for hours after the ballet was over, looking for the silky strands to preserve in their lockets as talismans. Fans waited at the theater entrance and pounced on her the minute she was out of the door. Eventually she realized that she needed protection from the Swooning Swans. That was when Mr. Dandré came in handy. The white lie of their marriage served as a very effective armor: thanks to Mr. Dandré, no one ever dared approach Madame beyond a certain point.

I never dared speak to Madame in public or get too close. It was as if she radiated perfection, not only through the movements of her body but through her onyx-dark eyes, and I didn't want people to see how ugly I was by comparison. I never missed one of her performances; I traveled in the same trains and stayed at the same hotels as Madame. Later, when I was lucky enough to be admitted into the troupe, I discovered that many of the other girls felt the same way I did toward her. But it took me three years of sharing the vicissitudes of a ballerina's life—of fasting in order to keep my figure, of taking care of my deformed feet and cramped legs and thighs; and most important, of observing her every movement at ballet class—to realize that I was part of a sacred order.

Madame was very pious—her dressing room was full of icons of the Virgin Mary, Mary Magdalene, and Saint Anne with candles flickering in front of them; before every performance she'd kiss them and ask for inspiration. But she was *our* saint, and we were her devout followers. We weren't at all interested in making a name for ourselves, we never wanted to be famous individually. Our duty was to spread Madame's doctrine around the world.

Madame loved children. Often I'd see mothers bring their daughters to the stage exit when they were no more than twelve years old. "Take her with you, she's yours," they'd plead, bowing respectfully. "We want her to be like you. Please do whatever you have to do to teach her your secrets." When someone brought her a prospective student, she'd stand before the child for a few minutes studying her, observing her poor or good turnout or the frailty of her ankles; she'd put her hands on the child's head and, on most occasions, advise the mother to take her daughter back home. "Girls have a difficult time making their way in ballet," she'd murmur softly. "They get paid very little—less than the boys. And since they have to dance on their toes"—boys dance in soft kid slippers, and on their half toes—"soon bunions sprout on their feet and their toes eventually overlap, so they often have to be operated on in order not to become crippled. Yes, classical ballet is a spiritual experience, but it's also very painful," Madame insisted, pulling her shawl about her a little bit tighter and tilting her head delicately to one side, as swans are wont to do. But the mother wouldn't listen, and the child, watching Madame with enamored, incandescent eyes, would listen even less.

The company was made up of twelve girls and six boys who danced in the chorus. The girls were taught personally by Madame and the boys were Novikov's students. Novikov was our ballet master and Madame's partner on stage. Madame had had a long string of partners who lasted only a few months until they were unceremoniously bounced out of the company by

Dandré once they fell in love with her. Novikov, fortunately, would never fall in love with her; he liked buns much better than breasts. Madame didn't have a generous amount of either, but it was the approach that mattered, as Madame once told me laughing.

Although our female dancers all had exotic Russian names—Katia Borodina, Maya Ulanova, Egorova Sedova, Nadja Bulova—two of them were actually shy English girls and had been trained by Madame in recent years. She had changed their names to Russian for appearances' sake. Nadja Bulova, Madame's understudy, was of pure Russian origin, but she only danced whenever Madame fell ill, which was seldom.

We Russians are a sentimental people—showing affection is natural to us; it's one of the things I have missed the most since I left my country. During our tours, the girls hugged and kissed and pinched each other's cheeks as if they wanted to reassure themselves that friends really existed, that they were not making them up because they felt so alone.

At that time it was still very difficult for girls from middle-class families to become dancers, and many of the students of the Imperial Ballet School came from the poorer families of St. Petersburg. The poor, like Madame's mother, didn't worry as much about their daughters' reputations. From the girls' point of view it was a magnificent opportunity to make their way in the world. To be free from all constraints of family! To fly around Europe like a flock of swans, in search of beauty, adventure, and romance, as Madame was able to do! She was always urging us to live full emotional lives which would enrich our art, but never to commit ourselves to a relationship that would clip our wings. This was the dream of every girl who wanted to become a ballerina. Our veneration of Madame was tacitly related to our struggle, as young women, to be at the helm of our own lives.

Madame was much stricter than the American dancer Isadora Duncan, who at that time was prancing around the world's stages clad in a semi-transparent tunic. It was very difficult to accuse Madame of being a "loose woman," as the press often did with the American. Isadora's horrible death, her fringed silk scarf caught in the spokes of the wheel of a red Bugatti, was considered by some to be suicide after her lover, the Russian poet Essenin, took his own life. But Madame was much stronger than Isadora. She was a survivor, and she outlived her lover, Diamantino Márquez, by many years.

Madame was the product of the Imperial Ballet School, where dancers lived under a merciless discipline; their training could only be compared to the drilling of army troops. The old czar, Nicholas I, who had founded the Maryinsky Ballet School, was very proud of this fact. The czar divided his passions almost equally between soldiering and dancing and liked to compare the Imperial Ballet to a cavalry corps. It was rumored that he loved to sit backstage and listen to the rumble of the ballerinas' toe shoes when they poured across the wooden floor of the stage, because they reminded him of a dragoon charge galloping across a field of battle.

The ballet school's pupils had to learn the choreography of Marius Petipa, the old commander-in-chief of the Maryinsky Theater, by heart. Petipa's ballets were very conservative; his scores were hieroglyphs pregnant with esoteric meaning only classical dancers could decipher. Isadora Duncan's art, on the contrary, was the result of improvisation; her dancing was far from the grueling discipline of the Imperial Ballet, and Madame always saw her as an amateur. Isadora danced, not only nearly naked, but also barefoot. "I would never submit my feet to those instruments of torture, the silk toe slippers," Duncan declared once to the press. And yet we, Madame's followers, knew it was the silk toe shoe, with its tiny base and the resulting near-frictionless contact with the floor, which made spiritual transcendence possible.

By the time the last dancer checked in at the reception desk, the Malatrassi Hotel was completely full. Thanks to Mr. Dandré, who had cabled reservations in advance from La Habana, we would all be able to sleep comfortably in beds that evening. The girls were all whispering and asking if anyone knew the name of the owner of the magnificent yellow-and-black Pierce-Arrow with honey-colored leather seats and whitewall tires that had whisked Madame away at the pier. But nobody did.

We were about to go up the stairs to our rooms lugging our own suitcases when Molinari, Bracale's sub-agent, arrived. He was tall and brawny, with a large nose—a Corsican who had come to the island fleeing an undisclosed crime in Italy, as we later found out. He was informing Dandré of the arrangements for the tour when two police agents with boots up to their knees and guns tucked into hip holsters appeared in the lobby and demanded to see our passports. Once they examined them, Dandré and Madame were unceremoniously escorted to the police station. I was asked to go along too, because I knew a little Spanish—which I had learned from the Gypsies in Minsk—

and could help translate. Molinari went as well. People on the street stared at us, especially at Madame, whose white lace skirt was very stylish, but a lot shorter than it should have been, judging by those worn by respectable women in the streets of San Juan.

The commissioner, a fat man with black hair on his fingers and crater-pocked cheeks, fired a barrage of questions at us. When had we arrived? Did we know that Russia had suffered a coup d'état and that the Bolsheviks were in power? We had evidently been at sea at the time and hadn't heard about it. In any case, since we were Russian citizens, our passports were now invalid, because Russia had ceased to exist.

"Russia ceased to exist? You must be joking. You have no idea how large and powerful my country is," Madame declared indignantly, a tilt of icy superiority to her chin.

"It's a fact, ma'am," a young man wearing sunglasses and a short-sleeved shirt standing next to the commissioner said. "The czar abdicated at Psok, and subsequently has been arrested. There are only Bolsheviks left in Russia now, and they are wiping out whoever's left. That's what I meant."

"These islands are full of spies because of the bloody war, and we don't want any more rabble causing havoc in our midst," the commissioner said, wiping his mouth with a paper napkin after swallowing the dregs from a coffee cup he held in his hand. "We may be a small island, but our secret service is first rate!" he thundered, as if implicating Madame.

Dandré tried to calm the commissioner down. He explained we had just been in New York before passing through Cuba, that we had appeared at the Metropolitan Opera House and at City Center, where the most exclusive audiences had come to see Madame dance. "Well, this isn't New York! We may be a part of the United States, but we have our own laws down here, and you'll have to abide by them," the little man declared, drumming his stubby fingers on the desk. "You can only remain here three days without a valid passport. On the fourth day you'll be deported and sent back to Europe on the first available ship." Dandré was furious. "Madame only cares about her art. She doesn't get mixed up in politics! And I am a conservative White Russian, a member of the Duma."

"The Duma doesn't exist anymore," the commissioner reminded him coldly, and he began to jot something down in a notebook, ignoring Dandré completely. Molinari, instead of trying to help out, remained silent, leaning his elbow on the commissioner's desk. Mr. Dandré was so angry he almost had a seizure. "We've had enough bloodshed as it is," he said. "Why do you think we're here, instead of in Europe? Because we're running away from the war, that's why, each and every member of this troupe. And you're going to send us back there!" And, he added, his face purple, "This company is *my* responsibility. The youngsters are innocent and several of the older dancers are British citizens. As to the invalid passports, I'm willing to sail back to New York as soon as possible and visit the English ambassador there, a personal friend of ours. Applying for English visas shouldn't be a problem." He dried his bald pate with his white linen handkerchief before replacing his bowler hat. Madame didn't utter a word; all the color had drained from her face.

The young man wearing sunglasses whispered something in the commissioner's ear. I guessed he was a journalist, and just managed to catch what he said: "Madame has been invited to a reception in her honor at the governor's palace this evening, sir, and maybe you should be more careful. She's internationally well known, and I've been asked to write a piece about her for a local magazine." The commissioner frowned and swore under his breath. He'd never heard of the famous dancer before, but he bowed stiffly. "Very well. Since our guest is a celebrity, we'll do away with our restriction for the time being. She can remain on the island for three weeks, until her husband gets new passports."

Once we came out of the police station Madame looked at Dandré in dismay. "The czar and his family detained! The government fallen under a coup d'état! Amazing!" she said, eyes wide with wonder. "What does it all mean?" Madame took Dandré's arm with a trembling hand. "It means," Dandré answered, "that we, as Russian citizens, are now pariahs without a country. We've become flotsam at the mercy of the waves." Madame bowed her head, as if a huge weight had fallen on her shoulders.

We walked out of the police station, heads reeling, and headed back toward the hotel. Molinari trailed behind us like a crow at a wake. Our spirits were in tatters, but thankfully our dance troupe was still together. And our faith in Holy Mother Russia and in our art was intact.

That afternoon we tried to keep our courage up as best we could. Talking about our beautiful city made us feel better; it helped us overcome the feeling that we were now unmoored and might drift apart. The company was our only family, and we needed desperately to hold on to one another. I never felt as close to Lyubovna Federovna as I did then, stern and dour as she was. I almost believed I could love her.

"Niura was a premature baby," Lyubovna said to me in her hotel room, as she poured a cup of tea from the samovar she had just unpacked. "You should have seen her when she was seven months old; she was no bigger than a baby rabbit. We lived on Kolomenskaya Street then, where I did the laundry for several well-to-do families. One of them was the Poliakoffs, a very wealthy Jewish family. Lazar Poliakoff's father was a banker on Nevsky Prospekt. They owned one of the largest investment houses in St. Petersburg, with branches all over Europe.

"One day I saw the son of the family come out of the house and he followed me to the apartment on Kolomenskaya Street. He was wearing a magnificent black astrakhan coat with matching hat of the same curly, jet-black fur. He closed the door after him and asked my mother to go out and get him a pack of cigarettes. As soon as we were alone, he pushed me on top of the bundle of dirty clothes I'd been carrying and raped me. He came back every week after that, and when I had my little Niura, Mother only had to see him from the window and she'd say: 'There's the black mutton that dropped little Niura on our doorstep again; he's come for another pack of cigarettes.' "

Lyubovna got up from where she was sitting and went over to light a votive candle in front of the Virgin of Vladimir. She crossed herself, as if asking pardon for what she had just said. "Don't worry, the Virgin knows what you're talking about," I said, trying to comfort her. "She doesn't mind." I laughed a little, but what she was telling me was embarrassing. I didn't stop her, though. I wanted to know everything about Madame.

"Things went on like that for another year, and then young Lazar stopped coming. Much later I learned that the Poliakoffs had found out about their son's 'mistake' and sent him to the university at Le Hague to get him out of harm's way. They paid me a small stipend, so I could adequately feed and care for the child, and they had a rabbi visit us, who taught her Scripture. Little Niura, as I always called her, had no idea who her father was but she knew she was different. One day, someone sent a photographer to the tiny apartment, and the man told us he was to take our portrait. He brought his camera with him, and the clothes we were supposed to wear for the shot: two black silk dresses with tight sleeves and narrow lace dollars. I was instructed to sit in a chair and Niura to stand a little away from me, as if we weren't related. She faced the camera with that expression of superiority I know so well.

"Niura was petite and finely boned. Her legs were long and her feet were beautifully arched. She had a great affinity with birds, quick, darting movements and a light step. The rich black silk of her sleeves made the long, tapered fingers of her hands look even more delicate. I myself am a large woman; I come from peasant stock. I was born in the village of Bor, on the banks of the Volga, whose waters are white as milk because it's the river that nurtures Russia—and my hands are as large as a man's. But I'm an honest woman. I've always worked for my keep. My knuckles are red from scrubbing the clothes of the rich, and I don't see why I should hide them. So when the photographer told me to slide my hands discreetly under the folds of my dress, I placed them squarely on my knees, to make sure they stood out in the portrait.

"Sometimes when I looked at Niura, I couldn't believe she was my daughter. I couldn't read or write, but thanks to the rabbi, Niura learned how to read Scripture and could write beautifully. Because she was always close to me and saw me pray every day, she became very pious and prayed to our holy icons, kneeling among the candles and kissing them.

"A few days later, the photographer came back to the apartment and gave me a print of the portrait in a cardboard frame. I liked it very much and put it on the living-room table. I wondered if the photographer had taken a print to Niura's father also, the black mutton who stopped coming to butt me. Maybe he was going to cut me out of the picture entirely, I thought, or maybe it's a convenient way for him to prove that his little girl's mother was Russian and if he were caught in a pogrom, it might help him survive. Lazar must have guessed I would never give up Niura, though, because he never offered to adopt her.

"Ever since Niura was a little girl she loved to dance: if it was snowing outside she'd copy the way a snowflake drifted down the windowpane. If it was autumn she'd sway like a leaf fluttering in the wind. Once, when she was in the park with me, she saw a dragonfly and began to imitate its nervous flight with marvelous precision. The rabbi saw her do this, and he must have said something to the Poliakoffs because a few days later he brought me a note from Lazar's father. The Poliakoffs were a cultured family, and they had influence in all the right places. The note said I was to take little Niura to the Imperial Ballet School on Theater Street, between Nevsky Prospekt and the Fontanka River—St. Petersburg's most exclusive district— and leave her there. I'd be able to visit her on Sundays, and she would be well taken care of. I was shattered, but I prayed to the Virgin and left little Niura in their hands.

"I had seen the Imperial Ballet School from the outside on my way to services at Vladimir Cathedral from Kolomenskaya Street. It was an elegant eighteenth-century palace, with many windows to let in the light and large salons with thirty-foot ceilings. When we arrived and I asked how much the tuition would be, a lady in a black shift said I shouldn't worry, everything was paid for in advance. She handed Niura two brown cashmere uniforms, four white muslin shirts, a pair of pumps, a pair of short leather booties, books, and study materials. I looked at the woman in wonder, but didn't dare ask questions for fear it would all evaporate like a dream.

"The pupils of the Imperial Ballet School were formally adopted by the czar; the parents virtually relinquished all rights over them. Niura was a boarding student for ten years. She loved it there. The school was run with an iron discipline based on military principles, the same that ruled the Imperial Cadet School. Niura's days were spent in rigorous exercise classes to develop her body, and she took courses on harmony, composition, and musical theory. She could read music and even direct an orchestra. I thought all this was wonderful, but my old fear hadn't left my heart, and I prayed every night that when Niura finished her studies she could stay by my side.

"The Imperial Ballet School owed its existence to the czar's subsidy, and the Romanovs considered the ballerinas their personal baubles. They went to the school often, to observe the students' progress or just to talk to them about art, music, or perhaps more private subjects, discreetly discussed. Niura saw the czar several times up close during the matinees given for the parents of the students. Like most Russians, she had ambivalent feelings toward him.

"Every year, on December sixth, there was a lavish celebration for Czar Nicholas's birthday. On that day the theater was full of small children and young people: tiers of boxes tightly packed with girls and boys in uniform from the Lyceum, the Naval Academy, all the popular St. Petersburg schools. Every child received a box of candies with a portrait of either Czar Nicholas, the czarina, or the czarevitch on the lid. During the intermission, tea and refreshments were served in several foyers, and the wait staff wore gala red uniforms adorned with imperial eagles on their collars. Cool almond milk, deliciously perfumed, was served. On one occasion they were all taken to kiss the czar's hand after the performance. Nicholas II was sitting in the imperial box next to Czarina Alexandra, and they must have been going to a ball afterward, because both were regally dressed. The czar wore a blue sash across his gala uniform and the czarina had on a coronet of stars. The czar inquired: 'Who was the little girl who danced the golden fish in *Le Roi Candaule*?' Niura stepped forward and curtsied gracefully before him. 'How did the shepherd's magic ring happen to be on you, when it was supposed to be at the bottom of the sea?' Niura was wearing a fish costume, modeled out of gold papier-mâché, and inside the fish's mouth was hidden a small box where the ring was put. Niura bent down and explained how it worked. The czar was enchanted. He smiled. 'I would never have guessed it,' he said.

"You can imagine Niura's amazement when the next day she heard that the czar had gone on a hunting expedition to the province of the Urals, where there was a terrible famine. He came back ten days later with one hundred deer, fifty-six goats, fifty boar, ten foxes, twenty-seven hares—two hundred forty-three animals shot within a week's time. 'Why did he shoot them? He can't possibly eat all that,' Niura asked. Poor heart, she was that innocent!

"The day of Niura's graduation I was very proud of her. Her grandmother came all the way from the village of Ligovo to be there, and Niura looked beautiful in the white tulle skirt and delicate diamanté wings in which she danced *La Sylphide*, her graduation ballet. All the dancers took part and the audience was mainly composed of parents, although the royal family was also present. They were sitting in the Maryinsky's royal box, just to the left of the stage, with the gilded crown carved on top and the gold fauteuils with blue velvet upholstery. They looked like a postcard: Czar Nicholas with his watery eyes; the czarina with her hard, unyielding German mouth; and their children, dressed in angel-white muslin. It was hard to see them as the oppressor, or a flock of devils in disguise.

"I had sewn the wreath of tiny roses that Niura wore that day around her head and she looked happy and carefree during her graduation exercises. That's why I was so surprised when, a few days later, she arrived at the apartment carrying two suitcases with everything she owned. She was moving back with me, she said, and we would have to change our lifestyle. 'At school we were taught that our progress in the world depended not only on the quality of our dancing, but on the magnanimity of our patrons. I'm tired of being poor, Mother. I should have made that my motto to start with.' I sighed with resignation. Now we would both have to survive on the small income the Poliakoffs sent us, which was barely enough for one person.

"When Niura began to get flowers from bewhiskered, portly gentlemen who brought her home from the theater in splendid carriages late at night, I began to worry. One evening I went to her room after she went to bed and said, 'You don't have to do this, Niura, I can go back to washing and ironing.' Niura looked at me with her large, luminous eyes. 'Thank you, Mama,' she answered. 'But my dancing will support us both; you have nothing to worry about.' That calmed me, because my little Niura was never wrong.

"Every time I saw Niura dance at the Maryinsky, I thought the same thing. Sitting high up in the gallery I could see the audience in the orchestra seats below, sumptuously dressed in lace and velvet and glistening with jewels. On stage the dancers wore similar apparel and jewelry. No wonder *Le Miroir* was St. Petersburg's favorite ballet. The aristocrats were convinced they deserved it all and were fascinated by their own spectacle. Meanwhile in the countryside the peasants continued to starve, because all the food was needed for the soldiers who were fighting a war against Japan.

"Matilde Kschessinska was prima ballerina when my Niura graduated. They danced together at the Maryinsky Theater a few times, and were always competing for the limelight. Matilde also had many followers who would have done anything to advance her career. Being older, she had much more experience than Niura. She obtained the favors of Nicholas II when he was still the czarevitch, and he bought her a magnificent house on the English Embankment, a very fashionable address. Matilde loved to dance wearing the jewelry the czarevitch gave her as a present. Sometimes she wore three diamond necklaces at a time, which made her look like a poodle because she was short and wore her curly hair cropped close to her head. She was not a great ballerina. She was very polished but she only danced 'on the surface,' to entertain the audience. She never danced from the depths, like my Niura did.

"Czar Nicholas had many artist friends, not all of them dancers. One of the most famous was a little girl, an American diva whose name I can't remember. She was ten years old, and created a furor when she appeared at the Winter Palace singing 'Ah! non giunge' from Bellini's *La Sonnambula*. She was warbling like a nightingale and standing on a little red plush platform with wheels when they rolled her out to the center of the stage. The ovation was so great that the czar and the czarina sent for her at the end of the performance. That was the same night my Niura danced in *Le Roi Candaule*. She was very young, but she never forgot the doll-like diva, dressed in a fan-like frock and wearing a hussar's red jacket, who threw her a rose as she went by. The czar presented the young prima donna with a coronet of diamonds that night, a smaller reproduction of the one that graced the czarina's head."

"At this time Niura took a large apartment in Anglisky Prospekt. I didn't know how she could afford it, but it was better not to ask. It was a new building, and we were to move in together. I was ecstatic. It meant I didn't have to be separated from my daughter again. I'd cook for her, wash and iron her clothes. No one was to know I was her mother, so my presence wouldn't embarrass her.

"The apartment was beautiful—big, lofty rooms decorated with white Empire furniture upholstered in blue silk. Niura's bed had a latticed headboard and footboard, with garlands of roses carved over them, and her bedspread was exactly the same ice blue as the Neva, which could be seen from her window. In what was once a salon for entertaining guests, Niura set up her own dance studio, with an immense mirror on one wall and a barre the length of the room on the opposite side.

"The income from Niura's friends and the Poliakoffs' stipend meant we could live with a certain degree of comfort. Niura also began to make more money dancing. Whenever she performed at benefits and galas people flocked to see her, because it was rumored that she came from a humble background. This was pleasing to people with Bolshevik sympathies. Matilde Kschessinska's imperial connections hurt her, and although she still held the title of prima ballerina at the Maryinsky, Niura was gradually taking her place in the public's eye.

"Niura never showed any interest in meeting the Poliakoffs, for which I was grateful, although I always suspected my daughter was secretly proud of her Jewish blood. It set her apart from the St. Petersburg haut monde we both despised. Although no one knew who Niura's real father was, one of Kschessinska's friends at the Maryinsky could dig up the secret by asking questions about my illegitimate daughter, which could lead to Niura's expulsion from the city.

"The Imperial Ballet was not exempt from the upheavals tearing Russia apart. Many of the dancers were students at the university and were thus very well informed about political developments. Niura began to attend Bolshevik meetings, and one day she stood up on a desk at school and made a forthright speech in which she poured scorn on an army that cut down defenseless people and saw innocent workers as the enemy. She was the daughter of the washerwoman from Kolomenskaya Street, she said, and she had everything to gain if the revolution was successful. She lent her apartment to the students of the ballet school who went on strike, so they could meet there. Then one day the Poliakoffs shut down their bank and unexpectedly left the country. Niura and I were left practically destitute.

"The night she found out about it Niura was dancing *La Fille Mal Gardée*—The Unchaperoned Girl—a ballet full of verve and playful coquetry, at a benefit gala for the families of the sailors who perished in the destruction of the Russian fleet. At the end of the performance she received a bouquet of roses in her dressing room with a card from 'the Honorable Victor

Dandré' attached to it. Each rose came skewered by a piece of wire and Niura couldn't bear the sight of them. She asked me to free them from their torture, taking out the wires and placing the flowers in water. I did so immediately, and put the vase on her dresser.

"The Honorable Dandré wished to invite Mademoiselle to a private dinner at his apartment after the performance, the card said. Niura received dozens of cards like that every night. This time, however, instead of ripping the card in two, Niura penned a quick answer on the back and had it returned to her admirer.

"Victor Dandré was a Frenchified Russian who had lived in Paris for a while. He was tall and bear-chested, with a red mustache that compensated for his bald head, and large, ruddy jowls that trembled when he laughed. He was known in St. Petersburg as a successful investor, and he had a comfortable situation. That night he invited Niura to one of the city's many luxurious restaurants with private chambers at the back. Afterwards they went to Dandré's plush apartment on Italiansky Street.

" 'Our economic problems are over, Mother: now we won't have to starve or sell our home because of the strike. I've finally found the protector the Maryinsky Imperial Ballet School always expected me to have,' Niura said. I began to cry; I understood well enough. I made her kneel down before the icon of the Virgin of Vladimir and ask for forgiveness. Niura kissed the lower corner of the icon and bent her head in front of it. The decision cost her a great deal. She'd always looked down on Kschessinska and the other ballerinas, who readily accepted the Maryinsky's patrons' demands in order to go on dancing.

"Mr. Dandré always kept his bachelor place in Italiansky Street; he never moved in with us. Niura didn't feel attracted to him, but he was a strong man and a shove from him would send any unwelcome admirer crashing against the wall. At the time, Dandré had a theater box at the Maryinsky, which he shared with a gentleman friend, and he went to see Niura dance every evening. He realized she had a unique talent, and that if she stayed in Russia she'd never be able to free herself from the 'shroud of the Imperial Ballet School,' as he used to say. She was stifled at the Maryinsky, where only old-fashioned ballets were produced. In Paris and London she could blossom into a true artist. One day he suggested she go on tour and visit Helsinki, Riga, Stockholm, and other cities of the Baltic coast. She could dance there accompanied by a small troupe and he would escort her part of the way. The tour was an enormous success, and after that, Niura began to go abroad more often. Dandré convinced her to buy a house in London, in the suburb of Golders Green—William Turner's famous Ivy House—so she already had one foot out of the country when the Russian Revolution began.

"Then we sailed off to America. Our first tour took the company across the whole United States by train. We visited forty cities, from New Orleans to Seattle, in a span of nine weeks, and sometimes Niura had to dance two performances a day. She earned thousands of dollars a week, but at the end of the tour she didn't have any money. Mr. Dandré mapped out pulverizing schedules for her and would disappear with the profits at the end of each month, although he insisted he spent it all on our traveling expenses, new costumes, salaries, and hotels. We stayed in New York for a while, where Dandré made Niura appear in all kinds of advertisements—Pond's Vanishing Cream, for instance—which was perfect for the image of Niura fading away in a swan costume. Dandré himself wrote a clever ditty for the publicity campaign in the States, which went: 'Wintry winds / frosts and fogs / have little effect or none / on a face protected by Pond's.'

"Mr. Dandré was already middle-aged when Niura met him. Some said he was corrupt, and it wouldn't have been surprising. In czarist Russia that was common, everybody was like that. But he was affectionate with Niura. He spent a fortune on her designer clothes because he insisted it was good for business. In his opinion, every little girl's dream was to be a ballerina, so Niura had to look exactly like a ballerina's dream.

"The ballet world was full of eccentric people. One of the most fascinating persons Niura met in Europe was Serge Diaghilev. He was a strange man. He liked male stars better than female ones, and in his ballets the male dancer always eclipsed the ballerina. A shock of white hair sprouting from his forehead gave him a diabolic air, but he had a passion for art, and could recognize true talent when he found it. He used to stroll down the Champs-Elysées with his monocled eye flashing in every direction as if defying the world, a red carnation in his lapel, arm in arm with one of his gentlemen friends. Once, years earlier, he did this with a famous Irish writer who visited Paris after having spent time in an English jail—Wilde or Wile was his name, I can't be sure—and their picture came out in all the papers.

"Diaghilev and Vaslav Nijinsky, the *dieu de la danse*, were lovers, they lived in open promiscuity. They say Diaghilev was obsessed with germs, and always kissed his friends through a handkerchief. When Nijinsky danced *L'Après-midi d'un Faune*, he wore a skin-tight leotard with rippling brown spots on it and mimed the sexual act on a scarf spread out on the floor. The silk scarf was supposed to belong to a nymph, but it could just as well have been Serge Diaghilev's opera muffler. The ballet, set to Debussy's music, was very avant-garde and shockingly beautiful, but even in Paris it created a huge scandal.

"Diaghilev was as corrupt as they come, but Nijinsky was as innocent as a child, he couldn't understand Diaghilev's obsessions. He wanted a normal life and married Romola de Pulsky during a tour of Argentina in 1913. Romola was the daughter of Hungary's foremost actress, she was wealthy and beautiful, but she was also ambitious and wanted to share Nijinsky's fame. What a tragedy that was! As a Russian, you must know what it means to be married to a Hungarian: they are like leeches and never let go, sucking your blood to the end. Nijinsky was still in love with Diaghilev, but he couldn't admit it to himself. Worst of all, he depended on the Ballets Russes to keep on dancing, but Diaghilev never forgave him for getting married to Romola and kicked him out of the company. Eventually Nijinsky went mad and was interned in Bellevue Sanatorium.

"But that was much later. When we traveled to Paris in 1910, Niura joined Diaghilev's Ballets Russes at Monte Carlo. For a marvelous season she performed with Nijinsky as her partner, but she didn't stay long. She was out of there like a bullet and returned to the Maryinsky. She's always been proud and never danced second to anyone. She was prima ballerina *assoluta* in every company she ever danced with. Vaslav Nijinsky, on the contrary, who came from a humble background, was easy prey for Diaghilev. Serge was the son of a cavalry colonel from the Urals, and he charmed poor Nijinsky into renouncing his contract with the Imperial Ballet and joining the Ballets Russes full time. Nijinsky reigned supreme in it, as Niura found out. But only for a short time. He was the perfect example of what happened to you when you let your heart get under your feet, Niura said.

"When we moved to London my daughter set out to create her own ballet company with Dandré's help, but it was a risky venture—the lamb bedding down with the wolf, you might say. It was around that time—June of 1912—when disaster struck. Dandré, who still lived part of the year in St. Petersburg, where he was chairman of the Commission of Inspectors to the St. Petersburg City Council, was accused of illegal use of city funds. He borrowed large sums, invested them, skimmed off the profits, and returned them to the fund a month later. But one day the operation took longer than it should have and Dandré got caught. He was prosecuted and put in jail. Niura had eighteen thousand dollars put away, the greater part of her earnings after her first grueling European tour, and she wired the money directly to Russia to get Dandré out on bail. When I found out about it, I was furious. I would have let the man rot in prison. Not a week passed before Dandré slipped away from St. Petersburg and secretly crossed the border over to Denmark, where Niura was waiting for him. She brought him to London, and he's been living off our backs ever since."

All through Lyubovna's story I sat listening as if in a trance, balanced on the edge of my chair. My tea had turned cold, and the cup stood on the table untouched. A storm of emotions was raging in my chest. I disliked Lyubovna for her groveling, but despised Dandré for having broken Madame's spirit.

10 I went to see Madame in her room at the Malatrassi the next morning. She embraced me and began to cry openly. Dandré sat on the bed, and went on thoughtfully smoking his cigar, a stern expression on his face. He was traveling the next day to New York, he said, to get all the members of our troupe English passports.

I told Madame she had to pull herself together, because if the dancers saw her fall apart, there would be no hope for our company. "This is only a temporary crisis, one of the many we've already had to endure, and the Virgin of Vladimir will protect us," I said, trying to raise her morale. But a premonition had seized me; I was afraid we'd be trapped on the island.

That afternoon we went out for a little sightseeing and Molinari went with us. He spoke French, Spanish, and English, and we were told he also worked for the government as a translator. I wondered at his versatility. He was dressed in black from head to toe, and his yellow eyes roamed about like a vulture's, ready to pounce on whatever caught his attention. If Madame lagged behind, or if I stopped to speak to people in the street, he'd be next to us in an instant, urging us to walk on. There was a lot of activity downtown, large crowds of people singing the American anthem and cheering at every turn, waving small American flags. A military band was playing on the corner of Calle Comercio, which led down to the piers. It was good music, gay and informal, and we let it flood over us so as not to think about what had happened. The American flag was flying in front of the schools, above the post office, at the entrance to the harbor; it even hung from the windows of the Municipal Theater and the balcony of the Casino of Puerto Rico. We wondered what was the reason for so much zeal.

A line of uniformed recruits marched toward the wharf, knapsacks on their backs, carrying Winchester rifles. The column was headed by still more flags, and a large band played a march by John Philip Sousa, the American composer. I recognized it immediately because the company had danced to it in New York's Hippodrome, where Sousa's band forgot all about us and went on playing until we almost collapsed from exhaustion on the stage. Once in a while, though, the Puerto Rican soldiers would break into a *paso doble*, a spirited Spanish dance accompanied by castanets and tambourines. They would fall out of step and begin to run a little to keep up with the fast rhythm of the music, and from the back of the column it looked as if they were dancing the rumba. This made Madame laugh.

"Where are they off to?" she asked.

"They're companies A and B of the Puerto Rican Battalion," Molinari replied. "They're sailing this evening for Colón and the Panama Canal, to defend it from possible German submarine attack." And he pointed toward the *Buford*, the ship anchored on the harbor, where it had docked that morning.

Madame was amazed. "And why should they defend Panama? It's not their country, is it?" she asked.

Molinari smiled ingratiatingly. "It is now, Madame! We were made American citizens only last month, and we have to defend our citizenship with our lives." Dandré agreed stolidly, while Madame stared at him in disgust. She had long ago given up trying to civilize him, but he always surprised her with his crassness. "That's impossible. How can you become citizens of one country if you live in another?" she asked. "That's exactly what you'll be doing, Madame, in order to survive," Molinari answered with an unctuous smile. Madame stamped her foot in anger, but couldn't deny what Molinari had said. She would soon be a British subject, whether she liked it or not.

Madame raced ahead of us to march beside the last soldier, who held a shorn lamb in his arms. "Where are you taking the poor thing? Is it going to Panama, too?" she asked. "Of course! It's the battalion's mascot. St. John's lamb is our country's national symbol." Madame laughed and clapped her hands. "I think I'm going to love it here, Masha," she told me. "How can you resist a people who have a lamb as their national symbol?"

As we crossed the city we looked around more carefully. Well-to-do women on the island dressed much as they did in Russia during the summer when they went strolling down Nevsky Prospekt: in white muslin or linen gowns, with elegant hats on their heads and parasols in their hands. Men wore traditional white linen suits and straw boaters. Adults in the street were very friendly, and looked at passersby directly in the eyes instead of avoiding our gazes, as they often did in St. Petersburg or, for that matter, New York.

Fortaleza Street was full of stores: hardware, textiles, shoes, bedding, children's clothes, all exhibited in the windows in an unsophisticated way. My favorite was La Casa de las Medias y los Botones, "The house of stockings and buttons." Madame and I stopped in front of it as we walked by. The display window looked like something out of *A Thousand and One Nights*: buttons made of ivory, of fake mother-of-pearl, of glass that shone like diamonds, fake gold, silver, all displayed on wooden drawers that rose all the way up to the ceiling. They also sold silk ribbons by the spool and all sorts of feathers: ostrich, marabou, pheasant. The rolls of lace, silk damask, brocades, wools, and linens recently arrived from Europe stood spilled over the mahogany counters like newly discovered treasures. The store was swarming with customers, all of them asking to be helped. Madame and I stood there, holding hands, and stared at what was going on. "People in San Juan must love to dress up," Madame said. "They're like me! We must come back here soon, to have new costumes made."

Fortaleza Street was narrow, and it had a chapel named after Saint Jude, one of my favorite saints because he intercedes for lost souls, and mine strayed long ago. His statue was in a niche, and Madame and I liked to pray to him. It was a nice chapel, with domino-marble-tiled floor and a gilded image of La Monserrate—a black Virgin—sitting under the altar dome. We didn't mind praying in Catholic churches because they resemble the Orthodox so much. They are dark and mysterious, so you can meditate on life's enigmas. We disliked Protestant churches, where everything was bare and cold, like the churches in New York where there wasn't a single saint and Madame and I got so bored we immediately started to yawn. Catholics love their saints, and on this island they seem to love them in a special way, because in almost every house we looked in there was a small altar with old saints carved in wood holding small, lighted candles in their hands.

Most of the buildings were dilapidated. Balconies with

wooden balusters or elaborate ironwork looked toward the Atlantic and took in the breeze. Walls hundreds of years old were
shedding plaster as if they were molting. The whole place
smelled of moss, and a dank humidity crept up from the slip-
pery cobblestones. And yet I liked it. In St. Petersburg, everything is old. When a city is new it feels uncomfortable. Trees,
sidewalks, houses are full of the sounds of the present and of the
past. The people who live there are listening to those who lived
there before. San Juan was like that, too.

Because of the military celebrations the streets were teem-
ing with automobiles: Studebakers, Peerless Eights, Franklins,
Willis Overlands. People had come from all over the island to
see the parade, and they went on arriving. It seemed as if half
of them were driving luxury cars, and the other half were
straggling barefoot down the cobblestone streets. But we didn't
see the magnificent yellow-and-black Pierce-Arrow that had
picked Madame up at the wharf anywhere, no matter how hard
we looked. As we went down San Justo Street a group of children, barefoot and wearing tattered, grimy smocks, skipped
over a hopscotch grid they had drawn on the street with chalk.
Many looked ill-fed and in poor health. They stopped playing
and began asking Madame for money. They broke her heart,
and she would have taken them back to the hotel with her if it
hadn't been for Mr. Dandré.

We were almost back at the Malatrassi when we passed a
large concrete building which was evidently a school. It looked
relatively new; the American flag stood in front of it also. The
windows that faced the street were open, and we could hear
the children singing in English. The school day was just beginning. First they pledged allegiance to the flag; then they sang
the American national anthem. Madame and I climbed on a
nearby bench and watched, fascinated. How could it be possible

that children on this island were taught in English when they only spoke Spanish? This was a mystery to us.

A very elegant gentleman entered one of the classrooms on crutches, apparently about to give a lecture. There was something remarkable about him: he seemed to exude an extraordinary energy, his eyes blazed from his pale face with a dark fire. He only had one leg. The other one had been amputated, and his pant leg, immaculately pressed and starched, was carefully folded around the stump. He was talking to a group of students, obviously a class. The youngsters listened reverently, and people on the street also stopped to hear. Suddenly the man raised his voice, and the whole school, the street packed with people, even the trees full of birds, fell silent around them—or so it seemed.

We couldn't understand a word he was saying, but we were sure he was reciting a poem. A police van pulled up in front of the school, siren screaming, and a group of officers ran up the front steps and barged into the classroom. They lifted the poet up unceremoniously by the arms and whisked him away. Madame was horrified and ran after them, wanting to stop them from roughing up the crippled man, but Dandré ran after her and held her fast. Molinari muttered angrily at our backs: "That's Manuel Aljama, reciting trash to our students again. American school principals are too lenient. The traitor should be shot!" Dandré hurried us on toward the hotel. "San Juan may not be as peaceful as it seems after all," I heard him say as he escorted us away.

We were all invited to La Fortaleza, and that evening we went to the governor's mansion to meet some of Madame's local admirers. She was to dance *The Dying Swan* in a private performance in the gardens. La Fortaleza was near the Malatrassi, so a few minutes before 7:00 p.m., we walked there single file wearing our evening finery, because the sidewalks were so narrow. Many of the shop and restaurant signs were in English, although everyone spoke Spanish in the streets. With Molinari leading the way, we turned right on General O'Donnell, formerly Calle San José, and then right again on General Allen, formerly Calle Fortaleza. Molinari kept translating the names from what they were before as if he enjoyed it, which made us cringe. We much preferred the Spanish names, which were several centuries old: San Francisco, San Sebastián, and San José, who are also holy in our Orthodox faith.

We passed a small chapel built over the city's ancient walls. "A miracle happened here some years ago during a popular feast," Molinari said. "Horse races are an important part of San Juan's Carnival celebrations, and dozens of horsemen partici-

pate in them. One day a runaway horse plunged over the
eighty-foot embankment at the end of Calle Cristo. They say
horse and rider hurtled into the rocks below, but the rider was
saved by the Virgen de la Providencia." Molinari told the story
with an ironic snigger, but Madame ignored him. "Look,
Masha! A sacred place!" she cried, kneeling in front of the
chapel's altar. Madame looked at the jagged rocks below, imag-
ining the poor rider's terrible fright as he tumbled through the
air. Devoutly, she crossed herself.

When we arrived at the governor's mansion, there were already
many guests waiting for us in the garden and almost as many
security guards. The guards stood around like stolid man-
nequins in their uniforms, staring with glassy eyes straight
ahead of them, their hands clasped behind their backs. We wondered if the reason there were so many police agents was because we were Russian and the governor was suspicious of us.
Political assassinations were common enough in our country
and Madame, they were informed by the police, was a Bolshevik sympathizer. The whole thing was absurd.

Governor Arthur Yager, tall and bewhiskered, stood next to
his slender daughter, Diana, in the receiving line of the Blue
Room, under a portrait of an overweight Queen Isabel II of
Spain, a huge dumpling wrapped in blue satin. Diana often gave
teas at La Fortaleza, and since her mother was ill, she graciously
performed the functions of official hostess. She was the one
who, upon hearing that Madame had arrived on the island, had
insisted that her father hold a reception in her honor.

Molinari informed us that Governor Yager was a graduate
and former president of Georgetown University and a good
friend of President Wilson's; he certainly looked the part. He

wore a white linen suit and the suede shoes that were his trade-
mark. His hair grew in tight silver curls around his head in the
manner of the Roman emperors. He was evidently a cultured
man and the mansion was decorated in good taste: colonial oil
paintings hung on the walls, and antique mahogany chairs and
consoles graced the corners holding up candelabra like oiled,
dark-skinned servants. He had heard about Madame's Ballets
Russes in New York, and was excited to meet its dancers. As
we entered the receiving room he bowed graciously before
Madame and kissed her hand.

Governor Yager was from Kentucky, Molinari explained, and
because he was familiar with the Appalachians, he understood
the problems of an agricultural island mired in poverty. In fact,
that was why President Wilson had named him to his post as
governor. I thought I detected a sarcastic tone to Molinari's
words but I couldn't be sure. Molinari was a puzzle—I didn't
know what to think of him. He was Bracale's sub-agent, but I
suspected he also worked for the police commissioner. The day
before, he had told us himself that he was a translator for the
government. Today he went on about how he "hated the grin-
gos' guts," because he had lost thousands of dollars in his coffee
plantation when the U.S. left Puerto Rican coffee outside its
tariff walls. His product couldn't be shipped to Europe as it used
to be, and on the mainland no one had heard about it. His coffee grains were rotting like drops of blood in the dense forest.

As a native Kentuckian, Molinari explained, Governor Yager
was familiar with the ins and outs of the liquor business, and he
was aware that the healthy revenues from rum production kept
the island from sinking completely into ruin. Yager opposed the
dry law vigorously, but Congress insisted that a plebiscite be
held; the law was applied to Puerto Rico, after all. In Congress's
opinion, the least Puerto Rico could do, in exchange for Amer-

ican citizenship, was vote for Prohibition. "And Congress was right!" Molinari told us. "Since Puerto Ricans are only semi-civilized, it's better if they don't drink rum at all, because it only makes them more ungovernable."

The whole story was incredible. "Russians drink vodka from the cradle, and pouring it into the Neva would not alter our taste for it," Madame snapped at Molinari, shaking a finger at him. But Molinari shrugged his shoulders and ambled on.

Madame made her way among the guests; her four principal ballerinas and I surrounded her in a tight little phalanx. We could feel danger throbbing around us, in the heat of the crowd. The men wore dinner jackets, and the ladies' evening gowns were ablaze with jewelry. Although most of the guests were Puerto Rican, it was considered impolite to speak Spanish because the governor and his daughter didn't, so everyone spoke English with a thick accent. We saw the police commissioner there, too, probably a fixture at all the formal affairs at the governor's palace.

Madame wore her black-draped chiffon Madame de Grès evening gown, which ended in a vanishing point at the waist, baring her back provocatively. The governor asked for silence and tapped his knife against his glass: "I wish to present to you one of Russia's greatest artists," he said. "Madame is one of the wonders of the world. Let us drink to her health and happiness." He lifted his champagne glass (the dry law didn't apply at the governor's) in Madame's direction and raised it to his lips.

Dandré drew near and shook the governor's hand. "Let's drink both to the Russians and to the Americans! May our people be friends forever!" he said. An awkward silence followed, as the governor made no answer but stared suspiciously at Dandré. It was rumored that soon the new Soviet government would ally itself with the Central Powers and Americans and Russians would become enemies: this was verified several months later, when the treaty of Brest-Litovsk between Russia and Germany was signed. But we weren't aware of this because of our recent isolation at sea. As usual, Dandré was making an ass of himself, and Madame innocently followed his lead. "The United States has so much and our country has so little. Almost ten million people have died in Europe since the war began. Americans and Russians must help each other and put a stop to this bloody war." The commissioner stood nearby and, lifting his glass to Madame's, he drank to the Russians' health without blinking. I gulped mine down, eyes shut, terrified of seeing Madame ridiculed.

Fifteen minutes later Novikov, Madame's partner, pushed his way through the crowd and asked if she wanted to dance a fox-trot. He was short and lithe—a perfect size for Madame on the stage—and he had a splendid physique. We were used to his eccentricities. He spoke with a lisp, lifted his little finger every time he drank from a glass, and was always on the lookout for new romantic conquests. Madame could dance with him as much as she wanted: Dandré was never jealous. At that moment we could see Dandré in the background still talking with Molinari; his tall, tuxedo-clad figure loomed darkly in the distance. Novikov took Madame's arm and led her to the adjoining ballroom, where a musical ensemble was playing. She looked over his shoulder and saw that several local young people were about to join them on the dance floor. Beautifully dressed girls were checking out their carnets with their partners to see who had the first dance.

Novikov whirled Madame around the elegant hall, decorated with gilded eighteenth-century mirrors and marble-topped consoles. I followed as unobtrusively as possible. He was keeping his eyes pegged on a brown-haired ephebe standing near the bar, who looked at him with lovelorn eyes. Madame noticed someone interesting also: the one-legged poet who had held her attention so thoroughly at the school that afternoon. He was sitting by himself next to a potted palm at one end of the room. Madame asked Novikov to whirl her in that direction. When they were near the gentleman, Madame stopped dancing and asked Novikov to get her a second glass of champagne. Novikov winked at her and went off toward the bar.

The gentleman was slender, his neck almost swimming inside his impeccably starched collar. His ears, which stuck out of his head like pale, almost transparent bat wings, gave him an alert and at the same time pathetic look. He trembled slightly, but the same fire was smoldering in his eyes we had noticed that afternoon. "Was that a poem you were reciting in Spanish at the school earlier?" she asked softly. "I heard you from the street, and it was beautiful, even if I couldn't understand a word. What was the title?" Madame spoke to him in French, convinced that the gentleman would understand her, and she wasn't mistaken. His eyes were the color of amber. "It's a poem about death and resurrection," he said. "The school principal didn't know I was going to recite it when they invited me to talk to the students, and when the police arrived, it was too late, they couldn't shut me up. Next time, however, it'll be more difficult. If there is a next time, that is. At least my daughter, Estrella, has promised to recite it at my wake." He looked directly at her, smiling under his huge mustache.

"Why do you write about death?" Madame asked him softly. "You should write about life!"

"Because I can't go on living when freedom isn't possible!" the poet answered vehemently.

Madame shivered and wrapped her shawl more closely about her.

 The crush of people milling about in the Hall of Mirrors began to make me feel claustrophobic. We were about to step into one of the enclosed galleries of louvered windows, which had fanlike, gaily colored panes of glass on top, for a breath of fresh air when Madame ran into a young man with a wide mourning ribbon tied around his upper sleeve. He was slender, with delicate hands and tapered fingers. He wore glasses, and behind them his eyes glowed like coals. He was very good-looking, and he knew it.

"Are you the famous Russian ballerina?" the young man asked eagerly, stepping aside to let Madame through. "I've been looking for you all evening. I'm the one who sent the Pierce-Arrow to pick you up at the wharf this morning. I wanted to receive you in style!"

Madame looked pleasantly surprised, and as they walked out onto the verandah together, I purposely stayed behind a few steps.

They stood looking toward the garden. A Moorish fountain spilled a jet of water into a mosaic basin, and its soft murmur echoed through the enclosed patio. The young man wanted to know everything about the company—where we were staying, how long we were traveling around the island, and what Madame was going to dance that night.

He'd lived in New York, he said, where he had studied journalism, and it didn't take Madame long to discover that he was very well educated. He had read Tolstoy and Dostoyevsky, and began to quote her a passage from *Das Kapital*, his voice full of enthusiasm, until she begged him to stop. Politics upset her, she said. He looked downcast at her lack of interest. Like many young men his age, he wanted to show off.

"I saw you talking to Aljama, our local poet, a minute ago," the young man added. "He's the Don Quixote of our independence movement, you know. Quite a picturesque character."

"I would have liked to talk to him longer, but he walked away. He seemed ill," Madame said.

"He *is* ill. He's a diabetic and lost his leg to gangrene recently. I hear that he's become addicted to morphine. He won't last very long."

"I'm sorry to hear that. Is he one of your well-known poets?"

"He is *the* poet; people travel for miles on foot, across rivers and mountains, just to hear him read his poems in public."

"This afternoon I saw the police manhandle and arrest him at a public school. Why on earth has he been invited here tonight?" Madame said, looking amazed.

The young man laughed softly and took off his glasses to polish them with a linen handkerchief. He shook his head.

"They weren't really arresting him. They pick him up and take him back home all the time. And of course, that's why he was invited here tonight. It's wise to keep your enemy in sight; that way he can do less harm." Madame listened with interest.

The young man had eyes with deep shadows in them, and he stared at her shamelessly. Half concealed behind a Sèvres porcelain urn that stood on a pedestal, I began to feel uncomfortable.

At that moment the governor approached with Diana and another girl accompanying him, one on each arm. Four uniformed security guards followed, a walking wall of muscle and sinew. "This is Estrella Aljama, our famous poet's daughter," the governor announced to Madame. "And this is Diana, my daughter. They are very good friends and they were looking forward to meeting you." The girls giggled, and it was obvious that Estrella, especially, was very shy; she hardly dared look at Madame. Madame turned on the charm and embraced them both, kissing them on the cheek. Then she called over Nadja Bulova and Maya Ulanova and introduced them to the girls, since they were more or less the same age.

"Now you go with them," she said. "You must join our corps de ballet." The girls laughed, immediately at ease, and the four of them went off, chattering away like magpies. I stayed behind eavesdropping, a necessary habit I'd picked up lately to protect Madame. The governor shook hands coldly with the young man and then turned his back to him. He asked Madame if the accommodations at the Malatrassi were adequate and then politely put himself at her service before he walked away.

"Estrella Aljama studies at Lady Lane School, in Norton, Massachusetts, the same finishing school as Diana Yager," the young man explained to Madame. "They are each other's best friends." Madame nodded and looked interested. "Do you know what *estrella* means?" the young man went on. Madame said no. "It means star; the poet named his daughter after the star on our flag. Since the Americans have forbidden us to fly or even to own the Puerto Rican flag, he named his daughter for it. Don't you think that's wonderful?" the young man observed ironically. Madame stared at him, baffled. "I find the lame poet heart-wrenching. He's not at all funny," she murmured.

"We don't get visitors from a country like Russia every day, where everything is being torn down in order to build a brave new world," the young man went on. He took out a silver flask from his vest and discreetly poured some of its contents into Madame's glass, then took a short nip himself. "I think what you're doing in your country is extraordinary. You got rid of the czar and his boyars at a single stroke. But here the American governor and the sugar barons are still very much in power." He took a sip from his glass and looked at Madame with interest. "I hear you sympathize with the Russian Revolution. Is that true?"

"I was a ballerina at the Imperial School of Ballet in St. Petersburg, and the czar was my patron," Madame answered noncommittally. "A revolution is something terrible. I hope you never experience it."

The young man shrugged. "You could be both, an ambassador of the czar *and* a Bolshevik agent! Or perhaps neither. Whatever you are, you're the most beautiful woman I've ever met," he said, bowing. I was so flabbergasted I couldn't move. There was no way I could approach them unnoticed.

"Tell me more about the lame poet," Madame said, purposefully changing the subject.

"I know him well," the young man answered. "He's published several books of verse. He's a toothless lion, though." And he explained how Juan Manuel Aljama, after swearing he would never adopt the enemy's citizenship, had decided to do so when he had to have his leg amputated. He traveled to New York, to Mount Sinai Hospital, to have the operation done there, because he didn't trust local doctors.

"You're very critical of your country, aren't you, Mr. . . . ?" Madame asked. The young man's tuxedo and starched shirt with diamond studs didn't exactly label him as working class.

"Diamantino Márquez, *mucho gusto.*" The young man shook her hand. "I'm a journalist and a poet, and I also play the violin. Forgive me for being sarcastic, but ours is a tragic case. We're the only Latin American country that never became independent: the little caboose at the end of the train, held up by American troops at the close of the Spanish-American War."

A shock of dark hair fell over Diamantino's forehead as he gesticulated angrily. He reminded me of a painting by Caravaggio I saw in St. Petersburg, in which an irate Christ, whip in hand, evicts the unholy merchants from the Temple. He was still wet behind the ears and here was Madame, the star of the Imperial Ballet, listening to him in awe!

It was getting late and Madame anxiously began to look around for Diana Yager. She would be dancing in less than an hour and still had to put on her makeup and costume. She stood on her toes craning her neck to see, and I took advantage of it to reveal myself, stepping out from behind the urn. Madame signaled for me to follow at a discreet distance.

"Well, thanks so much for sending your car around this morning to pick us up, Mr. Márquez. Please excuse me, I have to go now."

"It wasn't my car; it was my godfather's. I was living at his house until recently because my father passed away."

"I'm sorry to hear that. And who was your father?"

"Don Eduardo Márquez, Aljama's best friend. He died six months ago. Thankfully, before Aljama's betrayal." His eyes glistened when he said this, and his voice trembled with anger.

"How old are you, Diamantino, if you don't mind my asking?"

"Twenty. But I feel a lot older. In fact, I could easily be your lover."

Madame was caught completely off guard, and so was I. The idea was outrageous, considering she was almost twice his age. But I could tell she felt powerfully attracted to him because of the dark circles under his eyes and the shadow of a beard on his cheeks. "And have you equally been invited here tonight to be observed, and thus to prevent disaster?" Madame said archly.

"Oh, unexpected things may happen, unexplained accidents that are never solved. But let's talk about something more pleasant, Madame. What did you say you were dancing tonight?"

Two minutes later Madame was half running, half flying up the stairs behind Diana Yager to the governor's private apartment on the second floor. There she would change into her swan costume. I ran after her to help her dress, carrying her makeup case. The garment was made of real swan feathers, and it fit her like a second skin. I pulled the hooks at the back closed and helped her tie her hair into a chignon under the delicate white feather headpiece, which had to be fastened with bobby pins. Then we went downstairs again, where the gaslights in the garden had been turned down and rows of people were already sitting in front of a wooden platform, conversing animatedly. The troupe of dancers stood at the back, half hidden among the giant ferns and peace lilies that fluttered in the night breeze, waiting for Madame's appearance.

Madame stood for a moment next to the platform, took a deep breath, and put her hands around her waist as she collected herself. This was the most important moment of her performance, when she willed herself into becoming what she was going to interpret. Movements had to come from within; they couldn't be mechanical. Madame had danced *The Dying Swan* hundreds of times, but she always conjured up its vision in her mind before performing it.

A violinist, a cellist, and a harpist sat under a frangipani tree, its white blossoms filling the night air with their perfume. A cool evening breeze came up and made Madame's skin crinkle like old silk over her arms and across her exposed chest as she bourréed across the stage to Saint-Saëns's haunting music. The melody began to spin its silver thread into the tropical darkness as she slowly glided over the floor and fluttered her arms, just like a swan struggling to continue its flight. Her body was a ray of light wavering in the darkness. Eventually she fell forward and lay still, her arms stretched over her head in a gesture of surrender. The lights were extinguished, and Madame rose to the applause and received a bouquet of roses from the governor. The last measures of the tone poem lingered in the air.

All of a sudden a bolt of lightning flashed over our heads and a noise like a gunshot rang out. Gray clouds that were accumulating on the horizon collided like powder kegs over the fortress's ramparts, and it began to pour. The red ribbon tied around the bouquet dissolved in a crimson stream of water, staining both the governor's white linen suit and Madame's feather costume. They looked as if they were spattered with blood. Madame shuddered and crossed herself at the bad omen.

Everybody ran for cover under the arched gallery of the restored stables that opened onto the garden, but as Madame hurried offstage, her feet gave way. The crimson stain spreading over her dress *was* blood, after all. Someone had taken a shot at her, but the bullet had only grazed her. We all rallied around, crying out in concern, and helped her down the stairs.

Diamantino Márquez, like everyone else, had disappeared. Only one person stayed behind in the garden: the lame poet leaning on his crutches, completely heedless of the downpour. "You're a poet in your own right, Madame," he said, clapping slowly as the rain streamed down his face. And he bowed deeply as Madame went by.

We took Madame to a nearby hospital run by the Sisters of Charity. The nuns rushed about with sail-like bonnets on their heads and bandaged Madame's arm. They insisted on dressing it with gauze, although her wound was no more than a scratch. Dandré went with Molinari and several bodyguards to La Fortaleza's police station to report the accident. The next morning I rushed out of the hotel to buy the local newspaper, but to my surprise, there was no mention of the attempt on Madame's life. No shot had been fired at the reception; no panicked guests had run out of the garden gates or hidden under the darkened shrubbery the night before. It was all kept quiet.

I was astounded that something like this could happen, when I ran into Molinari on the street. He appeared suddenly from behind a building and loomed over me like a threatening shadow. "Could I have a word with you?" he said quickly, taking me by the arm as I was about to go back upstairs. He reminded me of the devil because of his black suit. He smelled of camphor and mothballs, like my stepfather, and I had a hard time breathing whenever he drew near me. We went into a coffee shop around the corner and he ordered ham-and-cheese *bocadillos* with *café con leche* for both of us. I was terrified, but I wasn't going to let on.

"I want to know what that stuck-up prig talked about with your mistress last night," he said. "She shouldn't be seen with him." I felt relieved it wasn't *me* Molinari was after. "They were talking about the weather," I said defiantly. He looked at me and smiled. "I like you. You've got spunk. Let's make a deal: you want to get rid of Diamantino Márquez and so do I. We should be allies from now on." I gulped down my coffee and *bocadillo*. "Fine," I said, pretending to agree with him. "As soon as I hear something interesting I'll let you know." *"Trato hecho,"* he replied, winking at me as he squeezed my hand.

The attempt on Madame's life made her so nervous that Dr. Malatrassi, the father of the hotel owner, had to be summoned to her room. He prescribed *bromuro* and valerian pills for her, and chamomile tea for the dancers. The whole company was on edge. Novikov refused to walk Madame's dog and wouldn't go out of the hotel at all; Custine began to give the dancers their daily exercises in his bedroom, after moving the bed out into the hallway. Smallens practiced his scores at the hotel's piano bar. The Malatrassi was buzzing like a beehive.

From my room, which was next to Madame's, I could hear her arguing with Dandré about what should be done. The commissioner of police had come by earlier and left a message that he wanted to see Dandré. Did he know what had happened? Would he be able to help us? If it weren't for the nick in Madame's arm, she would be hard put to convince him there had been an attempt on her life. They couldn't agree as to who was behind the shooting: the reactionary sugar barons, who pegged Madame as a Bolshevik, or the radicals who saw her as the czar's ballerina, a relic of Imperial Russia. Madame believed it was the former; Dandré the latter.

While they quarreled loudly in the bedroom, I went on with my duties. Dandré was always ordering me about, to keep me away from Madame, but I didn't mind. Ubiquitous Masha had to be everywhere. I ran upstairs and began to draw Madame's bath. I washed her underwear, polished her shoes, and ironed the dress she'd be wearing that morning. Then I had to go down to the kitchen to bring them their breakfast tray. I was anxious to finish my chores and go out as soon as possible. The atmosphere on the island seemed charged with danger, and I wanted to find out why.

I already knew why the governor's wife hadn't been present at the reception the night before. One of the waiters at La Fortaleza had informed me of her mysterious illness: Mrs. Yager lived like a recluse in the upstairs rooms of the governor's mansion and never came downstairs to any of the parties because she had a neurotic fear of the tropics. She lived in terror of being stricken with TB, typhoid fever, or malaria, all of which were rampant in Puerto Rico—especially among the poor. Whenever she went out, Mrs. Yager wore white cotton gloves to the elbows and a veil covering her face so as not to pick up germs. The situation didn't help the governor, who was a snob who seldom mixed with anyone.

 Two days later Juan Anduce joined Madame's troupe. The company needed to be replenished with new toe shoes, so on the second day after our arrival Dandré had put an ad in the paper asking for a cobbler to come to the Hotel Malatrassi, and three of them turned up. Juan didn't speak any Russian, but he spoke English quite well, and Dandré picked him.

Juan had large, coarse fingers, but he had a magician's touch with shoes. Madame herself taught him how to block the dancers' toe shoes, dipping them in rosin in order to strengthen them before shaping them into cylindrical molds of paste, then upholstering them in pink silk and sewing ribbons on them. He was so successful an apprentice that Madame used to say to me, "Thanks to Juan, our company literally dances on clouds." She broke in a new pair of slippers at every rehearsal, and during a performance sometimes used up to three pairs.

Juan and I immediately became friends and he invited me to visit his workshop, La Nueva Suela, which was on Calle San Sebastián, near the Plaza del Mercado. It was a shed where he had a charcoal stove, a hand basin, and a shower—everything crowded into one room. The shoe repair was two blocks away from La Casa de las Medias y los Botones, and the first time I visited Juan I asked him why that store was always so full of people. I had just passed it on my way over and was surprised to see a crowd already at the door when it was still early.

Juan looked at me, a curious expression on his face. "That's something you only understand when you live on an island, my duck. *Sanjuaneros* are always giving carnivals and costume balls and dressing up as something or other, because they're always trying to get away."

"From what?" I asked innocently.

"From themselves," Juan answered with a wink.

Another time, Juan told me the story of Diamantino Márquez. There was very little to do in San Juan and I visited him almost every other day; *el chisme*—good old-fashioned gossip—kept us entertained. One afternoon I was watching him block the toe shoes and spread the silk covers on them when he told me about El Delfín.

"Diamantino's father," Juan said, "was one of the most powerful political figures on the island. Don Eduardo Márquez was the island's prime minister, and he would have been the island's president if the Americans hadn't landed at Guánica. His son, with his magnificent mane of dark hair, was looked upon by many as El Delfín, the rightful heir to the throne on which the American governor now sits.

"A year after the Americans arrived, General Brooke banished Don Eduardo from San Juan. He'd struggled enough, trying to wrest independence from the Spaniards for years. Now he was too tired to start all over again with the Americans. He felt he'd been made the laughingstock of the island.

"Don Eduardo sold his tobacco plantation and went to live in New York with his family. Ten years later he got sick and had very little money left. He sailed back to Puerto Rico, and Don Pedro Batistini, a millionaire hacendado and the Liberal Party's vice president, welcomed him with open arms. He offered him his mansion in Miramar, and Don Eduardo moved in with his family. It was a grand gesture, although Don Pedro could well afford it: he owned the most profitable sugar mill in the north: central Dos Ríos, near the town of Arecibo.

"To have Don Eduardo Márquez convalesce at home offered the elderly Don Pedro and his wife an endless source of entertainment. They were both getting on in years, and growing lonely. But most of all, they had suffered a tragedy they were trying to forget: Don Pedro and Doña Basilisa had had a daughter, Ronda, and an only son, Adalberto, who was twenty-two, two years older than Diamantino is now. He had become infatuated with a young Spanish diva who had visited the island some years before. When the singer left the island, Adalberto was devastated and disappeared.

"No one knew where he'd gone, but the neighbors gossiped. Some swore he'd stolen his father's gold watch, and that with the money he had sailed to New York, where Angelina had gone with her father to perform. Others were sure he had committed suicide and that, because Don Pedro was so religious, he had kept the boy's death a secret to avoid a scandal: Catholics believe suicides go straight to hell. Don Pedro was furious and forbade his son's name to ever be mentioned again in his presence. 'You must erase him from your mind,' he ordered his daughter, Ronda, and his wife, Doña Basilisa. 'Forget we ever had a son.' This, for Doña Basilisa, was of course impossible. She could just as well forget her son as she could banish the sun from her eyes or the darkness from her heart. But she loved Don Pedro and tried her best to obey him. The story of what had happened was veiled in mystery and all their friends were told the young man had gone away on a trip. Eventually people forgot all about him.

"Don Eduardo's presence in Don Pedro's house proved to be an amusement which kept the couple's mind away from this tragedy, and it also gave them the opportunity to exercise their largesse. The house became a mecca for the island's intellectuals, the artists and writers who were always visiting. When Don Eduardo took a turn for the worse, politicians with the most controversial views came to stand, head bowed and hat in hand, next to the great man's bed, which was moved from the second-floor guest room to the front living room of Don Pedro's house.

"Those difficult days were not without their light moments, however. Don Eduardo, no matter how much he begged, wouldn't allow Don Pedro to hang over his bed a silver crucifix he had brought from Jerusalem during one of his travels. It was said to possess miraculous qualities because it contained, in the round crystal locket embedded at its center, wooden fragments from Christ's cross.

" 'Let the priest apply the Sacrament of Extreme Unction to you, my friend. These splinters from the Holy Cross may still cure you, and protect you from pain,' Don Pedro would say.

" 'Take away those rats nibbling, my friend,' Don Eduardo would reply. 'It's better to meet death in Spanish and face to face than mumbling spells in Latin no one can understand.'

"Diamantino, in spite of his grief, had the opportunity to mingle with the island's most gifted poets and musicians thanks to his father's illness. They all came to pay their respects at Don Pedro's house. He heard them play the piano and read from their works, and he took part in the heady political discussions that were held on Don Pedro's ample terrace overlooking the lagoon. Diamantino was a poet himself, and read voraciously— literature, history, and sociology. Over and over he listened to his father explain, in the slow, measured terms which befitted his aristocratic mien, the need to fight for the island's independence (autonomy he called it, so as not to seem too radical to the Americans, who immediately grew alarmed at the word) through a law-abiding, parliamentary process, and not through violent means.

" 'Our countrymen are a peaceful people,' Don Eduardo would say. 'Fighting for self-determination with guns would go against our nature. We'll gain freedom with a clear conscience by democratic means.' Diamantino would sit, head bowed, listening. He revered his father and had always obeyed him, but a secret anger seethed inside him.

"Don Eduardo's health deteriorated even further and his family realized he was going to die. On his last day, Don Pedro held his friend's hands and didn't leave his bedside until he passed away. He paid for all the expenses of Don Eduardo's funeral. The wake was worthy of the president of the republic. The caravan of automobiles, with the flagless steel bier covered with funerary wreaths at its head, wound slowly up the mountains, girding the island from end to end with its coils. Diamantino and his mother rode with Don Pedro and his family in Don Pedro's splendid Pierce-Arrow—the one that picked Madame up at the pier—all the way to Manantiales, the small town in the heart of the mountains where Don Eduardo was born and where he wanted to be buried. His tomb was a plain slab of marble with his name, two dates, and no cross carved on it.

"After the wake, Diamantino's mother left for New York. She preferred to live in Manhattan, where she could get minor roles onstage and would live with relatives—she didn't want to be dependent on a stranger's charity. Diamantino was about to depart with her when Don Pedro approached him.

" 'Stay here, Tino. You're already like a son to us. Basilisa and

I would like to make you our beneficiary when we pass away.'

"Diamantino decided to trust his father's friend and he canceled his plans for returning to New York. From then on he looked on Don Pedro as his new parent.

"His studies in journalism helped Diamantino find part-time work at *El Diario de la Mañana*, one of San Juan's most prestigious newspapers. He also loved music and played the violin. When his mother passed away unexpectedly from pneumonia in New York, Don Pedro adopted him legally and Diamantino relaxed. He knew he'd be expected to make a living eventually, but he could take his time. He thought he'd finish work on a book of poems he was writing. 'It's good to study,' Doña Basilisa told him reassuringly. 'But don't worry your handsome head about it. The purpose of education is to be able to enjoy life more, not to make your nerves sick!' Diamantino kept on freelancing for several newspapers, and spent the rest of his time writing poetry and getting together with his intellectual friends to play the violin in the cafés at night.

"Don Pedro waited for a year, and didn't mind bumping into Diamantino in the dining room at lunchtime, his hair tousled and his eyes puffy with sleep because he had just gotten out of bed. But one day he finally got tired of his bon vivant godson. 'The moon isn't made of cheese, you know. If I were you, I'd get a serious job. Don't press your luck.' And he took away the young man's allowance. 'Either he gets a job or he starves,' he told Doña Basilisa sternly. Her tears failed to move him. 'He can dig trenches or split stones by the road, for all I care. But he has to learn to live off the sweat of his brow!'

"Then, in April, the Americans joined the war in Europe, and Puerto Ricans were urged to volunteer. Don Pedro thought it was a wonderful opportunity for Diamantino to prove himself. It would turn him into a man, and he could also see the world. But Diamantino refused to even consider it.

" 'I'm not going to join the army if it kills me,' he said. 'I'd rather go to jail than fight someone else's war!' To Don Pedro this was the last straw. Soon after that, he told Diamantino to get out of the house.

"Diamantino disappeared from San Juan for a while and no one knew where he had gone. Doña Basilisa was hysterical, but then he turned up unexpectedly at the YMCA. He still didn't have a job, except for an occasional freelance piece at *El Diario de la Mañana*, and he would have starved if not for Doña Basilisa, who turned up every afternoon at the Y with a steaming *fiambrera* at the bottom of which there were always a number of folded dollar bills conveniently hidden under the large, blandtasting María biscuits. The boy was proud. He wore his linen suit and his father's diamond studs whenever he undertook a freelance piece at the newspaper, or just sat in a café reading. His linen shirts were soiled and crumpled and his fake collar and shirt cuffs were scruffed, but he didn't care. Then he appeared unexpectedly at La Fortaleza the night of Madame's reception. He hadn't been invited, but everyone knew who he was and no one dared turn him back at the door."

This was the story Juan told me about Diamantino Márquez, better known on the island as El Delfín. I found it fascinating, like everything else in his baroque, tropical paradise.

15

Mr. Dandré left for New York the next day and we all felt a huge weight lift off our shoulders. He stifled Madame, and she had been pulling at the bit for some time now. She was so pleased at being on her own, she forgot all about the sniper at La Fortaleza's garden. She wasn't the least bit afraid of being left alone. After all, she had Masha to protect her and her dancers to keep her company. We were all elated.

The governor sent Madame a message, inviting her to stay at his house for the duration of her husband's trip. He was worried that something might happen to her in the Malatrassi after the attempt, and at the mansion she would have police protection at all times. Madame was grateful—La Fortaleza had large, airy rooms and she would be a lot more comfortable there. "You'll have to go with me, Masha," she said. "You know I'm lost without you!" I moved our things to the mansion that same day, and the rest of the troupe stayed at the hotel. Dandré left in a dark mood. Now he had no recourse but to leave Madame with me.

We went shopping in the old city, which had many European-style boutiques and cafés, and visited the medieval forts. Every night she was wined and danced by the governor himself. What more could she want?

A few days later one of the secret-service men at La Fortaleza knocked on Madame's door to let her know she had a visitor. It was a reporter from the *Puerto Rico Ilustrado*, who wanted to do an interview. Madame herself opened the door: she was wearing her exercise clothes and I had just combed her hair, which she wore tied back at the neck in a chignon with a yellow silk handkerchief. Madame invited the young man to sit down and went on with her routine, doing pliés and ronds de jambe as she held on to the back of a chair.

The reporter was stylishly dressed, with a vest and a silk butterfly tie, and he was wearing sunglasses. Assuming a pose, he took out his notebook and gold pen. "Rogelio Tellez, pleased to meet you," he said.

"Is it dark enough for you?" my mistress asked maliciously.

Rogelio shook his head. "Cats can see better in the dark, Madame. And so do I," he joked conceitedly.

Rogelio was the son of a rich hacendado who wrote for the *Puerto Rico Ilustrado* as a hobby. He had his poems published there as payment for his work as a reporter. The magazine was enormously popular with the bourgeoisie, since they showed up in it constantly. Rogelio brought us a copy: there were photographs of all the elegant dinner parties, picnics, and *thés dansants* attended by the well-to-do. When I saw the magazine, I knew immediately our ballets were going to be a success in San Juan. The well-to-do on the island reminded me of the Russian nobility. They were living in a dream world, with palaces by the seashore and summer homes in the mountains, while everybody else starved. Maybe we ought to dance *Le Miroir* for them, I thought. They might wake up before it shattered.

Unfortunately, the young man hadn't done his homework and he asked Madame all the wrong questions, blinking behind his thick glasses like a myopic bat. What did she think of the Russian Revolution? Did Madame believe it was justified? Would she say that her art was an anachronism in a world of striking workers, violent coups, and peasant massacres?

So the red fox was out of the hole; the young man was a Bolshevik sympathizer! Madame didn't let him know she had caught on. She talked only about the weather, the impossible heat, the tasteless American food at the Malatrassi. The reporter had to come down a notch. Where did Madame learn to dance? Who were her mentors? Whom did she emulate when she danced? And then finally the worst faux pas of all: How old was she?

My mistress blanched and began to arch her toes, as she did whenever she got angry. "Madame has always been Madame," she said in an icy tone. "I don't copy anyone. When I was admitted to the Imperial Ballet I was already prima ballerina. And my age is a secret no one has ever dared ask."

The young man was so wrapped up in his role as "dance critic" that he didn't notice anything was amiss. Rogelio fumbled with his notes, looking for his next question, and silence followed, during which one could have heard a pin drop. "Tell the young man the interview is over, won't you, Masha, dear?" Madame ordered, turning her back to Rogelio and glancing at me over her shoulder.

Her right foot began to beat impatiently on the floor and I signaled to the young man that he had to leave, but a photographer squeezed in the door and began taking "flashlights"—as the recently invented flashbulb photos were called. Madame was furious. "How dare you!" she said, wrenching the expensive camera away from him. Quick as lightning, she ran to the window and let it drop four floors below. "I'm not going to let a provincial little twit like you snatch my image and publish it for free in your magazine when I'm paid thousands of dollars in Paris and New York to pose!"

I was screaming and dragging Rogelio out the door—fortunately he was at least six inches shorter and thirty pounds lighter than I—when the young man, who was hanging on to the doorjamb, turned around and begged: "Please sign my shirt cuff, Madame. I promise I'll never wash it." Instead of getting angrier, my mistress burst out laughing. And she signed the cuff before the secret service took Rogelio away.

 After the interview Madame rallied her troupe around her at the Malatrassi and gave each one of us something to carry—a wicker basket full of costumes, makeup cases, wigs, and all the ballet paraphernalia—toe shoes, rosin bottles, chalk. "Here, Lyubovna, you take my jewelry case and guard it with your life. Here, Custine, dear, you take Poppy's leash and walk him down the street all the way to the theater. Edgar and the other musicians, hurry, bring the violin, the viola, and the harp down to the lobby. Mr. Molinari, you'll be in charge of the cash register." Madame was wearing her amber necklace as usual and twirled the beads around her fingers nervously as she stood on the sidewalk waiting for us. I didn't feel comfortable with that arrangement, but something prevented me from informing Madame of Molinari's little cross-examination the day before. I thought I'd wait and see what was going to happen with Diamantino Márquez.

As we walked down Calle Fortaleza the heat was unbearable: sticky and viscous. Several of the girls wore bathing suits and cotton skirts, but they were still perspiring and complaining about the temperature. Madame didn't mind. She was as fresh as a handful of mint. "Isn't this heat wonderful, Masha?" she asked me as we walked out the hotel door. "This way we'll save time, because we won't have to warm up before we start rehearsing." All the houses had balconies and Madame loved the colors of their exteriors: garish yellow, blue, red, as well as many other hues.

Every morning of Madame's life was like this: she arrived at whatever theater she was going to dance in like a tornado and left in the afternoon like a hurricane in full gale. As soon as she got to San Juan's Teatro Tapia, she ordered all the windows and doors opened, to let in light and air. There was a strong smell of brine, as the building was near the wharf. Teatro Tapia was small, but it was nicely decorated, with burgundy velvet opera stalls all around the first tier and matching red velvet chairs and curtains. Smallens had placed an ad in the local paper and several musicians turned up. He hired them, and they squeezed into the orchestra pit as best they could. A number of musicians played outside the pit, sitting in the wings.

The theater dated from the eighteenth century. It had been built by a Spanish governor as a magnificent birthday present to his wife, who wanted to be an actress and who loved balls. The seats could be removed and a wooden platform slid cleverly from under the stage, covering the entire orchestra section to create a ballroom. Operas and dramas were performed there from time to time, but ballet was totally unknown on the island. It was a new art, and as such, our troupe was ambiguously described by the local press as a "group of demoiselles who go about onstage in semi-transparent skirts, with neck, arms, and legs daringly bared, and who perform athletic feats." But Madame didn't give a damn and neither did I.

We inspected the stage inch by inch, looking for holes or loose boards. The smallest knot in the wood, the tiniest upended nail was enough to twist an ankle and make us land like broken dolls on the floor. The carpenter began to hammer away to repair the wooden boards, and we chalked the places where we were supposed to stand at the beginning and at the end of each performance. Then the floor was swept clean and rosin dust was sprinkled over it.

We slipped on our toe shoes, tied the ribbons to our ankles, and began the exercise of the day, holding on to whatever was available—a chair, a wicker basket full of costumes, a theater flat. This was my favorite part of the morning, when I felt the power of dance throb beneath my feet. Our bodies became columns of energy; our legs rose up from the hip, strong and straight as iron beams; our feet were pink phalluses pointing toward the ceiling. At that moment I felt completely fulfilled. We didn't have to envy men anything; we had everything they had, only better, for in ballet, women always performed the leading roles. We worked all morning. The rehearsal couldn't begin until every single one of us was warmed up like a steam engine, practically whistling and raring to go. Once the class was over, however, slowly, like somnambulists entering a dream, we followed Madame out on the stage. Then we assembled around her to begin rehearsing the performance.

There was nothing we wouldn't do to please Madame. We were all celibate, in spite of the young men milling around us backstage at the end of each performance. We simply shunned them. This was something unheard of in a troupe of young ballerinas, but our company was special. We went without eating for days to keep our bodies slim and light. Hunger was cleansing, it purified us from desire. Pain meant we were working hard; we were doing things correctly. A ballerina is supposed to feel pain in order to make her art transcend the mundane, and so we put ourselves in Madame's hands.

Then a dreadful thing happened.

We had begun rehearsing when Madame suddenly stopped dancing midstage. I was standing a little bit to the right of her and saw her dark eyes flash with pleasure. She had picked out someone standing at the back of the empty theater, someone with very dark hair, dressed in a white linen suit and wearing a mourning band on his arm. Everyone stopped dancing and stared out into the darkness. My heart leapt to my throat: it was Diamantino Márquez. He smiled broadly and carried a violin case in his hand.

"Could you by chance use an extra violinist in your orchestra? I'd be willing to work for modest pay," he asked, a debonair look on his face.

Madame's face lit up. "We certainly could," she answered across the rows of empty chairs. "Come right up and join us."

Diamantino walked jauntily down the aisle and up to the stage. Madame ordered Smallens to accommodate him in the orchestra, next to the piano and the flute.

As soon as Madame began to dance to Diamantino's violin, she was transformed. I had never seen her dance like that, her sweat-slick body curling and uncurling, her body turned into a sign that could only be deciphered by another body's mute language. She forgot all about our sacred mission. Under Diamantino Márquez's appreciative gaze, Glazunov's *Bacchanale* burned sublime.

 Madame went everywhere with Diamantino, and she insisted that I go with them. She still hadn't fallen completely under his spell and was worried about what people might say. I was, as usual, blindly devoted, and went innocently tagging along. Diamantino insisted he wanted Madame to experience life on the island as it really was, and Madame fell for it, hook and line. We went to the casino in the evenings, to church on Sundays, to the meetings of poets and artists in the cafés of Old San Juan in the afternoons. Madame spoke French and English as well as Russian, but when they went out together, Diamantino often spoke to her in Spanish, as if Madame could understand him. At first, Madame found this amusing and enjoyed trying to guess what he said, but later it became a nuisance because the meaning of entire sentences escaped her. Fortunately it didn't matter because I could understand Spanish and I translated.

I suspected one of the reasons Madame felt drawn to Diamantino was because of her secret Jewishness. Her mother had feared pogroms in Russia because Poliakoff, her daughter's father, was a Jew. She commiserated with the *independentistas*

because she understood how they felt. "You lost your country, but I've never owned mine," Diamantino would say. "You're not the only one," Madame would answer in a low voice. "Think of the Jewish people."

"This island has been in chains for four hundred years; first because of the Spaniards and now the Americans," Diamantino would grieve. And Madame would try to console him: "Being so near to the United States is like living next to a boiling cauldron. Every time the heat goes up and it boils over, you get scalded." They went on and on about island politics until I had to stuff my fingers in my ears because I thought I was going to go mad.

Gone was our privacy, our marvelous days together when we enjoyed the small satisfactions of intimacy and catered to each other's needs. No talk of war, politics, or money had ever crossed our lips, only pleasing words about art, beauty and love. I realized that, with Diamantino present, I had lost Madame for good.

The evening of our first performance I had to make a huge effort to pretend nothing was amiss. Teatro Tapia was completely full and I picked out Diana Yager and Estrella Aljama sitting conspicuously in the first row. They were next to the governor, and were dressed in glittering gowns with orchid corsages pinned to their breasts. All of San Juan's bourgeoisie was present, and the gowns were again ablaze with jewels. Madame tore herself from Diamantino long enough to peek from behind the curtain, and gave a sigh of relief when she saw the large audience. When Mr. Dandré left for New York, he had taken most of the funds remaining from our performances in Cuba, and we needed the money from that night's show to tide us over until his return. Everything went smoothly at first. The music was adequate, and Smallens didn't have to whistle to remind the musicians of how the melody went, as had happened before on several occasions when provincial orchestras had played for us in the small towns.

We danced Glazunov's *Bacchanale*, one of the few ballets I truly dislike, because it's so chaotic, asserting the supremacy of tumultuous passion over reason's wise counsel. In it Dionysus is devoured by the wild bacchantes when he comes to take Ariadne away from the isle of Naxos. On stage, of course, this didn't actually happen; we merely pantomimed the drinking and the carousing. Many people found the story line shocking, but the ballet was very successful in Paris and New York, where audiences are more sophisticated and enjoy this sort of spectacle, not unlike what happens in their harlot megalopolises. Molinari joined us and his caustic commentaries were immediately forthcoming. He pointed out that cannibalism, after all, was relatively common in Western religious practices, and that Christ was devoured in the white communion wafer at the end of each Mass, be it Orthodox, Catholic, or Episcopalian. We all burst out laughing but were secretly terrified.

Clad in semi-transparent silk, Madame let her billowing veil drop, threw rose garlands at Novikov/Dionysus, ducked and twisted with almost animal vigor, and even went into kissing clinches with him. Novikov lunged at her like a satyr, following in leaps and bounds. Then a buzz rose from the back of the theater and rippled forward until it reached the front row. The satyr's costume was, unfortunately, very revealing; it clung to Novikov's masculine form like skin. The girls and I were the dancing maenads, and when we attacked Dionysus, cries of "Disgusting!" were heard from the crowd. People began to get up angrily and leave the theater. At that precise moment, however, Novikov fell through a trapdoor on the floor and disappeared. The audience clapped vigorously as the character's integrity was restored, and the god was chastised for his sinful behavior. Diana Yager and Estrella Aljama both looked relieved.

The second part of the program was more sedate. Madame's *Dragonfly* had nothing more risqué than a strapless chiffon costume which billowed around her like a cloud and a pair of narrow diamanté wings which trembled at her waist. The night was crowned with another perfect rendition of *The Dying Swan*. Halfway through it, however, the lyrical atmosphere was shattered by several gunshots. I ran to the back door of the stage to find out what was going on and opened it a crack only to see the empty, cobblestoned streets and the silent piers. Since the dry law had been passed, many bars in town had closed, while others had turned into shooting galleries.

Our troupe danced three evenings in a row, to dwindling audiences. Madame couldn't figure out what was wrong. There were no more protests about indecent exposure; we judiciously altered Dionysus's costume and now he danced with a short tunic over his leotard that concealed his conspicuous physique. Madame speculated that the revenue from the rum sales was an important part of the *Sanjuaneros'* income, and now they couldn't afford to throw away money on entertainment. In any case, by 6:00 p.m. the streets were empty and most restaurants and bars in San Juan were closed. Prohibition, which had been hanging like a shroud over the capital for months, finally smothered it.

During the day people were seen running to empty their rum casks on the wharves and at the beach to get away from the police. A cloud of sweetish, rum-soaked vapor hung over the city. Others were going around drunk from the fumes and mourning for the thousands of dollars they had literally poured down the drain. On the fourth night no one came to see us dance. Teatro Tapia remained ominously empty.

Huddled in front of the stage's back door, we argued for over an hour about what should be done. Molinari had collected seven hundred dollars in cash, the profits from the first night's performance, but part of that money belonged to the theater, and we needed the rest to survive until Dandré came back. The agent was mad as a hornet, and kept threatening us that Bracale would wreak vengeance when he heard his profits were wiped out.

Madame tried to appease him. "Dandré never dreamed we could be left out in the cold, unable to earn our keep. You must be patient," she pleaded. I rolled my eyes at her gullibility, but I didn't want to make things worse. I clearly remembered other situations when Dandré had left us in the lurch. I was trying to convince her that we should stick it out at Teatro Tapia and wait for the weekend, when audiences might be larger, rather than venture into the interior of the island, when that interloper, Diamantino, stepped in.

"We mustn't lose any more time in San Juan," he said, adjusting his glasses on his nose and drawing his arm protectively around Madame's shoulders, defying suspicious stares. "We should pack up and leave for the countryside immediately. In smaller cities like Arecibo, Aguadilla, and Ponce, the enforcement of the liquor legislation won't be as strict, and people will have more money to spend." Also, he had *independentista* friends in *el campo* who would be willing to help us, he said. Madame accepted Diamantino's plan.

On our way back to the hotel we discussed what was to be done. Neither Custinen nor Volinine could speak a word of Spanish, and they were afraid to leave the capital. They kept silent and hung their heads, but it was evident they wouldn't set out on the trip. Half the troupe would stay behind in San Juan. Custine would take care of Poppy, one of the ballerinas would see to the nightingales, and the male dancers would all remain at the Malatrassi. They would live on the three hundred dollars we left them until we got back. Lyubovna insisted she couldn't go, either—her arthritis had flared up because of the humidity on the island, and she was in pain. It was wiser for her to stay at La Fortaleza, where the governor had extended her an invitation for as long as she wished and where she could keep Madame's jewels safe. Her daughter could go traipsing around the country all she liked.

Only three musicians and six ballerinas would accompany Madame on her tour in addition to Smallens, the orchestra director; Novikov, her partner; Juan, the cobbler; and myself (for a moment panic struck at my heart like an ice pick, so afraid was I that she would leave without me!). Molinari said he would go too; he could help translate. We would take only our costumes in wicker baskets and no stage props, as we'd be traveling by train. Diamantino, of course, needed no invitation. He would be our scout and help Molinari contract the performances in the local theaters. The income from the tickets would tide the troupe over from day to day.

Once the journey took a concrete form we felt better. It would be an adventure, Madame said, and we'd survive thanks to our own ingenuity. "Now we can finally enjoy ourselves," she declared, laughing, "free of Dandré's stuffy constraints." Tears of rage welled up in my eyes.

18

I had to pack my bag, since we were leaving at six in the morning the next day. But instead of going to my small bedroom in La Fortaleza's lower quarters, I went to Juan's workshop, La Nueva Suela, on San Sebastián Street. I asked him if he could take a message to Lyubovna. I had to see her immediately, I scribbled on a scrap of paper, and she should come and meet me at the shoe-repair shop.

A few minutes later I was leaning out the window and saw a tall, bony figure come out of La Fortaleza's wrought-iron gates and walk, half limping, down the cobblestoned street. Lyubovna was wearing a black cotton scarf printed with red roses, tied under her chin Russian peasant style, because it was raining lightly and she didn't want her head to get wet. She was more than sixty, but she didn't look it; she was as straight and tall as a fir. Fortunately Juan wasn't with her; she was alone.

(When Madame passed away some weeks ago, I read in the papers that Lyubovna was living in Russia, and that she expected to inherit all the money from Ivy House because proof of Madame's and Dandré's marriage couldn't be found. I laughed at the irony of it. "She has me to thank for that, the old witch," I told myself, "though she'll never find out." But knowing what the Communist regime is like, I doubt the money will ever reach her.)

Lyubovna knocked on the door and I quickly let her in the shoe-repair shop. "I can only be a minute, Masha. Niura is driving me crazy with her packing and we still have a lot to do," she said hurriedly. Lyubovna embraced me cordially. We had had our difficulties in the past—once she had been jealous of how close my mistress and I were—but we were on relatively good terms then. She insisted I was like a second daughter to her. I didn't feel sorry for Lyubovna; traveling as Madame's personal maid must have been a lot easier than doing the laundry for her clients in the public baths of St. Petersburg, especially in winter. And I never opened my heart to her completely because of her close friendship with Dandré. When the chips were down, I knew she would side with him instead of with her daughter, and my goal was to defend Madame.

"Have you noticed the romance blossoming right under our very noses?" I asked her point-blank when she crossed the threshold, since I've never been one to beat around the bush.

"You mean that young violinist Niura is going around with? Isn't he the son of some local political chieftain?" Lyubovna asked. She was so preoccupied with Dandré's departure, she hadn't noticed anything was amiss.

"Yes," I said. "And he's also a revolutionary out to make a killing with your daughter, who, in spite of her thirty-eight years, is still a babe in arms."

I explained Diamantino's tactics to Lyubovna. Everywhere he went on the island people recognized him as Don Eduardo's son, and to be seen with Madame, who was an internationally renowned star, gave him a lot of prestige. If he could convince her to publicly espouse the revolutionary cause on the island, it would help him even more. Such support would give him recognition, and they might offer him an important political position. I had convinced myself this was the real reason for Diamantino's insistence that we leave San Juan and make the trip to the countryside. He wanted people to see her with him. Diamantino didn't just happen to meet Madame at La Fortaleza a week before. He sent her the Pierce-Arrow to fetch her at the dock and then came to meet her at the governor's mansion for a purpose.

Lyubovna sat down on Juan's working stool. The floor around us was covered with strips of leather curled around the edges, sawdust, and centuries of grime. It smelled of glue, wax, and turpentine; of people who had to pinch both pennies and toes, and had their shoes repaired over and over because they couldn't afford to buy new ones.

"It can't be. Has Niura gone crazy?"

"She hasn't yet, but she will if she falls in the arms of that rascal. I know his type."

"But he's a total stranger! And he doesn't even speak Russian. I'm sure Niura thinks of him as her son; you're exaggerating."

"No, I'm not. And lots of 'mothers' have made love to men young enough to be their sons—remember George Sand and Isadora Duncan. You must speak to Madame and remind her of her duties. It's not just her life; it's that of all of us."

"That's ridiculous. Niura would never do that." Lyubovna's voice was pebbly, and when she got nervous it rasped several notes higher.

"You know Madame when she gets something into her head. She's convinced that through patience and love, she'll be able to overcome the differences of age, belief, culture, language, and just about everything else that estranges her from her provincial Romeo."

I could tell Lyubovna was frightened. For the first time since we arrived on the island she saw there was a real possibility that her daughter might fall into Diamantino's clutches. "What can we do?" she asked, the blood drained from her face.

"You must stay here and keep an eye out for Dandré when he comes back. We must not lose contact with him. I'll go with Madame on the trip, and try to protect her from that scalawag." Lyubovna embraced me and we both went out hurriedly, afraid that Juan might be coming back.

There is only one train on the island; it runs all the way around the coast to La Concordia, then turns around and comes right back by the same route. We boarded it at seven-thirty in the morning at a very European-looking station, with clock tower, glass ceiling, and all—only everything built in miniature—on the outskirts of San Juan. The train was rustic but charming. It had a coal engine, two passenger cars with wide open windows, the mail coach, and one freight car. The passenger cars were of two kinds: first class—$1.50—had slippery straw seats, second class—seventy-five cents—had wooden seats made of slats, both equally hard on your derriere. Madame asked Diamantino to buy two first-class tickets for them and second-class for everyone else—as Dandré used to do—but Diamantino refused. Madame was traveling with *him* now, he said, and he was a gentleman. He took off one of his diamond studs, bought fifteen first-class tickets with his own money, and gave one to each member of the troupe. (Molinari paid for his own ticket, and traveled second class.)

The night before, Madame had left the Teatro Nacional with Diamantino and they walked on the Condado beach for hours. "The sand was strewn with jagged volcanic rocks against which the waves kept smashing," Madame said. (The next morning she wanted to share with me what had happened. I swallowed hard and prayed to the Virgin that she might spare me, but my prayers went unheard.) "We made love like a pair of playful octopuses crawling over each other," Madame half sighed, half joked as she lay back on her bed and I fluffed her pillows. "We wanted to know everything about each other, inspect every nook and cranny of our past lives." I forced myself to go on listening as I bent down solicitously to straighten her bedcovers, but her words were like hot coals falling on my skin.

"The sky was perfectly calm and the full moon spilled light over us like an overturned bucket," she went on dreamily. "It's a shame not to have met earlier, Masha, not to have been born at the same time. I'll never let him go!" I began to vigorously brush with a whisk broom the dress Madame would wear the next day, and looked uneasily out the window. The doves were cooing and nuzzling on the balcony's rail as if validating what she had just said. I could taste blood seeping up my throat and was sure it was coming from my heart, then I realized I had bitten my lips.

"When he turns thirty you'll be forty-eight; when he turns sixty you'll be resting quietly in your grave," I said dejectedly, without turning around to look into her eyes.

The next day, as we plowed through the steaming cane fields rustling on either side of the train, I spoke to Madame in private. Diamantino and Novikov had walked to the last car to get us some breakfast, and we were alone for the first time. "You're making a terrible mistake," I said over the train's nerve-racking clatter. "How can you behave like this? Everybody's judging you. You'll end up poor, alone, and unloved if this goes on!"

Madame looked at me, pale with anger, and the wind from the open window whipped her words around me like wasps. "How dare you, Masha!" she cried. "You don't own me. I can do whatever I want with my life." She slapped me, and her hand left an imprint, bright as a tulip, on my cheek. Just then Novikov walked in, a tray of steaming coffee in his hands. It spilled over the straw seats and we jumped away. "Christ! What's come over you?" he cried, taking hold of our arms.

"It's a relief to be away from Dandré," Madame sighed. "We've been together for eleven years—a lifetime—and everybody has a right to be free once in a while. But I can't even talk to another man without this calfless cow butting in to reproach me." Novikov understood perfectly. He smiled and nodded at Madame while I kept tactfully silent. Novikov was an expert in the science of love. "Make him suffer, darling," he said. "Dandré is an old alligator, enjoy yourself as much as you want."

I was always wary when Madame criticized Dandré, because she always forgave him in the end. Maybe that's why at that moment I turned into the devil's advocate and tried to defend her husband.

"Dandré is a kind man," I said to Madame. "He pampers you even more than your mother—always making you drink milk and eat meat so fresh it's practically breathing on the plate because it gives you energy. I see him take such special care of you. 'Your feet are your fairy wings, my dear, you must give them maintenance,' he keeps saying. It's true that he's like the front bumper on a train and understands life from only one perspective. In Dandré's eyes what's black is black and what's white is white—there's never a double take. But that's why he's so successful at everything and is such a good manager. He thinks the world of you and is a good companion because he's your own age." And I emphasized the last sentence, giving Madame a reassuring smile.

Novikov roared with laughter and agreed with me. "Of course, Dandré is my friend and he's everything you said. But one must live for the moment, dear. Don't worry about the future. It usually takes care of itself."

That same afternoon we made up. Our bickering was like a tropical shower—angry raindrops one minute, serene sunlight the next. We were the heart of the company. The other members came and went—they were always looking for romance, though usually, thanks to Madame's preaching, common sense prevailed. But Madame and I remained faithful to each other for years.

20

"I feel exhausted from so much traveling, Masha," Madame admitted, sitting beside me. "After a while you don't want to stop anymore; you just go on dancing until your feet wear out. The feeling of home evaporates; it doesn't exist at all. There's only the stage, where you disrobe your soul for others every day. It's a scary feeling—as if music took hold of your life and were leading you to your death."

I agreed. In the States alone we'd traveled for three whole months and visited forty towns by train.

We relaxed, looking out the window at the beautiful scenery speeding past us. Diamantino was still somewhere else; he knew many people on the train and liked to converse with everyone.

"You and the girls have sacrificed a lot for me, Masha," Madame went on in a conciliatory tone. "Your work is anonymous and thankless. Tulle skirts evaporate in an instant; there are so few testimonies of our art. But you mustn't worry. Thanks to the photographs Dandré is always taking of us, our art will become eternal, like Schubert's, Tchaikovsky's, or Chopin's."

She was concerned that when she was gone the girls and I would be left out in the cold. Many of us were already past our prime, and there was very little Madame could do to remedy the situation. How could she, an impoverished dancer from a country that had evaporated from the face of the earth, assure our survival? It was impossible for a ballet company like ours to have more than one star—it took too much money for promotion, costumes, clothes. The dancing was important, but it wasn't everything. "One must constantly give birth to oneself, become one's own creation," Madame said. As Niura Federovsky, the reserve officer Matvey Federov's illegitimate daughter, had struggled to become the great Madame. And that took guts, because it was easy to lead quiet, mediocre lives, but terribly hard to live up to an image of perfection all the time.

"My sari in *Pharaoh's Daughter*, for example, was made of twenty-four-karat gold lamé. It was worth thousands of dollars. My headdress, an ibis with turquoise eyes, cost another thousand. I designed both of them myself, because I knew that if I did, Dandré couldn't refuse me the money. We barely managed to raise it, and I had them made. Could you imagine what it would cost to dress all the girls like that? That was the secret of Serge Diaghilev: he had all the money in the world for his Ballets Russes de Monte Carlo; Prince Sergei Oblonsky and Prince Savya Mamontov's pockets were at his disposal and they were bottomless oil wells. Our company is very different. We dance for the poor and for the everyday citizen, as well as for the rich. Considering our meager funding, our Ballets Russes have done wonders."

And then there was Dandré, who was always a liability. Dandré's passion for Madame had caused his downfall in Russia. Madame had just graduated from the Maryinsky; she was still a virgin when Dandré saw her dance for the first time. She was doing the ghost scene in *Giselle* at the Imperial Ballet Theater, and after Dandré saw her, he couldn't get her out of his head. He couldn't afford to keep her, but he set her up in a beautiful apartment in St. Petersburg and then began to get involved in illegal deals in order to pay her expenses. My mistress didn't know any of this or she would never have permitted it. When she found out about it, it was too late. His petty thefts were discovered, and he was thrown in jail.

Madame immediately took out all her savings and had him released on bail. Then she gave him enough money so he could travel secretly to Helsinki on a fishing boat. She was still very young then, no more than twenty-four, and on her first ballet tour abroad. Dandré met her in Estonia and later made his way to England with the group. Madame helped him settle down in London. After that she could go back to Russia as many times as she wanted, but Dandré could never go back. He lost everything—his country, his estate, his relatives—all because of Madame. She couldn't help feeling grateful.

"Now Dandré has a lover in New York, I'm sure of it, Masha," she told me. "Every time he says he has to take a little side trip there for business, I know exactly where he goes. But I don't mind. He's a nobody, a commonplace impresario. I'm the one who's famous: I can bask in the glory of my reputation."

When Madame was young she had desperately needed someone like Dandré to help tide her over her difficulties. She was an orphan and he was like a father to her. Madame met him when she was seventeen and was about to graduate from ballet school. Dandré had a box at the Imperial Ballet Theater which he shared with a young friend, handsome Prince Kotschubei, who came to see the girl dance every night. She had recently begun an affair with Prince Kotschubei, but the prince was very young also, and he didn't have independent means. So when Madame met Dandré at the Imperial Theater, she clung to him like a gull to a rock in midocean.

At intermission they invited her to come up to their box, and she sat between them and drank her almond juice like any other schoolgirl, since dancers couldn't touch alcohol. But she was far from innocent. She had an erotic talent at an early age, an extraordinary sexual energy. "I danced naked for them, Masha," she said guiltily, "my feet sliding over their naked bodies like soft, silk stars. I had the physical configuration of a child and hardly any pubic hair, my sex floated above my smooth legs like a delicate triangle of flesh, my breasts were twin moons, rising pale from my chest. During these extravagant, wild afternoons we made love untiringly on the prince's bed, our limbs sprawled over his linen bedsheets, and I felt wonderfully loose and relaxed as I floated above both my lovers, light as a dragonfly.

"Mother has never forgiven me for these intemperate meetings, Masha, when the Eleusinian spirit took hold of us. That's why she never speaks to me, even though she follows me around the world like a shadow and I take good care of her. With all the playing and frolicking, I became pregnant and had to have an abortion. I was too young to bear children, and the abortion made me sterile. That's why I can't see a child walking down the street without wanting to hold it in my arms. Even now, years later, Mother kneels before her icons every night and prays to God that a bolt of lightning may strike Dandré dead when she remembers, although I have long since forgiven him." I shushed her and told her to close her eyes and rest. But she persisted. The affair with Diamantino had stirred up dregs I would never have dreamed of.

"These early bacchanals with Prince Kotschubei, Dandré,

and myself were a great sin, and they were never repeated. We were all upset by what had happened and mended our ways from then on. Dandré and I were secretly married a few months later in the small Orthodox church of Ligovo, where my grandmother came from and where I was baptized as a child. But I didn't want anyone to know of our marriage; I agreed to it just to keep Dandré happy. That's why I gave you the marriage certificate right after the wedding, Masha, with strict instructions that you burn it. How could I belong to Dandré and at the same time give myself to my art? My duties as a dancer were sacred. As an instrument of God, my body had to be free. Just the same, for ten years Dandré and I have been faithful to each other, drawn together by the terrible secret we share: the sad memory of a child unable to give birth to a child.

"After my terrible sin I went about with a newspaper clipping in my handbag and took it out from time to time to read it. It's the story of a woman in Russia, a poor peasant from Tilsit, who had fourteen children. She sat on the corner of the town square with her children all around her, and gave them away to people as they went by. Isn't that unfair? When I would give my life for a single one.

"During all the years we've spent together, I've accepted Dandré's attentions, but I never loved him. He's too masculine. Everything about him is so big: his bear paws; his shoulders, wide as a stevedore's; his penis, as overpowering as a judge's mallet. I cringe when he lies down next to me in bed. He could easily crush my arms like the wings of a bird if he accidentally put his weight on them. I can't let myself go; I can't experience any womanly pleasure. But after I met him, I slept soundly every night, knowing Mother and I were financially secure. Now Dandré rarely presses me for anything. He still solves all my problems, but he's content just to be near me, to have me kiss him on his bald pate or on the tip of his nose. But it's not a good arrangement because I feel so empty. Is it sinful to want both?

"Our dancers are normal, middle-class young women from Russia, England, the United States; I'd do anything for them. They dream of Prince Charming every night, though they don't tell me about it. But you're different, Masha; you worry me the most. It makes me sad that you dislike men because of what you've had to suffer. I try to comfort you as much as I can so you won't feel that way. My father didn't beat me like yours did, but I never got to meet him—he left a void in my life. When I was a child, I used to dream about a dark, empty closet and that I was locked up inside it. My father was waiting for me there, squatting in the darkness. The dream terrorized me, but when I met Dandré I stopped having it. I'm grateful to him for that."

Madame was getting drowsy and I thought she would stop talking, but her voice droned on, hovering like an insect above the pounding of the train.

"It's amazing how much my life has changed since I met Diamantino. Every time I look at him, I blossom inside. His face has a softness about it I love; it's so different from the stone-cast expression Dandré wears at all times. Diamantino is a poet and a musician. I love to dance for him, Masha, I know it's difficult, but you must understand. His violin sets me free.

"I'm a melancholy person by nature; that's why I wear this ring with a black opal on my index finger. It was a present an admirer from Australia gave me. The black opal is like the Russian soul, at the same time dark and radiant, with rays of light glowing from its mysterious depths. Before, when I looked into it, I thought love simply wasn't in the cards for me. God had given me talent, professional success, beauty, and good health.

To complain would have been ungrateful. Today I look into the shimmering black stone and Diamantino's face emerges from its depths: dark and dangerous and fascinating; powerful as a magnet.

"I know you think Diamantino is too young for me, but I don't agree. He's very sensitive to other people's feelings. He doesn't dictate his opinions like Dandré; he asks you what you think. Diamantino and I are kindred souls, Masha. We both dream of the same things.

"Dandré, on the contrary, is like a blob of putty. You punch him and your fist goes in all the way and then you can't pull it out. Dandré never risks anything, never gets excited about anything. God! How have I been able to bear him all these years?"

I was impressed by her confession, and only disagreed with one thing. I didn't dislike men: Madame was, as usual, taking me for granted. But I didn't have the heart to contradict her. I just took her in my arms and cradled her until she fell asleep.

21

The girls jumped off the train and began jogging next to it, calling out to Madame to join them. She woke up in her seat, but was content just watching them. She couldn't help feeling proud at how beautiful and strong they were. That morning they hadn't had their exercise class, so they decided to race the train. Six amazons, their golden manes trailing in the wind, ponytails flicking from side to side, the muscles of their legs rippling under their short exercise tunics. The train was traveling slowly because there were cows crossing the rails, men pulling carts loaded with sugarcane stalks, barefoot children playing at every junction. The passengers, their heads sticking out the car windows, were all watching the crazy Russians, mouths agape at the spectacle.

People on the island were easily amazed by us. They weren't used to Russian women, who are often as brawny and strong as the men and capable of any physical feat. Everything here seemed minuscule to us, coming from the Russian steppes, where distances are measured in thousands of kilometers. It gave us a feeling of power and made us believe we could do anything.

As the train went through the poorer areas, urchins in rags ran alongside it, calling out to the girls to throw them pennies and sometimes hopping on the steps of the last car for short rides. A lone vendor was going up and down the aisle selling fish fritters—*empanadillas de chapín*—and goat cheese wrapped in plantain leaves. Madame promptly bought some of each and distributed them among the girls.

Madame dozed off, her head on my shoulder, and when she opened her eyes we had left the city behind and were picking up speed, riding out into the countryside. A breeze came up and dried the perspiration on our faces and necks. I racked my brain wondering how I could make her understand how important she was for me. I had sacrificed much more than she had because in leaving Russia I had betrayed the revolution. I was a member of the working class and I had everything before me—but Madame, in spite of being the daughter of a washer-woman, was identified with the nobility. She was a White Russian, and her solo *The Dying Swan* was the personification of the aristocrats' agony.

I loved her and hated her for it. In Russia, the czar's family is sacred; the czar is head of church and state. He is our pater-familias and we love him almost as much as we love God. Even Nicholas we felt affection for, in spite of his weaknesses; the country blamed Alexandra, who was German, for the mass murders he committed. Madame, because she had met the czar personally, shared in the mystique of his family. This didn't keep her from being democratic. As in the train, when she began to hand out tidbits to the dancers, and Nadja and Marina both curtseyed to her.

Diamantino returned and sat next to us in our compartment. If what he said was true, everything we saw belonged to the sugar barons. On the left a caravan of *mogotes* rose from the cane fields like a school of green humpback whales. I had read about these exotic rock formations in some magazine; they also existed in the China Sea and were many millions of years old, among the oldest mountains in the world. The clouds above looked like lambs shedding fleece. On our right the sea stained the lower part of the sky a darker blue, like melted oil paint.

Five hours later the train neared the town of Arecibo. Several sugar mills appeared on the horizon, their funnels smoking like huge cigars. "That's Dos Ríos over there," Diamantino said, pointing to a red-brick building. "My godfather's sugar mill." Madame got up from her seat to get a better look. A large house with a gabled roof stood on the plain; it had a verandah and a wide, fanlike staircase leading up to the front door. Suddenly the train lurched and threw them off balance. Diamantino put out his hands to steady Madame and I heard him whisper: "I want you more than anything in the world; just the two of us, going deeper and deeper into the cool interior of the island."

Arecibo's train station was on a tongue of land overgrown with hyacinths on the far side of the Río de la Plata. The main street went along the coast; its houses all stood with their backs to the ocean and faced the narrow streets of the town, as if the islanders were afraid of the wide open space through which foreigners always reached them—first the Spaniards, then the British, the Dutch, and finally the Americans.

"Everybody out!" Diamantino cried as we reached the platform, and we clambered stiffly off the train. A few minutes later the engine whistled and started up again, going on toward Ponce. Our troupe walked to the center of town in a little caravan, the girls skipping ahead of Molinari, a dusty giant dressed in black who fanned himself with a piece of cardboard. Everyone was complaining about the heat. Grigoriev, the flute player, was perspiring so much and was so red in the face, he looked as though he were about to have a stroke. Juan Anduce and I carried heavy baskets full of costumes which Madame ordered us to balance on our heads.

I didn't like it one bit that Diamantino had now become the leader of our group, and that even Molinari and Novikov were taking orders from him. Diamantino did everything: he checked the luggage to see that nothing was left behind on the train and directed the group toward the Hotel Las Baleares, on the main square. Most important, he never left Madame's side, not even for a second. It was as if everything we had shared until then—our spiritual as well as our material adventures—had gone up in smoke. I was so angry at my mistress, I kicked the stones on the road and muttered under my breath. How could she be so blind? Didn't she realize she was being used?

No more ideal of perfect beauty; no more swan acting out the rite of death for the destitute to accept it more readily. Madame was sick with love. She was thirty-eight; her milk-white flesh was beginning to curdle on her bones. She should have been thinking of retiring and going back to Ivy House in London, where she promised me she'd found a school for young dancers. Instead, she'd fallen head-over-heels in love with a stuck-up Spanish grandee's son. How could she preach the sanctity of art to her followers when she was fucking away happily with that Young Turk? I'll stay awake all night if I have to, I told myself, in order to prevent it. How could she dare insist that her only purpose in life was to take the joy of ballet to the unfortunate of this world? Claim that "dancing is a form of prayer, a reaching out to God," and that "nothing should come between the dancer and her sacred task"? She's a hypocrite and a libertine, I murmured to myself as I sat down angrily on a large tree trunk by the road. Madame saw me hanging back. She came over, sat down next to me, and put her soft, white arms around my shoulders.

"What's the matter, Masha, darling? Is that basket too heavy for you? Here, let me help you carry it."

I only hated her more.

22 I picked up the wicker basket with the costumes and toe shoes and set off determinedly down the road, walking between Madame and Diamantino, although I could tell I wasn't wanted there.

Why is it that in mature women lust is always offensive? An older man with a young girl is immoral, but there's a celebration of life implied in the relationship—death and infirmity are vanquished. An older woman with a young man, however, is unforgivable. It means the triumph of death over life: the woman can't conceive; the seed is lost, sown on sterile terrain. When an older woman falls in love with a handsome swain, it's an insult to nature. She turns into a clown—her wrinkled, made-up face becomes a mask of death next to her lover's blossoming countenance. And that's exactly what will happen to Madame, I told myself.

The town of Arecibo—which Diamantino absurdly called a "city"—was small, it couldn't have had more than fifty thousand inhabitants. The streets were mud; there were no pavements anywhere. And instead of the luxurious Studebakers, Peerless Eights, Franklins, Cadillacs, and Willis Overlands that teemed in the streets of San Juan, the well-to-do here went about on horses and tilburies, or in covered carriages of all sorts. The poor, of course, went barefoot.

When we walked in from the train station, a military band was playing and a large group of soldiers marched down the street, which opened onto a spacious, beautifully kept square. This was Arecibo's Plaza Mayor, where the Spanish battalions had held their parades and military maneuvers in the past, and now the Americans did the same. Teatro Oliver very conspicuously faced the Plaza Mayor at one end, its back to the open sea. A whitewashed church stood at the other end of the square, with a three-tiered facade, a clock over the main door, and a strong, squat belfry with a red-brick dome which echoed the square design of the plaza.

A dozen handsome oak trees planted in front of the church spread their pink blossoms on the ground. An octagonal wrought-iron gazebo of Moorish design rose in the middle of the esplanade where the military band performed. A regiment of U.S. Army troops marched to the music, the same one we had seen in San Juan: battalions B and C this time. The army was recruiting Puerto Rican soldiers from all over the island, and they brought them together at the main towns like Arecibo. The next day they would board the train to San Juan and from there sail on to Panama on the *Buford*.

People streamed into the square from the side streets to listen to the band and watch the parade. A sea of women in white uniforms, with wide red crosses sewn to their starched caps, marched into the square to the same music as the soldiers. Some of them were matronly and had children in tow; the younger ones came from Arecibo's Central High School, or so their banner read. Behind them were at least a hundred children, also dressed in white. They lined up around the kiosk singing "America the Beautiful" with thick Spanish accents. Another battalion, the Home Guard, brought up the rear of the parade. These young men were dressed in civilian white pants and shirts, with *jíbaro pabas* on their heads and machetes secured to their belts. Once they walked past, the spectators lining the street followed behind in a formless mass, swaying and dancing to the music. A powerfully built man with a red shock of hair falling over his forehead marched in front and waved to Diamantino as he went by.

"That's Bienvenido Pérez; the son of Arnaldo Pérez, Don Pedro's overseer," Diamantino said. "Don Pedro is his *padrino* also—his godfather. Now that the troops are leaving, he's the leader of the Home Guard. They're supposed to defend the town from enemy attack after the soldiers leave."

"With machetes?" Madame asked, raising her eyebrows.

"You'd be surprised what they can do with them. Cutting sugarcane is good military training. They can't use guns, in any case. Puerto Ricans aren't allowed gun permits."

"Bienvenido grew up in Dos Ríos," Diamantino added, "and he's my best friend. When I was a child, whenever my parents came here on weekends to stay with the Batistinis, he'd play with me. He's just come back from Río Piedras, where he's studying to be an engineer, thanks to Don Pedro's generosity."

A tall, thin man wearing a white linen jacket began to give a speech in front of the orchestra—Arecibo's mayor. He was explaining the purpose of the volunteer movement of the Red Cross: since Puerto Ricans were being recruited into the army, it was only natural that they should donate money to buy Liberty Bonds and provide food for the troops overseas. And if they couldn't buy food, they could certainly grow it. The mayor was urging citizens to plant corn, tomatoes, sugarcane, and coffee in their backyards and to take the proceeds to the offices of the Red Cross every week. A cargo ship bound for Europe, the *Liberty Bell*, would dock near the town in a few months to take the food to the soldiers. I couldn't believe my eyes. It was almost as bad as Minsk, where I once saw the mayor take food from the starving peasants to feed the czar's troops.

"We'll win the war with food instead of with bullets!" the mayor cried, as if cheering on the home team. By which I suppose he meant that, since the *Arecibeños* couldn't pay for ammunition, they could at least grow food for the soldiers. Children began to mill around the mayor, who was giving away hoes—they'd soon be taught how to use them at the agricultural camps to be set up on the outskirts of town on government land. Women were selling lemonade, cookies, and all sorts of sweets made of coconut and molasses in order to raise money for the army. When the mayor stopped talking, nobody clapped. A heavy silence fell on the crowd.

Suddenly one of the men from the Home Guard ran to where the mayor was standing, leaped over the banister, and landed on the platform. He wrenched the mayor's megaphone away from him and began to scream: "The Red Cross, the Boy Scouts, the Liberty Bonds are all part of the same campaign. Who are we? Nobodies from nowhere. We have no citizenship, no political rights, no civil rights. The United States won't give us independence, but they refuse to give us statehood because of prejudice!" At this point, the man was overwhelmed by the police, who clambered onto the dais and pinned him to the floor. The rest of the Home Guard, evidently restless, was surrounded by soldiers in navy blue uniforms and marched toward the train station. "The idiot!" Diamantino cried. "We'll all have to pay for this!" The soldiers looked his way but no one dared move. We stood there flabbergasted.

The audience, however, didn't seem surprised at what they'd seen. Molinari drew near and explained that *espontáneos* were a common sight in the local parades, but that Americans never shot people for this sort of thing. The man would be locked up for a few days and then let loose.

"Americans are much more careful than the Spaniards about their image," Molinari said with an ironic little smile. " 'We are bringing democracy to the island,' General Miles proclaimed grandly in 1898 when he landed here. But Spain never had qualms about turning rebels into martyrs."

Molinari led us to a small square behind Arecibo's cathedral, the Plaza del Corregidor, where public executions used to be held. "Many men died here after conspiring against Spain," he said. We could see a series of trees planted equidistant from each other, with a seat at the base of each. "The condemned men were tied to the seats, eyes covered with black hoods, ropes lowered over their heads, and tourniquets rapidly tightened until their necks snapped. Thus they sat corrected."

We stared at the gruesome sight. Molinari actually relished telling us such stories. "It's amazing that people on the island haven't rebelled," Molinari added. "They're just a bunch of cowards with no pride; no wonder the lamb is their national symbol." When Diamantino heard this he went pale. Molinari looked at him with pursed lips. "I'm glad I'm not a Puerto Rican. I was born in Corsica," he said. And he smiled, baring his rotten teeth.

Arecibeños did everything differently: it was as if every house in Arecibo were trying to sail inland, toward the mountains, instead of away from them. In contrast to San Juan, the town had no walls around it. For centuries it had been the target of the pirate ships that plied the Caribbean by the dozen. While in the narrow cobblestone streets of San Juan you heard only the Castilian Spanish of the king's ministers, in the dusty alleys of Arecibo you often heard French, Dutch, German, Italian, and Portuguese. In San Juan, people looked to Spain, *la madre patria*, for their material well-being and spiritual sustenance. But in Arecibo the whole world was *la madre patria*, and immigrants from all over Europe settled in its environs.

Diamantino took us to a modest, two-story house next to the church and knocked on the door. Beethoven's *Emperor* Concerto came pouring out of the house and practically drowned out the John Philip Sousa march the military band was blasting at that moment. Diamantino wrote down something on a piece of paper and gave it to the girl who opened the door. "Give this to Doña Victoria Tellez, we'd like to say hello," he said. Doña Victoria soon came to the door and opened it wide herself. "How wonderful to see you, Tino!" she said. And she ushered us in graciously.

She was a small woman with unruly snow-white hair that surrounded her head like a halo. She led us into an inner patio shaded by a lemon tree, with hibiscuses in bloom everywhere. We were all introduced. Then we sat in rocking chairs under the shady arcade, gratefully fanning ourselves and drinking cool lemonade.

Diamantino began to make rapid movements with his hands, as if he were playing an invisible instrument; I realized it was sign language. Doña Victoria was totally deaf. She got up, leaving me with my mouth open in midsentence, so amazed was I at her abilities, and walked over to the piano in the adjacent living room. She sat down on the bench and began to pound the keyboard. Beethoven's *Emperor* silenced Sousa's dutiful little march again. The old lady went on playing until the band finished, and then, as the last measures of the brass instruments reverberated from the walls, Doña Victoria lifted her hands from the keyboard and smiled smugly. There was complete silence in the room.

"She always plays that whenever the U.S. Army marches around the square," the young servant girl who opened the door told us with a laugh. "She does it to drown out the Americans." We laughed politely, but were left totally in the dark. I began to suspect there was a lot of resentment in Arecibo toward the army. But this wasn't our country, and I didn't see why we should get mixed up in someone else's war.

The maid went on picking up the empty glasses and putting them on a tray as Diamantino spoke quickly with Doña Victoria. Then she carried the tray out to the kitchen, her sandals flip-flopping after her.

Exasperated, Madame went over to the window to look out. I could guess what she was thinking. She missed the Maryinsky and the Neva, London and her beautiful house at Golders Green. She had managed to escape from the Russian Revolution and had fallen from the frying pan into the fire. I stood at her back, my hands on her shoulders to try to calm her, but it was no use. I sighed, and wished with all my might that we were back in St. Petersburg.

23

We were looking around for the hotel when Madame opened her handbag and dropped a coin into a Red Cross box. An automobile insistently honked its horn. She turned around and couldn't believe her eyes: the yellow-and-black Pierce-Arrow that had picked her up at the wharf was right behind us. The top was down and an elderly gentleman with a white mane of hair in a double-breasted suit had his hands on the wheel. Diamantino stared incredulously. It was Don Pedro Batistini, and it was too late to slip away. Don Pedro was already waving at him, and Diamantino had no choice but to wave back.

"We'll have to go and say hello," he told Madame with a frown, and, taking her by the elbow, he propelled her through the crowd in the car's direction. Don Pedro had come to pick up his wife, who was participating in the parade. Doña Basilisa heard him and hurried over. She saw Diamantino before the couple reached the car and threw herself into the young man's arms.

"Tino, darling, where have you been! Six weeks without a word from you! I was so afraid something terrible had happened!"

Diamantino kissed the woman's cheek and tried to calm her, turning around to introduce Madame. "Maite, I want you to meet a friend of mine. She's here with a group of artists to perform at Teatro Oliver during the next few days."

"To perform? How?" Doña Basilisa asked in wonder.

"Madame is a world-famous ballerina, Maite. And I'm playing the violin in her orchestra now. It's a good job."

Doña Basilisa couldn't believe her ears. Diamantino had never held *any* kind of job, and playing the violin in an orchestra was not exactly the kind of employment the son of a well-to-do Puerto Rican family would be caught dead in, no matter what Don Pedro said. But Doña Basilisa was so glad to see him, she forgot all about it and kissed the young man on each cheek. Then she leaned toward Madame and embraced her too. "How lucky to have a beautiful lady like you as a friend!" she said as they walked together toward the car, with Doña Basilisa holding on to Madame's arm. Don Pedro opened the car door and the couple insisted that Madame and Diamantino ride with them to the house in Dos Ríos, which was just out of town. The dancer got in the backseat with Doña Basilisa, and Diamantino sat in front with his godfather. Madame opened a frilled pink umbrella over her head and Don Pedro started up the car. They were about to drive off when I waved at them. I planted my basket in the middle of the street and they had to either run over me or stop. Diamantino reluctantly opened the car door and I elbowed my way into the backseat. He stashed my basket in the car's trunk and we all drove away together.

24

"How wonderful to meet you, Madame. But of course, now I recognize you! I saw your picture in the *Puerto Rico Ilustrado* just a week ago. That young reporter who's a friend of Tino's, Rogelio Tellez, interviewed you, and he was most improper, asking you your age! I think you were absolutely right not wanting to answer. These young scalawags just get too big for their britches sometimes, don't you think?" Don Pedro winked at Diamantino. "Madame is a world-famous ballerina, *mija*," he turned around and explained to Doña Basilisa. "In fact, she's probably the most famous dancer in the world! We're very fortunate to meet her." The old man was acting as if nothing had happened between Diamantino and himself. He evidently wanted to patch things up.

Diamantino began to explain to Don Pedro what their plans were—they were going to stay in the Hotel Las Baleares, which was just in front of the plaza. It was a two-story building, with the rooms on the second floor and a balustered balcony around them. It had a restaurant, a soda fountain, and a bakery on the first floor, and a large American flag waving out front. Diamantino still had to go to the theater and speak to the manager, to arrange for a performance which they hoped would take place the following week—but Don Pedro interrupted. "What do you mean, the Hotel Las Baleares? Surely you'll be staying with us."

"Madame is not alone, Don Pedro, she brought a number of dancers with her, and they all want to stay together," Diamantino explained.

"Don't worry about anything, my dear," Don Pedro said to Madame. "I'm a friend of Don Andrés Oliver, the owner of the theater. You'll be able to dance there as much as you like. And the hotel will not charge you for the rooms because they'll be my guests, also. If I had known Tino was with you, I wouldn't have worried so much about his whereabouts these last few weeks!"

Don Pedro loved to have famous artists visit him, and he wasn't going to let Madame get away from him. "You'll have a wonderful time at our house, we'll see to that," he insisted. And he began to honk the horn, squeezing the black rubber bulb to make the people crowding the street scatter like geese to get out of his way. Madame sank back into her seat and tied her red chiffon scarf around her head. She was too tired to argue.

Doña Basilisa broke the silence: "I can't believe this coincidence! Yesterday I asked Pedro to bring me to Arecibo because the Red Cross began its campaign here, and since we're still official residents, I had to come join the volunteers in town. We had to pose before rolls of bandages and scissors and make believe we were going to cure wounded soldiers at the front. It was funny because, of course, there wasn't a wounded soldier in sight. I felt like an actress, with the war so far away. But now that we're American citizens, we must participate in all these official acts. My husband and I have been living in San Juan now for ten years, you know," she explained to Madame, "but people always keep their hometown close to their hearts and it's good to see one's friends again."

Doña Basilisa was now talking about her parents, who were Catalonian and French. They had a large business of importing cotton cloth, with which sheets, tablecloths, and all sorts of clothes were sewn by local seamstresses. Before their workshop was established in Arecibo, these items were very expensive because everything had to be imported; the common people wore crudely made clothes, cut from the white cotton bags in which flour was brought to the island. This was why the Red Cross had contacted her family—they were asked to donate several hundred yards of cotton to make bandages to be shipped overseas.

Doña Basilisa had an affable disposition and was very plump: she had a double chin that hung from her face like a coconut flan. And like most women from the provincial bourgeoisie, she had been schooled only up to eighth grade with a private tutor. Since her daughter was away studying in the States—as she was now informing Madame—she had very little to do during the day. That was why when Diamantino came to live in Don Pedro's house, she was so glad to have him there, she said. She loved him like her own son.

"So you're from St. Petersburg?" Doña Basilisa asked Madame in wonder. "The city of the czar! Tell me about the imperial family! I saw their picture in the paper once. Are they as rich as they say? Do they give each other Fabergé eggs every Easter?"

"Eggs are a symbol of life, and they are also healing instruments," Madame intervened. "That's why the czar and the czarina exchanged eggs at Easter. They were such elegant people and now they're all in prison like common criminals!"

Madame was almost in tears, and Doña Basilisa seemed taken aback.

"Is there a war in Russia? How amazing!" Doña Basilisa said.

"Maite doesn't read the papers, Madame," Don Pedro said apologetically. "I read them for her and then tell her about it. I forgot to mention the Romanovs' unfortunate fate."

Doña Basilisa looked sheepishly at Madame and giggled. There was definitely something wrong with her, I told myself. She wasn't all there in the head.

"You remember Rogelio, the young man who did the interview about you? He's a friend of Tino's," Doña Basilisa said. "He's staying in town for a few days and wants to do an in-depth article about you; that's why he's following you around. Tino would like to be a writer, like he is, but Rogelio's father has a lot of money, and he can afford to pay for his son's magazine, which of course is very bad business."

"Yes, I remember the reporter very well. He was wearing sunglasses inside the hotel, and my room was quite dark. I couldn't understand how he could take notes. I suspected he was *très gâté*."

"He was what, excuse me, Madame?" Don Pedro asked. Until then they had spoken English, but he didn't understand French.

"Very spoiled," Madame explained.

Don Pedro laughed. "We have a different term for that here, *alfeñique*, a young man made of almond nougat. You know what that means, right, Tino?" Don Pedro asked, winking at my mistress on the sly. Diamantino didn't answer, but scowled at the road ahead.

"So, when will we be seeing more of our reporter friend?" Madame asked.

"He'll be arriving tomorrow; he's staying with Doña Victoria, the piano teacher. She gives free piano classes to all those in town who have a musical aptitude. She lives in the house right next to the church."

"Doña Victoria Tellez is a piano teacher? But she's totally deaf!" Madame couldn't contain her amazement.

"Have you met her?" Doña Basilisa asked. "Her father used to be the mayor and they lived in the biggest house in town, which is the Alcaldía today. But when General Williams arrived, he asked the mayor to move out. The soldiers took over their house, and it became his official residence. Doña Victoria can't forgive him."

I knew then what Doña Victoria's banging on the piano was all about, and I smiled smugly. The rich were the same all over, in Russia or in Puerto Rico. Rogelio with his sunglasses, vest, and silk butterfly tie; Doña Victoria in her balconied house playing Beethoven to drown out the Americans; Madame keeping her eye on her jewelry case while she danced "for the people." I despised them all! None of them were Bolsheviks, no matter how much they posed. A Bolshevik was a turd, a bastard, a barbarian. A Bolshevik didn't have a cent, scratched himself in public, smelled bad, and farted all the way to Asia. Like me.

Madame was telling Doña Basilisa how Doña Victoria was so kind as to offer them something cool to drink when they had just gotten off the train. "We'll have to ask her over to our house for dinner, then, to return the kindness," Doña Basilisa said, and patted Madame's hand.

"Why did you come to our little town, Madame?" Don Pedro asked, straining his neck to look around at the dancer. "I can see why you traveled to San Juan, which is a rich city. But Arecibo! There's absolutely nothing here, except a few families who own run-down sugar mills like our own, and a lot of hungry peasants."

"Dancing is my vocation, monsieur," Madame said. "The purpose of my dancing is to give joy to the people, and help create a better world."

"Really?" said Don Pedro, looking askance at Doña Basilisa. "Well, we'll be more than happy to help you. Maite likes to do things for the common people, too, right, Maite? How much money did you raise for the Red Cross during the parade?" he asked his wife.

"We raised sixty dollars already. We feel so proud that Puerto Rico is soon to be involved in the European conflict! We're a part of the modern world now, and will give our blood in defense of the holy principles of democracy and liberty."

"Well, at least some of us will," Don Pedro said, not particularly to anyone.

"Puerto Ricans are not going to be fighting next to the Americans anytime soon," Diamantino answered, staring at Don Pedro over the top of his sunglasses. "They don't trust us."

Don Pedro laughed again, this time a little forcibly. "What do you mean they don't trust us? We're American citizens, aren't we?"

"We're citizens, all right, but not like they are. We're second class, and they know we know they know. That's why, when they need to have their backs covered, they'll get a hillbilly from Kansas to help them out, not a *jíbaro* from Cayey. And as to the food they're making us grow, we should give it to our starving population instead."

"The boy is crazy! Youth is wonderful, isn't that so, Madame?" Don Pedro turned toward Madame, laughing condescendingly. "You think you can get away with anything."

"I'm sorry, but I don't believe in war," Madame answered

solemnly. "I believe in beauty as a healing force, and I'm opposed to all kinds of violence. So, if anyone refuses to join the army to fight a war, I would have done the same."

"Oh, you mustn't talk like that, either of you, you really mustn't!" Doña Basilisa whispered as she fanned herself with her wide-brimmed straw hat. "It's very dangerous to say things like that in public around here. The police have ears everywhere, and you could both be put in jail. Thank God we're in the car, and what you've both said will stay in the family!"

A silence followed during which I wondered about the different ways the term "good for the people" was interpreted. To Madame it meant art as spiritual inspiration—her head in the clouds, as usual; to Doña Basilisa and Don Pedro it meant becoming prosperous American citizens and helping the army and the Red Cross; and to Diamantino it meant political independence for the island. But none of them belonged to the "people" except me! I was the only one who knew what the people really needed, and that was decent salaries. I was about to open my mouth to say so when we arrived at the house and I was made to get out of the car.

Two beautiful Airedales, yellow and light gray, came to say hello, barking and proudly swinging their tails like banners. "These are Oro and Plata. They were a gift to us from Governor Yager a year ago, when he stayed at Dos Ríos for a few days," Don Pedro said jovially. And he led the way to show Madame a very pleasant room opening onto a verandah, with a comfortable "rainbow hammock" of woven maguey fiber hanging just outside the door. Inside, the bed was a four-poster, and it had something like a wire colander hanging above it, covered by a mosquito net tied into a large knot. "I'll sleep in the hammock if you wish, Madame," I blurted out, picking up my wicker basket and placing it next to the hammock.

Madame gave a sigh, went into the bedroom, and resignedly locked the door. I was exhausted, but I wasn't going to give up. I wearily took up my lookout post outside her door.

The next morning Don Pedro, Diamantino, and I went into town in the car. We were going to pick up the rest of Madame's luggage and check on the troupe at the Hotel Las Baleares. "I don't suppose you're considering this little escapade seriously?" Don Pedro asked his godson in Spanish, thinking I couldn't understand him, and arching his eyebrows as he put the key in the ignition. "She's not only old enough to be your mother, she's a *vedette*, a stage *bataclana*. It's all right to have her as a 'friend,' but you don't have to proclaim it to the world."

"I thought you admired her, Padrino," Diamantino said. His voice dripped with irony.

"Of course I do. And Maite likes her too. But it's one thing to like sweetsop and another to get the mess all over you."

"I'm twenty years old, and I don't have to ask you who I can spend my time with, Padrino."

A heavy silence followed during which Don Pedro rolled down the car window. The heat was sweltering, and his shirt was soaked with perspiration. "Well, we were worried to death about you all these weeks. It was most inconsiderate to leave without any explanation. Maite, especially, has gone through a lot. Where were you hiding? Someone said they'd seen you in the mountains a while back."

"I'm sorry, I didn't mean to hurt Maite's feelings. But I can't say where I was staying. I was with friends."

"Be careful what you're getting into, Tino. The war is at our doorstep and Americans don't fool around. Political agitators, like terrorists and draft evaders, are sentenced to life at federal prisons on the mainland." But Tino kept stubbornly silent, and Don Pedro looked away.

"So, did you find a job in San Juan? I mean, a real job. Not playing the violin in a vaudeville company, like you've been doing these past few days."

"Yes, I found a job," Diamantino said quietly. But he refused to volunteer any more information.

 "My godfather is obnoxious, but you'll be more comfortable staying here, because the Las Baleares is definitely not the Ritz," Diamantino told Madame solicitously when we got back from town with the luggage. I was sitting out in the hammock, but I could hear their voices clearly through the louvered windows. "It'll only be for a few days, and we can simply ignore him and enjoy the amenities."

That evening, after dinner, they left the house and took a narrow path between the sugarcane stalks which ended at the seashore, a mile and a half ahead. I followed them, ducking behind the shrubs of beach grapes as subtly as I could. It was a cool night, and the sea was tossing restlessly, rolling long arms of foam up and down the beach as if trying to dispel insomnia.

"I've booked the theater for three nights in a row. You'll start performing on Friday next week," Diamantino was saying. "And as soon as we've collected the money we'll take off on our own. I can't bear to be separated from you any longer." His words were like a thread of fire winding itself around her heart. She let him kiss her, and shamelessly agreed to the plan.

They were reclining on a sand dune, and Diamantino was

leaning over my mistress, propped up on an elbow. I saw the
emotion alter the expression of his face. I sighed and told myself I'd seen enough. But something—a primeval jealousy or
maybe my own solitude—kept me there. I wanted to test my
endurance, to be a witness to the ritual of love. Would I have to
look away? My heart was racing, and I wondered how strong I
really was.

I had often seen Madame naked when I helped her bathe,
but her nudity then was as unselfconscious and innocent as
Eve's, the kind we all experience in childhood. She had a beautiful body in spite of her age; her skin was a dusty pearl, the
color of powdered snow at dusk, and she had lean arms and
legs that glimmered softly as she moved. But when Diamantino
began to undress Madame, her nakedness was different—it was
a deliberate address to the eyes, a command to envelop and
bring close in a consuming embrace. "I love you," I heard
Madame whisper faintly. "I'll do anything for you."

And I, who had never loved, felt weak with yearning and at
the same time defeated, as if a wave of mythic proportions had
rolled over my head and left me stranded on the beach. My
flesh trembled as if I had an ague and I sought refuge against
the bristly side of the dune like a poor, ungainly mollusk that
had suddenly lost its shell. When the lovers dozed off, I crept
silently away.

That night, after Madame turned out the light, I hardly dared
to breathe. All Madame's life had been a struggle between love
and art: Prince Kotschubei, Dandré, Nijinsky, all the leading
men in her life filed before me in their elegant attires: the
prince in his golden vest and lace-ruffed shirt; Dandré in his
dark suit and black bowler hat; Nijinsky in magenta rose petals,

as he appeared in *Le Spectre de la Rose*. I knew that, after becoming temporarily infatuated, Madame had rejected all of
them. I couldn't believe what was happening. For the first time
Madame was insisting that Love was more important than Art.
The world had turned on its head.

I lay in the hammock perfectly still, crossing its woven
maguey folds over my arms and legs to keep the mosquitoes
from biting. I may have looked exactly like a tamale wrapped in
a corn husk, but I kept an eye out for any suspicious janglings
or rattlings that might indicate a visitor had slipped into
Madame's bed. Thankfully, the house remained as silent as a
tomb.

 At lunch the next day Don Pedro was talking about a band of wild riders called Los Tiznados, who had laid waste to several of the neighboring towns. Their faces were rubbed with sugarcane soot so they couldn't be recognized, and they carried Mauser rifles as they crisscrossed the mountains shooting at everything in sight. In town they had set fire to the brand-new American post office and to a National City Bank branch. No sugarcane mill was safe from them, and at night, little tongues of fire were often seen licking the mounds of dry sugarcane chaff on the fringes of the pressing installations. One or two choice fields burst into fire every day at dawn, after having been doused with gasoline.

Don Pedro hardly slept, trying to keep an eye on things. "They should wring their necks like chickens—*el garrote vil* to all of them, and save the bullets!" he said, pale with anger. "People are talking about the marines coming to help us but nothing happens. As usual, we'll have to take care of things ourselves." He patted the gun he was carrying in his holster.

Molinari was invited for dinner, and he came over from town early. He agreed with Don Pedro wholeheartedly. Even though he was déclassé, Molinari was a coffee hacendado and the Batistinis were glad to have him at their table. He had gone off to town the day before and had just come back with a letter from Dandré, which Madame read during lunch. It was from the Gotham Hotel, and she wondered if Dandré had snitched the stationery or if he was really staying there. She had pictured him at his girlfriend's apartment. Dandré was well and sent his love. Thanks to Mr. Hinojosa, the Cuban ambassador, who was a lot more powerful than the Puerto Rican resident commissioner in Washington, the U.S. government had finally agreed to help him get the English visas. He'd be back in two weeks at the latest. Madame's hands trembled slightly as she folded the letter and put it inside her handbag. By that time, she was sure, Dandré would never be able to find her.

I was surprised to discover that Molinari knew Bienvenido Pérez, and that apparently they were good friends. They had met while Bienvenido was studying at the university and Molinari had helped the young man out with a loan of some sort while he was still a student. The two men stepped out on the verandah to smoke cigars and converse amicably.

When we entered the dining room for lunch, Molinari sat in front of Madame and wouldn't take his eyes off her. "Good news, Madame?" he asked, leaning toward her in his buzzard's suit, as she began to read Mr. Dandré's letter. He sat with the sunlight at his back, so his shadow slid over her arms. Madame shuddered at the contact. "Of course. Mr. Dandré will be back soon, and we'll be able to sail on to Panama."

"Mr. Dandré is a very able manager. You're lucky to have him," Molinari said to her.

"Yes, I know. We make a good team," Madame answered, looking down at her plate. She was certain he'd read her thoughts if she looked into his eyes.

"Things here are volatile, Madame," he rumbled ominously. "You and your ballerinas don't belong here. I wouldn't stay on long, if I were you."

Juan came up to the hacienda that afternoon, and as soon as Doña Basilisa saw him she ordered him to go to the kitchen to help Doña Basilisa's maid, Adelina, peel the potatoes and gut the guinea hens, after plucking them in a bucket of scalding water. Juan was an educated man, but because he was black, Doña Basilisa sent him straight to the kitchen. He kept quiet about it, however, and I was lucky he did, because Doña Basilisa let him spend the night at the house so he could help the servants out.

I liked *arroz con guinea* immensely; the fowl had the same smoky, bitter taste our game meat had in St. Petersburg, and as I sat at the table during dinner I kept thinking of Madame's beautiful dining room in Anglisky Prospekt, which was decorated with blue velvet curtains. We often ate partridges there, because Madame's admirers sent them as presents. I was helping serve at the dinner table when I felt someone step close to me. Juan held the silver platter with the rice and guinea hen to pass it a second time, and he stood so close to me, the heat of his hips and lower abdomen radiated right through my muslin blouse. I felt a delicious shudder as the aroma of the wild meat mixed with the odor of his perspiration. When Juan approached with a new dish, he repeated the operation until a suspicious bundle began to swell beneath his white cotton pants. I gave a start and looked away embarrassed, just in time to catch Molinari staring at me with lecherous eyes. I had to laugh! In St. Petersburg nobody looked at Masha, but here men were flocking to her like flies!

Juan wore a very handsome pair of shoes which he had made himself before leaving San Juan, but the rest of the servants in the dining room were barefoot. They didn't make a sound as they moved around the table, serving the wine from cut crystal carafes and other delicious tidbits from silver platters. I was depressed by their presence—pale, thin zombies dressed in rags.

After dinner, Madame disappeared from the house. She was spending more and more time by herself, and never wanted me to accompany her. I supposed Diamantino was to blame, every time she went for another "walk on the beach." Juan and I sat in the hammock after we finished picking up the table and clearing the dishes, swinging to and fro on the balcony. Juan was feeling very romantic, but I was too worried about Madame, who was probably rolling at that very moment over some dark sand ridge, catering to her own pleasures, to pay him much attention. My innocent flirting was naive; I could never behave like Madame and throw decency to the winds.

The hammock's movement made the jasmine bush growing next to us smell more fragrant, and as I inhaled its perfume my head rolled back over the woven straw and the angle of my vision changed. The door to Madame's room was slightly ajar, and a thin ray of faint light, only slightly lighter than the night wrapped around us like a mantle, came from inside her chamber. Suddenly I saw a shadow flit across it. Quick as lighting, I jumped out of the hammock and flung the doors open. There was Molinari, standing with his back to us, searching for something in Madame's open suitcase. He leaped away, agile as a cat.

"I'll kill you if you come any closer," he said, flicking out a shiny blade and waving it at us. I was petrified and couldn't move. Juan barged into the room in front of me, but it was too late. Molinari jumped out the window, which opened onto the garden, and then he slithered down the mango tree.

27

The next day we kept what had happened to ourselves. Juan was convinced Molinari was an agent and that he was under the police commissioner's orders; it was better if we didn't meddle with him. The commissioner still suspected Madame was a Bolshevik and was probably having her followed. That morning Doña Basilisa took us to see her orchid grove, where she grew her rarest specimens that clung like spidery stars to the stems of pygmy coconut palms. As we strolled among the white cattleyas and phalaenopsis, we couldn't understand why Doña Basilisa kept praying in whispers.

After a while I got tired of her mumbo-jumbo—her pious Ave Marias and Paternosters—and I asked Doña Basilisa if I could pick some of the blossoms and take them up to my room. But Doña Basilisa refused. "In Russia you have cherry orchards and in Puerto Rico we have orchid groves," she said. "An orchid should blossom and die on the plant, it must never be cut off. Orchids are sacred to us. But we won't have them for long if the revolution breaks out! God save us." And she crossed herself. When I listened to this I felt my Bolshevik

blood rising. What gall! To talk about the Russian Revolution
as if it were unfair.

Doña Basilisa's admiration for Madame stemmed from her
connection to the Old World, and she didn't see anything
wrong with Diamantino's infatuation with the dancer. It was
simply a passing fancy, a *romance a lo divino*, which would leave
them both with beautiful memories once Madame's dance tour
moved on and the swan again took flight.

Later that afternoon at Dos Ríos everybody had a siesta. I
managed to doze off in the hammock after I put Madame in
bed and tucked the mosquito net around her. When we got up
around four, Doña Victoria had just arrived from town with
Rogelio Tellez, riding in her nephew's Willis Overland. They
were sitting on the verandah drinking tea and fanning themselves with large *panderetas* made of pale green braided palm
leaves. Diamantino was explaining to Doña Victoria with sign
language what the *Bacchanale* was all about. She disapprovingly
shook her head. Diamantino repeated her answer out loud:
"You mean Madame and you will actually dance the myth of
the God Dionysus and Ariadne of Naxos? But nobody will understand what it's all about! Do you think people in Arecibo
know anything about Greek mythology? It'll be Greek to
them, my dear!" I scowled at her, but since I couldn't talk with
my fingers, I didn't answer.

Rogelio began to ask Don Pedro about Los Tiznados, and if
they had committed any terrorist acts lately. Doña Victoria read
his lips, immediately sat up in her rocking chair, and stopped
fanning herself. Her hands moved incessantly: "They're not
terrorists. They're freedom fighters. That's what you should
be choreographing, my dear," Diamantino interpreted. "Stra-
vinsky's *Firebird*, dressed in workers' overalls, instead of Saint-
Saëns's *The Dying Swan* in musty, moth-eaten feathers. Art must

be committed and denounce injustice if it's going to be any good."

I couldn't believe my ears. In Russia, Madame had renounced her belief in Bolshevism precisely because she wanted to remain loyal to her aesthetic values. She remained bound to the czar and his court even when she knew Nicholas was a tyrant and his generals were butchers, and we Russians pardoned her because she was a great artist. And now she was letting this half-demented old hag, with hair as straggly as an ancient lion's, accuse her, in this two-bit town on this two-bit island, precisely of the nightmare we were running away from. "Go to hell!" I yelled at the needling little woman, who was now leaning forward, shaking a finger at us. Madame got up and left the verandah, but instead of going to her room she went angrily down the stairs and took one of the paths close to the house that led to the mill.

I followed Madame, walking behind her as quickly as possible and holding an open parasol over her head. Her skin was very delicate and she couldn't stand the sun, so I always went with her when she went out—especially at noon. Suddenly we heard steps coming down the gravel path. It was Molinari.

I walked on rapidly, but Madame stopped by a hibiscus hedge. My heart beat like a snared bird's. I hadn't told her about Molinari's sinister visit to her room the night before because I didn't want her to know I'd been secretly meeting with Juan.

"You mustn't mind Victoria," Molinari said, drawing closer. "Her deafness has made her resentful and she's a bit off her rocker. She's mad to defend Los Tiznados; there's a price on their heads, you know. But why am I worrying you with all that? Please forgive me. Would you like me to take you on a tour of the grounds? All the hacienda's machinery was made in Scotland and it's fascinating to see how it works."

Molinari looked at me, as if sizing me up. His invitation, after what had happened the night before, made me go cold. He guessed I hadn't told Madame about it.

Madame tartly refused. She had a headache, she said, and wanted to go somewhere quiet to be alone. When Molinari insisted, she turned around and walked quickly back to the house. I shut the parasol and tucked it under my arm like a weapon. I should have run away then also, but I didn't. Maybe it was the thrill of danger; maybe it was something darker, the need to experience evil at first hand, as I had in my childhood. Most of all, I didn't want him to think I was afraid of him. I was about to turn back when Molinari clamped his hand on my shoulder.

He gave me a lecherous look, dragging his yellow eyes over me like a vulture. I just stood there, rooted to the spot.

"And how is my hefty Russian milkmaid?" Molinari asked, smirking. "You promised you'd cooperate with me in San Juan, remember? You wanted to get rid of Diamantino too."

I said I had no idea what he meant and tried to shake him loose, but he had me in a vise grip. He propelled me toward the mill, a huge building built of corrugated zinc sheets, and we walked past dozens of roller presses, vats, and vacuum pans and several huge Catherine wheels. I couldn't have cared less if they were made in Scotland or Finland. I was terrified. The roar was deafening and there was febrile activity everywhere. After a few minutes, a thin film of sugarcane chaff was sticking to my arms and face. None of the laborers had shoes on, and they wore their pants tied at the ankle with *bejucos*, dried strips of plantain leaf, in order to keep the centipedes from crawling up their legs and into their crotches. They all looked away as we walked by, pretending they didn't see us.

Molinari pushed me toward a shed at the back, where the

discarded roller presses, their grooves eaten by rust, were stored. He made me go in, shutting the door behind him. I was as tall and strong as he was, but the smell of camphor and mothballs overwhelmed me as he pushed me against the wall. All of a sudden I was back in Minsk, locked up in a closet in my father's house. I closed my eyes.

That night I sat next to Madame under the mosquito net while I tenderly massaged her feet. I was still shaken, but I put my anger about what had happened with Molinari aside and managed to control myself. After I came out of the shed that afternoon I had dragged myself to a deserted stretch of beach, removed my clothes, and soaked in the salt water for nearly an hour, hoping to cure my wounds.

Madame lay back on her bed and looked reproachfully at me.

"Where were you this afternoon, Masha? I looked all over for you."

"I took a walk down the beach, Madame. But I'm here with you now, so you mustn't worry." She was suspicious, but I could easily fool her. I knew her weaknesses.

It took me a long time to quiet her down. She complained that she still had a migraine, and I rubbed her temples with eucalyptus oil as delicately as I could. "Where is Diamantino? Have you seen him?" she asked.

"He went into town with Novikov, Madame, he had errands to do," I answered quietly, not rising to the bait. I knew she wanted to talk about him but refused to comply.

I should have been thinking of myself, of the terrible thing that had happened to me that day, but I could only think of her. I wanted to bring her out of her depression and didn't know how. "The roly-poly ladies of Arecibo never wear red because they say it's the whores' favorite color," I spoke out like a parrot as I got up to hang her clothes in the wardrobe and began to look for her nightgown. "They say it makes bulls aggressive when they go for a walk out of town!"

But Madame didn't laugh at my halfhearted joke. She sat up on the bed, incensed. "This time I'm not going to throw my lot in with the oppressors as I did in Russia, out of loyalty to the czar!" she cried, with no small measure of melodrama. She was going to help that zealot, Diamantino Márquez, bring justice to the world.

"We can't get rid of the past that easily," I cautioned her. "In the eyes of the world you'll always be the czar's ballerina." Madame didn't answer. It was as if a sheet of ice had formed between us.

The next morning Madame, Diamantino, and I rode into town in Don Pedro's Pierce-Arrow for the first rehearsal at Teatro Oliver. Novikov and the girls looked haggard, as if they hadn't slept all night. They complained that the beds at the hotel were iron cots, and that they were full of bugs; the rooms were separated from each other only by low wooden walls, so there was no privacy. At least the beach was very near to the hotel, and the girls went swimming in the morning. When they saw Madame they greeted her icily, and I wondered at how fast news got around about what was going on at the house. I was sure they would have returned gladly to San Juan if they could have done so.

We rehearsed at the colonial theater, which was surprisingly large and elegant for such a small town. Spaniards have no sense of proportion; when they build something they do it to last forever, even at the bitter end of the world. Madame immediately felt the influence of her grand surroundings, and as she lifted her arms in an arch over her head and let Novikov circle her waist, she became transformed. There was an old stand-up piano at the back of the stage and Smallens sat down before it. "Order and you shall be obeyed!" he said to Madame with a little bow. "Monteverdi's *Orpheus*," she said with a thrill, "because today Eurydice has risen from the dead." She danced as I had never seen her dance before. The arpeggios rose and fell under her feet like silver ladders from the bowels of the earth.

When the rehearsal was over, we went back to Dos Ríos to rest. "Do you think it's wise to go on wearing your tunic when you dance the *Bacchanale* on opening night?" I asked, trying to be as diplomatic as possible. "People may think you're wearing it for political reasons." But Madame didn't heed my warning, and the costume for the *Bacchanale*—the red chiffon tunic I loved because it made her look like a Communist Venus—was kept as it was. She only asked me to repair the hem. That night I knelt in front of the icon of the Virgin of Vladimir and prayed that the days might go by fast and that Dandré, the lesser of two evils, would come back to us as soon as possible. Madame knelt by my side and, I am sure, prayed that he would never return.

29

On Sunday, Doña Basilisa's daughter came home from school to spend summer vacation on the island. Ronda Batistini arrived from the States early; her ship dropped her off at Arecibo's wharf at eight in the morning. Don Pedro was crazy about his daughter and went to pick her up in the Pierce-Arrow himself.

"This is my daughter," Doña Basilisa said to Madame proudly as she took the girl to meet the dancer. They were all sitting in rocking chairs out on the verandah, drinking cold *guarapo*—silvery sugarcane juice—spiked with a little rum in tall glasses. Ronda was refreshingly spontaneous; she pumped my hand vigorously and then gripped Madame's, defying Puerto Rican custom, which dictated that women never shook hands. "I saw posters of your performance at the Metropolitan Opera House, but I couldn't get tickets. And now you'll be dancing in my hometown," the girl said, clearly elated to meet the famous ballerina.

Adelina, Doña Basilisa's maid, told me the story of Ronda that morning, as we were preparing lunch. The girl was the apple of her parents' eyes, she said as she gave me a bowl of *gandules* to clean, picking out the dry ones. The tender smell of the fresh peas reminded me of spring in the Russian countryside, and I breathed it in so that it would cure my lungs. Since her brother, Adalberto—the one no one ever talked about in the house because of Don Pedro's religious beliefs—had vanished, Ronda would be Dos Ríos's sole heir. This made her feel she had a great responsibility resting on her shoulders.

Her brother's disappearance made a deep impression on Ronda, who grew up to be sober-minded and thoughtful. Perhaps because she tried desperately not to dwell on her brother's absence, she had developed an intense passion for healing. She loved animals and was always bringing sick dogs and cats to the house, which turned into a regular animal hospital because she would bathe, feed, and minister to them. She became famous all around Dos Ríos for her gift and people would travel for miles to bring her their sick pets. Many brought them when they were terminally ill and knew they were going to die. "I want my dog to die with you," they'd say to her. "After being my companion for fifteen years, it's the least I can do for him." And Ronda became used to looking death in the face.

When Ronda turned sixteen Don Pedro insisted she go to high school in the States. He wanted to get her away from the turmoil at the farm, from the yapping dogs and lowing cows she was always taking care of. At first Doña Basilisa was adamant and refused to be separated from her daughter, but when she learned that Diana Yager, the governor's daughter, was attending Lady Lane School in Massachusetts, she condescended to send Ronda to the same school, where she would learn proper manners.

At Lady Lane, Ronda discovered how different she was from the rest of the girls. The housemother boxed her ears because she sliced meat and ate with the knife in her right hand and the fork in her left, "as stevedores do," instead of putting the fork down and picking it up again with the right in a routine polite young ladies were supposed to observe; because she reached across the table for the bread, or threw salt over her shoulder for good luck whenever it spilled over. Her roommates laughed at her because she doused her bedsheets with bay rum every night to keep away bad dreams and drank tea made from soursop leaves her mother sent her in little brown paper parcels, to use whenever she had menstrual cramps. But Ronda patiently stood their teasing because soon she would be returning to her pets.

When she came to Arecibo for vacation in the summer she scandalized everyone with her American tomboy independence. She wore bell-bottomed khaki slacks in public, smoked unfiltered Chesterfields, and took her pets riding with her in her father's Pierce-Arrow. She went to the beach alone at night with her boyfriends to roast marshmallows on an open fire, and never went to Mass on Sundays. Tongues wagged, but she was headstrong and went on doing what she pleased. She was very pretty, with light brown curls that framed her oval-shaped face and made her look like an ivory miniature. Don Pedro and Doña Basilisa were crazy about her. They forgave her rebellious behavior and kept her on a pedestal.

When she graduated from high school that spring, Ronda said she wanted only two things: to be able to go on to veterinary school and to own a *pura sangre*, a *paso fino* horse she wanted as a graduation present. She dreamed it would be all white, its mane and tail the color of *guarapo* spilling all the way to the ground, and its glossy pelt rippling under the sun. She planned to name it Rayo, and would love it for as long as she lived. But Don Pedro, in spite of his preference for his daughter, refused both. There were no women veterinarians on the island—it was a career for men. And owning a spirited horse was

dangerous, she might have a serious accident. They had already
tragically lost her brother, and they couldn't risk losing her also.
Don Pedro had written Ronda a formal letter at school informing her of all this—Adelina the maid had heard him read
it out loud to Doña Basilisa before he mailed it—but as they
still hadn't talked about these matters in person, Adelina was
sure Don Pedro would eventually give in. "What Ronda wants,
Ronda gets," Adelina told me, shaking a sheaf of freshly picked
lettuce out the kitchen window as she began to make the salad
for lunch.

Ronda got along better with her mother than with her father. Don Pedro's family was Spanish; his father had been born
in Majorca, at a little town called Soller, where he built a magnificent stone house with the money he sent back home from
Dos Ríos. Don Pedro was very strict with Ronda, and expected her to get married and start a family as soon as she graduated from high school. Doña Basilisa, on the other hand, saw
her daughter's veterinary career as an actual possibility. Don Pedro should consent to let the girl pursue her studies, since later
she could lend a hand at the mill. She could help cure farm animals—the cows, the heifers, and above all, the valuable oxen,
with their horns bound in strips of mud-spattered cotton sacks,
that pulled the sugarcane carts up and down the slushy country
roads.

Doña Basilisa wasn't religious like Don Pedro. Her family
was half Spanish, half French—great admirers of encyclopedists
like Montaigne, Voltaire, and Montesquieu. They were skeptics
and rationalists, and Doña Basilisa was also, if only by family
tradition, because she certainly hadn't read them. But she never
dared express her own opinions or contradict her husband in
any way. At the dinner table, when Ronda argued with Don
Pedro and ran sobbing to her room, Doña Basilisa would follow

and simply sit next to her on the bed, stroking her daughter's hair without saying a word. Doña Basilisa's comforting presence, her soft arms that always smelled of powder, and her cool hands eventually helped Ronda regain her self-control.

Doña Basilisa couldn't even begin to imagine what would happen if Don Pedro found out that Ronda and Bienvenido Pérez were attracted to each other. When Ronda came back from school that summer looking so beautiful and full of life, Doña Basilisa became even more apprehensive. She knew Don Pedro was capable of anything; he would be furious with Bienvenido when he found out. He had helped the young man acquire an education partly to get him away from the farm. But Bienvenido, instead of staying in San Juan once he graduated, where he had many more opportunities as an engineer, had, incredibly, come back to Arecibo.

Madame was pleased to meet Ronda. She liked young women who knew what they wanted. When Madame learned Ronda was going to be a veterinarian, she thought it was wonderful. She told her all about the exotic whiskered nightingales she had received as a gift in Cuba, and about Poppy, her American bull terrier, who looked just like her husband. "I often get along better with my pets than with many of my friends," Madame confessed to Ronda. "Most animals are more trustworthy than people." Ronda, on her part, hit it off with Madame from the start because of her passionate nature.

At first the girl was a heavy cross to bear. I found her conceited and spoiled—being her father's pet she was used to getting her way—and I couldn't understand why Madame found her so charming and went out of her way to be nice to her. But then, Madame always did all she could to gain a hold on her young female admirers. At first she thought she could do the same with Ronda. The girl admired Madame to no end and wanted to know all about her, but she was already in love with Bienvenido when they met. Madame could never control her.

Madame went everywhere with Diamantino now, and they were often seen at the beach swimming or visiting Doña Victoria's parlor in the evening, where they sat together listening to music. When her love affair with that Young Turk became evident, a rift opened between Madame and the girls. They refused to come to the house to see Madame, and spent most of the time on their own in Arecibo. Madame, on the other hand, liked to be with Ronda when she wasn't with her lover (she was almost never with me anymore). Ronda entertained her and took her mind off the animosity that had sprung up between her and our troupe. To feel rejected and unloved, after being the center of attention for so many years, was a calamity Madame could not accept. Furthermore, when Ronda found out about the rumors that were going around about the dancer—that she was almost forty and had fallen for Diamantino Márquez, who was twenty—"an old hag embracing a pink-cheeked cupid," as her backbiting students put it—Ronda was incensed. "I don't care how old she is! If she loves him, all the more power to her."

One afternoon, Madame and I decided to walk to town with Ronda instead of waiting for Diamantino to drive us there. We strode down the road, enjoying the sunshine and the sweet breeze which combed the cane fields. Oro and Plata ran beside us. "In Philadelphia once I got to see Isadora Duncan dance barefoot," Ronda said. "I liked her very much," she added candidly. "Why don't you dance barefoot, Madame, instead of with your feet bound like Chinese women? It would make you much closer to nature." And when Madame laughed and insisted she was wrong, that classical ballet made the liberation of the spirit possible precisely by disciplining the body, the girl answered: "Isadora's art is far more advanced than yours."

"That may be so, my dear," I retorted in defense of Madame. "But *I'd* like to see Madame dancing barefoot and au naturel if she began drinking vodka with her caviar in the company of poets with golden locks and baby blue eyes, like Isadora did with Essenin, her Russian Ganymede."

That exchange was worthy of the trenches of Verdun, and I felt proud of myself. But when Madame heard what I said, she turned and stared back at me accusingly. "How about the pot calling the kettle black?" she shot at me. And I knew then she had caught me making love with Juan, who was ten years older than I was, on the verandah's hammock.

Doña Basilisa wanted to have a picnic on the beach for Ronda. She asked us to help out, and we carried everything we needed down to the seashore: towels, canvas chairs, umbrellas, tablecloths, napkins, paper plates, and cups. Adelina brought out steaming cauldrons full of delicious food that Doña Basilisa had prepared: rice and guinea hen, roasted pork, *pasteles, hayacas*, rabbit fricassee, and we all went merrily over to the nearest palm grove looking for shade. Diamantino was wearing an oil-black bathing suit which fit him like a glove. It was the first time I had seen him partly without his clothes on, and I must admit I felt jealous. He was very attractive; under the circumstances, Madame's folly seemed more understandable.

Don Pedro had picked out a special wine from his wine cellar—a golden amontillado which we cooled at the water's edge, inside a lobster trap. The day was clear as a glass bell, as they often are in December on the island. I was feeling happy and looking forward to the outing when I saw Diamantino and Madame kissing shamelessly in public, a bit further down the beach. They were leaning into the wind and Madame's clothes were billowing around them; they looked like a pair of sloops sailing full gale.

Food was the only magic raft I could hold on to so as not to sink in an ocean of sorrow. My appetite has always been my impending nemesis, and I've finally succumbed to it in my old age. Now I'm fat and have stopped worrying about my weight, but when I was young I used to remind myself: "A minute on the tongue, a lifetime on the hip, Masha," trying to resist temptation. Doña Basilisa was an expert temptress, and the day of the picnic I ate everything in sight. It was the most effective way to combat depression.

Doña Basilisa had invited several of her friends from the War Relief Association: twenty ladies, all of them as plump as she was, with flanlike double chins and pink elephant legs and arms, all wearing white uniforms with red crosses sewn on their caps. After lunch they planned to cross the canal, Caño Tiburones, in a towed barge and visit Piñales, a hamlet with several poor neighborhoods. They meant to make speeches to the people there, asking for Red Cross donations and instructing the children as well as the adults on how to plant manioc roots and breadfruit and plantain trees, fast-growing staples which traveled well. They would pick up the produce themselves in a few months in several wagons, they said, to ship them to the soldiers overseas.

It was obvious Doña Basilisa had her heart set on making a good match for her daughter: Diamantino was just the right age for the girl, and he was from an excellent family. With time he would inherit part of Don Pedro's fortune and maybe go into politics, as Don Pedro wanted him to. "Things have to happen naturally," Doña Basilisa told me with a wink that afternoon, when she asked Ronda to spread the gay, red-checked tablecloth on the sand with Diamantino's help. "They can't be forced." But it was obvious where Diamantino's interest lay, and he only treated Ronda like a good friend.

I had to wheedle and plead, but I finally convinced our

dancers to come to the party. They arrived a little later with Molinari. Juan was at the beach also, and was helping me carry the cauldrons of food to a shaded spot under a sea-grape shrub when we saw them. Molinari brought with him two bottles of rum and he said hello as if nothing had happened. Juan and I did the same. Where was he staying? He wasn't at the hotel, and he certainly wasn't at Dos Ríos; he had disappeared for three or four days. Neither of us dared question him about his little night visit, however, and we decided to wait until we could corner him alone.

The servants passed the rice and guinea hen around and we all began to eat and drink. Our girls wouldn't join the rest of the company; they kept to themselves in a little group, grumbling and complaining about the heat, the sun, the mosquitoes—whatever they could think of to spoil Madame's happiness. I walked over to them and heard them discussing how much money they would need from the sale of the tickets to go back to San Juan after the first few performances. Madame pretended she didn't hear, and went on sitting next to Diamantino and sipping white wine under a large-leafed almond tree to keep out of the sun. Doña Basilisa and her Arecibo friends sat at a long wooden trestle table the servants had set up under the palm trees, shaded by large black umbrellas.

After lunch, Doña Basilisa called out to the boatman to ferry her over to Piñales. The girls all dove into the shallow waves and were cooling off in water up to their chests when I saw them whispering among themselves. A mischievous gleam had appeared in Nadja's eyes. She was the most talented of the dancers, and since Madame and I were staying at Dos Ríos she had become the leader of the pack. Doña Basilisa and her friends were standing placidly on the barge, letting themselves be rowed to the other side of the canal, when the girls began to wade determinedly toward them. Madame, Diamantino, and I stood on the shore, wondering what was going on.

Nadja, Katia, Maya, and Egorova, together with Ronda, who now joined them and was laughing hysterically, pulled themselves up on the barge and sat on it until it began to sink. The fisherman who was shoving it with a long pole across the canal began to shout for them to get off, and we ran forward to try to help him. But the girls wouldn't budge. Doña Basilisa and her twenty plump, powdered friends slowly sank to the bottom of the canal like so many waterlogged pink elephants. Fortunately, the canal was shallow at that point and the water only came to their waists. Their snow-white Red Cross uniforms ruined, they had to give up their plans to collect money from the poor and to teach the starving people of Piñales how to plant manioc root and plantain to feed the soldiers overseas.

I wondered if the girls had had too much to drink in the heat, or whether they were following someone's orders. I remembered seeing the servants passing around jiggers of Molinari's rum with tall glasses of lemonade, which the girls drank avidly. Fear filled my heart. The devil was punishing us for our sins, stirring the pot with his tail.

Doña Basilisa wasn't angry at what had happened; she took the whole thing in stride. "You wanted to teach us how to swim, isn't that so, dear?" she asked Ronda and the dancers as she came out of the water, laughing good-naturedly and dripping from head to toe. Her friends from town didn't laugh, however, and they all angrily left the party, heading toward the house to dry themselves before driving back home. Suddenly I felt sorry for Doña Basilisa; she was all sweetness but she had no core, a chubby, gray-haired little girl everybody made fun of. To prove that she didn't hold anything against Ronda and the dancers, she invited us all to dinner at the house that evening. But Nadja, Katia, and Maya began bickering among themselves about who was going to dance the leading role in the chorus. Madame had to intervene and ordered them all back to town with Smallens and Novikov. Molinari went with them; he said he had something important to do in town. Madame said she would stay on at Dos Ríos with me.

That evening Bienvenido, Don Pedro's godson, was invited for dinner, and as he arrived early I welcomed him into the house, making small talk while everyone finished dressing. Doña Basilisa was in the kitchen giving the last touches to her suckling pig basted in Madeira wine. My mistress was taking a long bath. I needed a respite from so much tension and we sat out on the balcony admiring the star-studded sky.

I had heard a lot about Bienvenido and his family from Adelina, Doña Basilisa's maid, the day before, when we were making the beds and scrubbing the bathtubs. Arnaldo Pérez, Bienvenido's father, was a very competent mulatto who ran Dos Ríos when the Batistinis were away at the capital. Both he and his son came to dine often at the house—Don Pedro prided himself on the fact that his dark-skinned overseer sat next to him at his table. Aralia Pérez, Bienvenido's mother, had passed away several years earlier, but his father had done a fine job bringing up Bienvenido by himself.

Adelina knew how many lovers Don Pedro had had in town and how many illegitimate children—in spite of his religious devotion. None was so beloved as Bienvenido Pérez, however. The boy was not only his godson, but his own flesh and blood. Although few people knew the secret, on the day of his christening Aralia had insisted that he be named Bienvenido B. Pérez. Tongues wagged that the mysterious middle "B" stood for "Batistini." The mother used to come to the house to take up the hems of Doña Basilisa's dresses, alter gowns, and turn the collars of Don Pedro's shirts around when they became frayed. In spite of her humble origins—Aralia came from a family of poor farmers on the mountain—she was beautiful, with very white skin and eyes the color of mint. One day, when Doña Basilisa was away in Ponce visiting her family, Don Pedro raped Aralia. Adelina saw what happened and took care of the girl, seeing she got back to her family. When Aralia gave birth to the child and brought him to the house to show him to Doña

Basilisa, Doña Basilisa had immediately recognized that he was Don Pedro's because of his hair, which was red and curly, exactly like her husband's. That was the reason Don Pedro worried so much about the boy and had given him the opportunity to study engineering at the university.

Bienvenido and Diamantino were practically like brothers. When Don Pedro and his family came to Dos Ríos to spend the summer months, Don Eduardo sent Diamantino with his godfather, to get him away from the city. Bienvenido, as the overseer's son, was treated with a lot of respect. It was not a calculated thing; people were simply incapable of forgetting—even for an instant—that he belonged to both worlds, that of the owners and that of the peons. Even as a teenager Bienvenido tried to help the workers receive just treatment. Whenever he saw one of them maligned—if a worker's pay was withheld because of illness, for example—he would stomp over to the overseer's office, his red hair flaming like an angry banner, and demand from his father, Arnaldo Pérez, that the wrong be redressed. Diamantino was very conscious of this and admired Bienvenido, although he considered himself his superior.

At the farm, the food was always fresher and more plentiful, and there were few of the epidemics which periodically decimated the population in the capital. When Madame visited Dos Ríos, however, relations between Bienvenido and Diamantino were not what they had been in the past. The previous summer, when Ronda had just turned fifteen, Adelina had caught sight of Bienvenido and the girl kissing in the orchid grove as she leaned out the kitchen window behind the house to scrub some pots and pans.

"If you don't watch out, your Ronda will be spirited away from you faster than a silver spoon from a rich man's table!" she told Doña Basilisa.

"What are you ranting about, Adelina? You're always gossiping and knitting cobwebs, as if you had nothing to do. That's what I get for having kept you with us until you're too old to do any real work." But Adelina pulled Doña Basilisa to the window and pointed at the couple embracing in the orchid grove. Doña Basilisa dropped the pillowcase she was embroidering and let out a horrified cry.

"Oh, my God! It can't be. I must be seeing things."

"I told you so," Adelina exulted. "That's Don Pedro's own flesh and blood down there, multiplied by two!"

Basilisa didn't know what to do. She was certain that Aralia's son was her husband's, and she had done the seamstress and her child many good turns. But Aralia hadn't explained anything to her son.

Doña Basilisa was panic-stricken at the possibility of brother and sister falling in love, but she couldn't show it. She had to keep the secret for Ronda's sake, or the girl would despise her father. Doña Basilisa told Ronda in no uncertain terms that she shouldn't get too close to boys like Bienvenido, because even though Bienvenido was sweet and a fine boy, he wasn't of their same social standing, and in life one did many stupid things, but the stupidest thing one could do was marry beneath one's station. Doña Basilisa didn't want to go beyond that, because she knew that Ronda was headstrong and that if she was too strict and forbade Bienvenido's presence at the house, her prohibition would backfire. Teenagers breathed counterclockwise, and what they most wanted to do in the world was exactly the opposite of what their parents told them. So Doña Basilisa had been nonchalant about Bienvenido, had counseled Ronda as if she weren't too worried about him, and had given a deep sigh of relief when, at the end of the summer, the red-headed young man got on the train and left for the university in Río Piedras and Ronda went off to Lady Lane School in Massachusetts.

Doña Basilisa had also tried to exert her influence on Bienvenido, but here the maneuver was more complicated. Since Aralia had passed away when the boy was twelve, there was no one to caution him regarding his kinship with Ronda. Doña Basilisa thought about it and decided to ask Diamantino to warn Bienvenido. He should suggest, with as much tact as possible, that Bienvenido leave Ronda alone. The boys were very close and Ronda was still very young; Doña Basilisa hoped it was just a case of puppy love.

Bienvenido was older than Diamantino, but Bienvenido revered him. It wasn't only because Diamantino was a city boy and Bienvenido came from a small town; Diamantino had studied philosophy and literature and he was a gentleman, while Bienvenido was a farmer's son and would always remain one, even though he was studying for a college degree.

Diamantino had read Rousseau, Locke, and Leibniz, and was convinced that no country could belong to another, or even subject itself willingly to another country—as some local politicians insisted the island had done—without violating the most basic of human rights: the right to be free. Bienvenido didn't know anything about philosophy or political science, but when he heard Diamantino speak about inspiring ideas like that, he felt lit up from within. He began to believe everything was possible, and his mood, which was usually despondent and morose for no apparent reason, lifted immediately. He felt sure that once the Americans were kicked off the island, Diamantino, the charismatic son of Don Eduardo Márquez, would be the republic of Puerto Rico's next president.

It was a bright summer day when Diamantino approached Bienvenido with Doña Basilisa's message. The boys were on vacation and they had taken their horses out for a ride across the lush cane fields spread out like a shimmering carpet all the way to the sea behind the house. They arrived at a stream at the end of a field, shaded by a cluster of bamboo shrubs that rustled like clouds of dry rain around them, and were letting the horses drink next to each other. Diamantino couldn't be a hypocrite. "I know this sounds strange," he said. "But Maite has asked me to tell you to 'leave Ronda alone,' whatever that means. You know how I feel about you; you're my brother. I have no idea what's going on between Ronda and you and under normal circumstances I wouldn't intervene. But it's about time you learned what everybody else at Dos Ríos knows: Ronda is your half sister."

Bienvenido threw his head back and laughed. He was sure Diamantino was lying. He loved his father deeply: Arnaldo Pérez, the overseer, was an honorable man and he had always looked up to him. Don Pedro couldn't be his father because Don Pedro was fat, bald, and lazy; he got out of bed at nine in the morning and lived half the year in San Juan with Doña Basilisa, spending the money his peons sweated blood to earn for him at the farm. The mansion in Miramar; the magnificent yellow Pierce-Arrow; the artists' soirées the Batistinis loved— since he had studied at the university Bienvenido was aware of what all that cost. He wasn't a country bumpkin anymore.

But Diamantino insisted. Maybe Don Pedro couldn't be his father because Bienvenido didn't *want* to be his son. He wouldn't respect himself if he were. And what about his mother? What had Don Pedro done to her? Or had she consented to his advances? Did his father, the overseer, know about her disgrace?

Bienvenido felt revolted. His blood went to his head and his fist came up like a jackhammer. He gave Diamantino a punch in the jaw which sent his glasses flying, and almost tumbled him off his horse. "You and your big talk of democracy and equality. You're just another liberal hypocrite. And I thought you could be this country's champion! I was wrong!" He galloped away in a fury.

Diamantino didn't say a word of what had happened to anyone. But Bienvenido stopped coming to Dos Ríos, and Ronda Batistini didn't see him again that summer. She was utterly crushed, but was too busy to dwell on it. She would soon be leaving for the States, to begin her first year at Lady Lane School.

Bienvenido decided to shut his ears to the infamous rumors that were circulating and decided it was better not to mention anything to his father. If what Diamantino said was true, it would make Bienvenido's father suffer to have to admit it to his son. And if it wasn't true, his father would suffer just as much, hearing what people were saying about his late wife. So Bienvenido pretended he hadn't heard. He went on preparing his clothes and books for his trip to San Juan, and a few weeks later he left for the university in Río Piedras. Nonetheless, after his conversation with Diamantino he was never the same. He lost his gaiety and debonair look, appearing instead serious and morose. Try as he would, he couldn't erase Ronda from his mind. When the Batistinis invited Bienvenido and his father to their house for lunch one day to say good-bye to the boy, they noticed that Diamantino sat stonily silent at the table all through the meal. Don Pedro suspected the boys had quarreled, but he had no time to try to get them to make up.

Bienvenido went off to the university and Diamantino traveled to San Juan with his family, to spend the autumn months in town. The following year Diamantino's father passed away, but Diamantino stayed away at Don Pedro's house in the capital, without coming to Dos Ríos even for a short visit. Now, Bienvenido had arrived in Arecibo for summer vacation just a few days before Diamantino. Bienvenido had heard that Diamantino was back in town. His friend said he was traveling with a motley crowd of foreign dancers—led by a ballerina who was supposed to be from St. Petersburg and had danced at the czar's court, the most decadent in Europe—and that he was playing in their orchestra like a common musician and making an utter fool of himself. Bienvenido was amazed when he found out. He had no desire to meet with Diamantino, but he had to admit he'd love to see him just for a minute, so he could land another one on his jaw.

 Diamantino was still in his room getting ready for dinner. He took forever to dress, shave, and comb his hair with eau de cologne. When he finally appeared on the verandah, he greeted Bienvenido cordially enough. I stood there making small talk, but when I saw the disapproving look on Diamantino's face I immediately excused myself. I didn't go far, though, and tarried behind a jasmine vine that grew nearby.

"It's good to see you again after such a long time," Diamantino said, smiling broadly. Bienvenido didn't smile and shook the young man's hand reluctantly. He was dressed simply, in a cotton twill suit and brown leather boots. Diamantino wore the traditional hacendado's white linen outfit, vest neatly buttoned under his jacket and golden watch chain attached to its pocket. The manners of both young men were impeccable, and I wondered whether Adelina hadn't made up the whole story about the handsome Bienvenido being Don Pedro's son just to keep me on pins and needles.

Don Pedro came out on the porch, wheezing and puffing and carrying two bottles of champagne. He'd been down to the half-cellar, the room under the stairs and the only place con-

structed of cement in the old wooden house. It was here Don
Pedro kept his wine bottles and his safe-deposit box. In case of
fire, everything else could go up in smoke except his liquor and
his money. "Well, I'm glad you boys have made your peace!
Now you know why Basilisa and I planned to have this little
dinner party. We wanted to see our little family together again.
After all, your father has been my right hand for the last thirty
years, and you're like a son to me," he told Bienvenido. "And
Diamantino is also like a son." Bienvenido let Don Pedro hug
him. He didn't expect this and would rather have shaken hands;
he couldn't help feeling tense. His father, Arnaldo Pérez, was ill
with a cold and had had to stay home, but he sent Don Pedro
his greetings.

Doña Victoria arrived, all dressed up in lavender silk and accompanied by our reporter friend, Rogelio Tellez. Apparently
the young man was an old friend of Bienvenido's, too, and they
immediately struck up a conversation. Rogelio began teasing
Bienvenido, who, in his opinion, had made a spectacle of himself in town the day before by letting the man from the Home
Guard address the spectators at the plaza like a common rabble-
rouser. "What got into you? You should have stopped the man
immediately! Do you want us to be a banana republic like the
Dominican Republic or Nicaragua? We're just starting to get
out from under the despotic boot of Spain and you have to insult the Americans." Rogelio Tellez wasn't just a Bolshevik sympathizer; he was an American sympathizer also. He seemed to
be running in a popularity contest.

"Desiderio is a hero," Bienvenido answered gravely. "Right
now he's being questioned—perhaps tortured—by the secret
police. I won't have you criticize him." He spoke slowly and
deliberately, so that everyone listened. Bienvenido was shy, but
his intensity reminded me of a Russian commissar's. He had a
glass of sherry in his hand, and as he spoke, he put it down

carefully on a miniature French ormolu table, as if he were afraid of breaking it.

Rogelio changed the subject to ease the tension. He told the story of the Russian peasant who had broken into the czarina's apartment. He was holding up the czarina's toilet seat, Rogelio said, which was upholstered in blue velvet, when a reporter took his picture and it came out in the paper. The peasant was laughing and holding his sides; he found it hilarious that anyone would shit on a velvet cushion. "He was shot the day after he broke into the palace," Rogelio said. "Let's hope Desiderio doesn't suffer the same fate." Bienvenido was incensed, and he was about to grab Rogelio by the lapel of his jacket when Madame stopped him.

"We lived through the Russian Revolution," she said. "You two don't know the first thing about it."

"I know how to take care of my friends," Bienvenido answered. "Don't get mixed up in this."

Doña Victoria couldn't hear a train go by, but she immediately guessed what her nephew and Bienvenido were arguing about. Rogelio's father was Governor Yager's press aide, as well as the publisher of the *Puerto Rico Ilustrado*, and he favored statehood. But Doña Victoria never quarreled with her brother, Rogelio's father, because of that. Like so many families on the island, theirs was divided politically, but that didn't prevent them from being always cordial and affectionate with each other.

Bienvenido's face had grown a deep purple. Doña Victoria pulled her nephew by the arm and sat him between Don Pedro and herself on the medallion-backed living-room sofa to keep him out of trouble. Fortunately Rogelio was as thin as a reed and sat obediently between them, not saying a word. Don Pedro began to make small talk with Madame.

I heard Adelina calling me and I went into the kitchen to

get some hors d'oeuvres—Spanish *jamón serrano* and fried *quesitos de Arecibo*. I came back as fast as I could because I didn't want to miss anything. Bienvenido had walked out of the room and onto the verandah, where Ronda was smoking a cigarette.

"The more this island changes, the more it stays the same," Bienvenido said angrily, shaking his head. "It's people like Rogelio who do the most harm: *'tira la piedra y esconde la mano.'* He likes to throw stones and then hide his hand," he complained to Ronda. "Rogelio's magazine is full of patriotic poems and songs, but when things come down to brass tacks—or to lead bullets—he scuttles away and nothing happens."

Ronda looked up at him and smiled. "And are you the type that scuttles away too? It's been a while."

They hadn't seen each other since the kiss in the orchid grove three summers before, and Bienvenido hadn't even said hello that evening. He hadn't acknowledged her presence yet. I crept up softly to where they were talking and stood behind the balcony's louvered doors.

The young man gave up. "How are you, Ronda? You've grown up; you're even more beautiful than I remembered," he said. Ronda leaned toward him, her arms on the balcony's railing, her brown curls falling over her shoulders like an unruly mantle.

"Really? I wouldn't have thought you remembered me at all. Not after the way you behaved." She took one more pull from her cigarette and extinguished it in a flowerpot.

Bienvenido protested that she was being unfair. He was terribly busy getting ready to leave for San Juan, and his studies at the university had been grueling. "Of course I remember you; in fact, I thought of you often."

"Three years. Has it been that long? It seems it was yesterday," Ronda said. They looked at each other as if they were on opposite banks of a river and not on Don Pedro's moonlit verandah.

"Why did you run away, Bienvenido?" I heard Ronda ask. "I know! 'No country should belong to another without violating the most basic of human rights: the right to be free.' Your famous motto," she said, speaking in a loud voice and gesturing with her arms as if she were about to give a speech. "Is that why you can't love me?" She had meant it as a joke to ridicule him, but her voice shattered, and it came out like a plea.

It was like striking a match to a wick—Bienvenido suddenly put his arms around her and kissed her passionately on the mouth. "You're like a curse I can't get rid of!" he whispered, and kissed her again.

I left my hiding place and walked hurriedly into the living room to ask people what they wanted to drink. Then Adelina came in from the kitchen and handed me a tray of delicious hot codfish fritters which I quickly passed around so no one would venture out into the terrace.

Don Pedro went over to Madame, who sipped a glass of sherry. She had gone into the dining room, where Doña Basilisa's lace-covered table awaited the guests, set with Baccarat crystal goblets, Limoges porcelain plates, and a gorgeous centerpiece of white orchids. A portrait behind it showed a beautiful young woman dressed in white tulle. She had hair the color of midnight and amber eyes that shone softly. Something about the girl caught Madame's attention, but she couldn't put her finger on it. She took a step forward to examine the portrait more closely, and noticed a coronet of stars adorning the girl's head. She half remembered seeing it a long time ago, but she couldn't say where.

"What a beautiful painting!" Madame said. "Who painted it?"

"You've no doubt heard speak of Angelina Bertoli, the extraordinary diva born in Spain of Italian parents, haven't you?" Don Pedro asked. Madame was startled; she hadn't noticed that Don Pedro had crept up on tiptoe and was standing next to her. "Angelina and her father visited the island some years ago and stayed a whole month at a nearby hacienda."

Suddenly Madame remembered walking into the Imperial Box at the Maryinsky, where everything was blue and gold, and bowing before Czar Nicholas II. She had been a little girl then and was disappointed by the unassuming presence of the czar, who stood next to his wife and was shorter than the czarina. He had the look of a timid, large-whiskered mouse, while Alexandra looked like an empress even sitting down. The czar had questioned her about her fish costume, and asked about the magic ring hidden in a little box on top of her head. It was then that Madame had noticed the coronet on the czarina's head.

"Angelina came to Arecibo during her first singing tour of America," Don Pedro said. "She was only fifteen, but she had already traveled in Europe as a child prodigy, performing at several imperial courts. It was rumored that she even sang in St. Petersburg, and that the czar was so taken, he had his jeweler make a replica of the czarina's tiara for her." Madame looked at the painting in wonder, and told Don Pedro her story. "The world is no larger than a handkerchief!" she said, smiling.

"La Bertoli was no less a prodigy than you are, Madame, and she also appeared at Teatro Oliver, which you will soon grace with your presence," Don Pedro exclaimed grandly. "Felix Lafortune, the famous pianist and composer from New Orleans, accompanied Angelina, and he was a spectacle, too. He was a young man in his twenties, thin and long-maned, with a silky mustache and arms as agile as a spider's legs. When he played the piano, it was as if he had four hands instead of two."

Bienvenido and Ronda had come into the dining room and stood listening to Don Pedro. Bienvenido looked uncomfortable. He had evidently never heard of La Bertoli and didn't care a fig about opera.

The other guests were entering the dining room. Rogelio walked over to the painting to examine it more closely. "The gallant young pianist and the doll-like diva apparently put on a magnificent show together," he said. "I was too young to see them perform at Teatro Oliver, but people in Arecibo are still talking about them."

"Angelina's experience was a good example of the charm of our island, Madame," Don Pedro said, a malicious smile on his lips. "You must beware of it. It could also weave its spell around you, and then you'll never want to leave."

"Would you find that a disagreeable prospect, Madame?" Diamantino intervened, looking at Madame with lovesick eyes. I was furious. "Oh, she'd love to stay!" I piped in before Madame could answer. "Except Madame is thirty-eight, not a fifteen-year-old nightingale!" Everybody burst out laughing and my cheeks were smarting, but I didn't give a damn.

Doña Basilisa announced that dinner was served, and the guests approached the table. I pulled out a chair for Madame and she sat down at one end of the table, while Don Pedro sat at the head. Bienvenido sat down last, making it a point to sit as far as possible from Ronda. Doña Basilisa evidently didn't relish the conversation or the idea of Madame extending her stay on the island, and she tried changing the subject several times, but Don Pedro persisted.

"If it hadn't been for Salvatore," he rambled on, "who looked after his daughter like an eagle after his young, La Bertoli might have stayed longer. During her visit to Arecibo

she met Adalberto Ríos, the son of one of our neighbors. He
was a no-good loafer; he didn't like to work and twiddled his
life away painting. One evening the young man went to listen
to Angelina sing and fell head over heels in love with her. When
the Bertolis went on their way, Adalberto followed them to San
Juan. Once there, and just before La Bertoli's ship sailed off,
Adalberto asked Salvatore for Angelina's hand in marriage. The
old man was wise enough not to say no; he simply begged
them to postpone the wedding. Angelina had engagements in
New York which she couldn't break; she had signed contracts
to sing at several charity fund-raisers. The girl had a terrific
tantrum and had to be wrenched from her lover's arms, but Salvatore finally managed to sail away with his daughter."

Don Pedro's voice was steady and without a quaver, but
there was something unreal about his story. I looked at him
keenly over the top of the cut-glass wine goblets and noticed
that his right eyelid had begun to twitch. He saw me looking at
him, and went on impassively. "Adalberto Ríos never got over
the affair. After Angelina and her father sailed away, he locked
himself up in his room with his oils and paintbrushes and no
one but his family saw him again for months. One night, after
everyone was asleep, he went up to the attic where he had his
atelier and hung himself from a rafter."

The suspense was so great I could hardly breathe. I wondered why Ronda hadn't mentioned the story to me before,
but nobody dared to contradict Don Pedro. Everyone at the
table had grown silent. Only Doña Basilisa was sobbing quietly
into her linen handkerchief, her pink, round shoulders quiver-
ing and her gray curls bobbing on her head like an old doll's.
Ronda got up from her chair and walked over to Doña Basilisa.
She put her arm around her mother's shoulders to comfort her.

"The name of the young man wasn't Adalberto Ríos,"

Ronda told Madame in a melancholy tone. "It was Adalberto Batistini, and he was my brother. The painting was done by him. We found it in his studio after he hung himself. Like all devout Catholics, Father considers suicide a capital sin, so Adalberto couldn't be buried in consecrated ground. He had him buried in our orchid grove, and forbade us to ever talk about him."

"May his soul burn in hell!" Don Pedro whispered, as he got up from the table and left the room.

So that was the reason for Doña Basilisa's nervousness, for her silly laughter and her ceaseless chatter! That was why she kept praying in whispers when she had shown us her orchid grove, and forbade us to pick a single flower!

By Friday everything was ready for opening night at Teatro Oliver. Madame had carefully gone over the stage floor, and all the imperfections were taken care of. The dancers had rehearsed their numbers meticulously: the program included a segment of *Les Sylphides*, then a scene from *Giselle*, both of which Madame would dance with the girls. Then came the *Bacchanale*, which she would perform with Novikov, and finally Tchaikovsky's Violin Concerto, played by Diamantino. In the morning, however, Nadja Bulova came down from her room to the hotel lobby looking agitated. Novikov had come down with a fever and had trouble breathing. "The doctor examined him and diagnosed pneumonia," she said. "It's impossible for him to dance."

Madame turned to Diamantino in despair. "Don't worry about it," he reassured her, "I can take Novikov's place in the *Bacchanale*. I've watched him dance it enough times, and the role is not difficult; I'll just do more miming than dancing. I can easily act out the role of Dionysus and hold you by the waist as you do your arabesques and pirouettes."

The Dying Swan was very obviously missing from the program. "I'm tired of dancing it, Masha," Madame had told me. "I want to dance about life from now on, not about death."

Ronda spent the day sitting at the back of the empty theater, chain-smoking and nervously watching the rehearsals. She had asked Bienvenido to come to the theater to help out and at first Bienvenido had said he was busy. But he couldn't stay away. He turned up after the musicians began to play and joined Juan in helping to move the theater props and adjust the footlights. Ronda was sure Bienvenido loved her in spite of himself, in spite of his silly conviction that he had to remain single in order to serve his country in its struggle for political independence. One day he would tell her so, and they'd be happy forever.

Arecibo is on the northwest side of the island, and in the summer, when the sun sets, churches, houses, roads, even the air one breathes take on a special glow. On the night of our performance the sky became flamingo pink and then a deep indigo blue as the evening fell over the sea that bordered the town. Arecibo's upper class began to arrive at Teatro Oliver, dressed in its best silks and laces. It was a hot night, and all the doors and windows were left open so that the night air might circulate. A lace-covered banquet table was set under the brick arches of the entrance hall, because Don Pedro was throwing a party after the ballet ended. The air was heavy with jasmine, as profuse vines crept up the theater's columns and hung from its eaves in delicate clouds sprinkled with white stars. This spectacle was completely new to us, used as we were to the disquieting white nights of St. Petersburg, when one walks in a haze for months.

I stood with the dancers to one side of the stage as Madame patiently went over some of the steps with Diamantino. I could see she was worried about the reaction his appearance might trigger. The *machista* conventions of the town could make him the butt of cruel jokes when they saw him dance the role of Dionysus, a crown of laurel leaves on his head, but Diamantino insisted. He told Madame he wanted to prove to his godfather and to his Arecibo friends that he was taking his career as an artist seriously. In any case, once Madame finished dancing, it would be his turn to show them what he could do with Tchaikovsky's Violin Concerto.

That afternoon I had seen Madame stashing away some clothes in a duffel bag in her dressing room, and I sensed that something was afoot, but I kept my suspicions to myself. I went on doing my exercises as usual. "You're a peasant girl from Minsk," I told myself sternly. "You've gone through much worse and have managed to survive."

The girls were aware of the situation, too, and their animosity was mounting. At first they didn't want to discuss it in front of me, but I heard Nadja Bulova whisper bitterly to Maya Ulanova that Madame was planning to leave us in the lurch and take off with her lover. They feared that they'd never be able to get back to San Juan, much less to civilization in New York or London. When anxiety reached a fever pitch, they begged for my help. They wanted me to talk to her, but I shook my head—there was nothing I could do. Madame's destiny was in God's hands.

Katia Borodina, Maya Ulanova, and Egorova Sedova—were sentimental and were more hurt than angry. But Nadja was furious. She had turned down several suitors in order to become a professional dancer and now that would be impossible. Without Madame, there was no company; it would melt like a dream. "She's an old bitch. I hope he breaks her heart," she whispered to one of her friends.

At eight o'clock sharp Smallens, the orchestra director,

walked to the podium. He tapped the music stand with his violin bow to demand attention, and darkness enveloped the theater as the curtains rose. Doña Basilisa and Don Pedro sat complacently in the audience, their plump arms and legs stuffed into their chairs like rubber limbs. Ronda was deathly pale and kept nervously fanning herself with the program.

Adam's music wafted onto the stage like a ghostly mist, and the girls and I ran out to begin our performance of *Giselle*. At first everything went smoothly; the local musicians were much better than any of us had expected, thanks, no doubt, to Doña Victoria's music school. A few seconds later, Madame joined us, wearing Giselle's costume. She danced the maiden who falls in love with Prince Albrecht and commits suicide when she can't have him. I danced the Queen of the Wilis, commander of the squadron of chaste virgins, who, ash bough in hand, orders Giselle to leave her lover and join them. I thought the ballet, produced by Marius Petipa in St. Petersburg thirty years earlier, was a fitting good-bye to our beloved Madame, who was about to sever herself from our company and take off with a scoundrel without a hint of regret. But we were in for a surprise.

The performance seemed under control and we were beginning to relax, anticipating the extravagant party we were going to afterward. At least we could get drunk on champagne and eat all sorts of fattening delicacies cooked by Doña Basilisa without having to worry about our weight anymore, since this was the company's Waterloo and we would never dance together again. Then Glazunov's *Bacchanale* began to throb under our feet like the beating of an uncontrollable heart. The atmosphere of the theater became charged with a mysterious energy.

I swear I didn't foresee what was going to happen. The music made us dance so feverishly and so fast that, after a few minutes, we didn't know what we were doing. Smallens had ordered the brass instruments and the drums to play increasingly louder, until I thought my ears were going to burst. The scherzo was already swirling around Madame and Diamantino, who, as Ariadne and the god Dionysus, were curling and uncurling around each other in a frenzy of lascivious movements, when I saw that the girls had fallen under the spell of the music. Slowly they advanced toward the couple—Katia, Maya, Egorova, Nadja—and began to encircle them. The choreography didn't call for such a development, and Madame looked up in surprise. Before she could do anything to prevent it, however, the maenads threw themselves on Diamantino and began to claw him. Six fiery dragons couldn't have been more fierce: they ripped his costume apart and tore at his flesh with their nails. They flew at him like witches, borne by their tulle skirts, aiming their grands jetés and their battements tendus at him. They yanked out his hair and screamed obscenities at him until the trapdoor yawned unexpectedly beneath Diamantino's and Madame's feet, and they both plunged into the darkness.

I cried out in anguish, and we all rushed backstage and down to the murky cellar. The girls were weeping and begging me to forgive them—it wasn't their fault, they insisted as they trailed behind me. The frenzy of the music had taken hold of them and they didn't know what had happened—it had all come about so quickly.

I couldn't blame them. They had given up so much for her!

Fortunately, no one in the audience noticed that anything was amiss, and the end of the performance appeared to go as planned. Everybody thought the attack on the god Dionysus was part of the choreography and thus a scandal was avoided. As soon as the curtain went down we began to look all over for Diamantino and Madame, but they had vanished. The police were summoned and agents swarmed all over the theater.

They looked in the dressing rooms, behind the scenery, even under the orchestra seats once the theater was empty. But they couldn't find them.

Instead of seeming upset, Molinari went around pinching the corners of his lips, trying not to let a smile of satisfaction slip out of his mouth as he observed the commotion. I was sure he had had a hand in the disappearance, but I had no proof.

"Congratulations. You finally got what you wanted: now Madame and her lover are safely out of our reach," he said, trying to pin the vanishing act on me. I was furious. I had no idea where Madame and Diamantino were: they could have been kidnapped or assassinated, or might even have left of their own accord—if what Madame had said to me about wanting to spend the rest of her life with him was true.

I walked to the back of the stage in a daze. The girls had to take off my toe shoes and help me undress. They tried to console me as best they could, but it was no use. Madame had fallen into Diamantino's clutches. She'd never return to England with us; never found the Imperial Ballet School in Turner's mythic Ivy House on a hill above the lake as we had dreamed, or teach young ballerinas how to dance their way to immortality.

Doña Victoria and young Rogelio came backstage to congratulate Madame, but the place was in turmoil. The ballerinas were whimpering and sobbing, people were running here and there. Rogelio carried his notebook in his hand. He was taking notes to write a feature article about the performance and began to jot down the details of the pandemonium around us when Molinari approached him and snatched away the notebook. Don Pedro and Doña Basilisa were incredulous when they were told their godson couldn't be found, and desperately fired questions at the police officers on the scene.

Molinari was the only one who kept his head, and ordered

everyone to calm down. Don Pedro joined Molinari and the police in their search around the theater and the adjacent streets, but it was useless. The couple had been spirited into thin air. Then Ronda approached me, as pale as a ghost. "Bienvenido has disappeared also," she whispered, trembling. "I can't find him anywhere." I took her in my arms and tried to calm her.

The Batistinis took me back to the house with them, and Don Pedro offered to pay for our troupe's accommodation at the hotel. I was grateful—I didn't relish seeing myself slaving as a house maid at Dos Ríos to pay our expenses. The next day Arecibo's *Ultima Noticia* published a heinous review, mercilessly cutting up our company for its "shoddy" performance. At the end, the author commented maliciously that Madame's rendition of Ariadne was much more pragmatic than her Giselle, because she had skipped Naxos with her lover Dionysus, instead of joining him in the grave. The review was couched in ballet jargon, and the police didn't censor it because they had no idea what the critic was talking about. How had the author discovered the truth? It was probably a malicious guess. The article was signed with the improbable pseudonym of Pubilus Cornelius Naso, a way to indicate that he smelled a skunk. This made me suspect the author was Rogelio Tellez, the only one pedantic enough to gossip about our art in those terms.

The other two performances of our Ballets Russes scheduled at Teatro Oliver had to be canceled. Doña Basilisa cried her heart out, and Ronda did her best to console her. She didn't mention that Bienvenido was missing, and her parents weren't even aware of it. Bienvenido was like the sea, here one day and in San Juan the next. And she wanted to be free to act as she saw fit the following weeks. We waited at the house for three days, but since we had no news of Madame, Don Pedro offered to pay for our train tickets, and we returned to San Juan.

Ours was a sad little caravan as we boarded the second-class car. Molinari brought up the rear, swooping behind us like a vulture and picking up costumes and slippers, whatever was left behind. None of the girls wanted to be near him; they kept skipping ahead, so I had no alternative but to sit next to him. He stank of camphor and stale clothes, and he looked at me menacingly, but I wasn't afraid of him. I only had to think of the *muzhiks* at home, or of Rasputin, the czarina's lover—who was a neighbor of my father's in Minsk—to feel that, by comparison, I was safe by his side. I was a *muzhik* myself. I could make pacts with the devil also.

Molinari accompanied us all the way to San Juan and then he too disappeared.

When I think back to those days, I still marvel at the intensity of Madame's feelings, at the total surrender of which she was capable. Only a woman approaching the barren steppes of middle age does insane things like that: give everything up for a young rascal she has just met. After struggling all her life to transform herself, from the daughter of a washerwoman on Kolomenskaya Street into the Maryinsky's prima ballerina, how could she throw away her life that way? Maybe she was tired of her fame, bored with *The Dying Swan*'s agonizing over a world that had been mercifully wiped out. But if you ask me, it was desire that was mostly to blame for her fall. As Sappho, the great poet, said, desire is catching; it makes our legs give way and loosens our limbs, just as the mortal blow of a spear doubles up a seasoned man in battle. Pity the blow, which I had received from Madame but could never return in kind, so that I was condemned to see her harnessed to Diamantino Márquez like a swan to a ballroom tiger.

After swearing she'd live free of lust, a vestal virgin devoted to the spiritual glories of ballet, Madame had fallen for a two-bit hacendado with heroic ambitions. Everything she had promised about the body being the harp of the spirit, the medium through which we achieved oneness with nature, was nonsense. It was simply a way to keep us in line so we would dance for practically nothing and not make trouble for the company. The body was the body and pleasure was pleasure, and Giselle shedding tears at her lover's star-crossed grave was a frothy white lie. We had sacrificed everything for Madame, led lives of hunger and sacrifice so she could go on impersonating the Dying Swan all over the world. But if Madame could fall in love, so could we. We weren't going to swallow the story of the happy demoiselles embracing prudish spinsterhood any longer.

After our return to San Juan, Juan Anduce and I kept on seeing each other at La Nueva Suela. Juan didn't speak any Russian, but he spoke English quite well. "It doesn't matter that you are Russian and I am Puerto Rican, or that you are large, white, and blond and I am slender and dark-skinned, my duck. The important thing is that we are both tender-hearted and fight for the common good," he'd say, winking at me puckishly. He called me his duck because I was always running after Madame, who was the swan. I had never fought for anything in my life, but I liked to hear him say that. No one had ever noticed I was tender-hearted before, or that I sacrificed my life for others. I liked Juan.

Juan answered all my questions about the island: about its mountains, its rivers, the towns that peppered its valleys. He loved to talk about the capital more than anything. "San Juan is a very old city," he told me once. "Centuries ago, it made the English and the Dutch green with envy. They sat on their ships looking at its sparkling ramparts, its houses and churches full of

gold and silver, and they drooled. It had an incalculable mer-
cantile value; it served as safe harbor for hundreds of merchant
ships which plied the ocean between America and Europe.
At the end of its deepest cove there was a huge fortress with
four solid towers with battlements on them—Santa Catalina—
where the gold from Mexico, the fabulous *situado* that was
shipped every year to Madrid, was kept. At night, a pale glow
could be seen rising from its towers miles away."

He also loved to talk about the bay, about its many lagoons,
linked to each other by mangrove labyrinths and whispering
canals. "White herons, pelicans, falcons, manatees, and turtles
inhabit them," he said. "When the first Spaniards arrived, they
decided to settle around it. The bay was more valuable than the
whole island put together and well worth fighting for. It had an
abundant fresh water supply, deep coves, and easy access to the
land from several points. Best of all, it was easy to defend from
enemy ships because the smaller island, where San Juan was lo-
cated, served as a natural barrier.

"Some people call San Juan Bay 'Señorita Bay,' because it's
guarded both by El Morro Castle and El Cañuelo Fort, which
make it almost impossible for an enemy ship to enter it. As you
sail in, it widens on either side like the hips of a beautiful
woman and ends in San José Lagoon, El Caño de Martín Peña,
Los Corozos, and Piñones. These canals are completely free territory, a no-man's-land. They are always in motion, and will
change overnight in accordance with the tides. It was here the
cimarrones, the escaped slaves like my grandmother Zambia, hid
when they fled the whistling whips and the sniffing dogs of
their masters.

"Zambia escaped from her master's house, and she went
through a terrible experience. For many years under the
Spaniards, we suffered a cruel embargo, and no foreign ships

were allowed into our bay. All trade had to be done with Spain, and as it was having a great deal of difficulty with its colonies in South America, Spanish ships never stopped in Puerto Rico. People survived because they could grow their own food—manioc roots, yuccas, plantains—and there was plentiful cattle, but they lacked two things which were vitally important: cloth and steel.

"My grandmother Zambia was a beautiful woman, and when she ran away and had to make her way through the mangroves, her dress ended up in shreds. She made a shift out of a burlap sack for herself and wore it resignedly for a year, until the day she met my grandfather, Ezequiel Carabalí, a handsome fisherman, who made a living selling fresh water to the smugglers' ships that hid in the estuaries of the bay. When Ezequiel saw her, he fell in love and asked her to marry him. Zambia was the happiest woman on earth, but she swore she wasn't getting married in a burlap sack.

"One day Zambia swam absolutely naked to one of the Dutch ships, called out for help as if she were drowning, and was brought on board by the sailors. Using sign language, she begged them to give her a piece of cloth and a few knives, because she was getting married soon and had absolutely nothing to wear. The sailors called the captain, who, amazed at Zambia's beauty, fell in love with her also. The handsome captain took her to his cabin, made love to her with Zambia's consent, and later had her put in a rowboat dressed in a beautiful robe and with several knives as a present. Zambia hid the robe and the knives, and kept the secret from Ezequiel.

"On the day of the wedding Zambia appeared dressed in an elegant silk gown at the door of her palm-thatched hut in the mangroves. Ezequiel asked no questions—he knew Zambia and her rebel ways; she never let anyone tell her what to do—but when they entered the church in Martín Peña, unfortunately there was a *guardia civil* there. The guard became suspicious that a black woman should be marrying a poor fisherman in such an elegant gown, and made her a prisoner. Zambia was taken to El Morro Fort, made to confess under torture that she had acquired her dress from a Dutch ship, and condemned to two hundred lashes in San Juan's Plaza de Armas. Before her punishment, Zambia was taken around San Juan on a mule, naked from the waist up and with her hands tied with rope. A town crier preceded her, announcing that she was being punished because she had 'obtained illegal cloth from a smuggler' and was being made an example to all those who thought they could do the same. While the ride through the town lasted, the neighbors could add their own whipping to the official punishment and many did so, beating Zambia with brooms and dry twigs as she went by, so afraid were they that they might be accused of the same crime.

"Just think of it, Masha! Because of what happened to my grandmother Zambia, the poor women on the island wore their clothes until they were in tatters and rich women left their robes to their descendants in their wills, as part of their inheritances. Which may be another reason why *Sanjuaneros* are so crazy about clothes. They still haven't gotten over their old deprivation.

"After the public disciplining in San Juan was over, Zambia and Ezequiel went back to their palm-thatched hut in the mangroves and never visited the city again. My mother, Altagracia Carabalí, was born nine months after her parents' marriage. She was black but had blue eyes, a fact that Ezequiel never noticed because, fortunately, he was color-blind. Mother wasn't happy living there, however, and when she was old enough, she emigrated to Cayey to work at the tobacco plantation where she met my father."

When Juan finished his story he blushed a deep red, so ashamed was he of his grandmother's follies. But I embraced him, and assured him that I admired Zambia and would have done the same.

Another time Juan told me the story of how the Americans conquered the city San Juan. I was very interested, since everyone on the island had a different version of the event. Some said the Americans had come to save the island from backwardness and Spanish tyranny; others that they were carpetbaggers and buccaneers.

Juan's tale about the marines' arrival was by far the most interesting, since he had been visiting his grandmother at the time in the mangroves and was an eyewitness of the event. "Eleven warships appeared on the horizon," he recounted, "and stood a few miles away from the city walls. It was still dark, and the ships bobbed up and down in the mist, unseen by the sentinels of El Morro Fort. As the sky lightened, the destroyers became perfectly visible from the rooftops, but nobody was afraid of them. For hundreds of years pirate after pirate had tried in vain to occupy us: Sir Francis Drake and that scoundrel Captain John Hawkins, the first to bring a shipload of African slaves to America, were soundly trounced by El Morro's cannons; George Clifford, Earl of Cumberland, perished near San Jerónimo's Fort. They all spent their ammunition in vain. The Spaniards had invested millions of *maravedies* strengthening the city's fortifications, so we weren't at all worried when this new pirate, Admiral William T. Sampson, and his fleet appeared on the horizon.

"At dawn we were awakened by a barrage of cannon shot the likes of which we had never heard before. Luckily, American guns were so powerful that, although many shots were fired, most flew over the city. San Juan's buildings are built very low—ancient Spanish law required that they not be more than two stories high, so that cannonballs would sail over the houses when fired by ships out at sea. Even so, many in the city perished. The population had to run for cover, most of them barefoot and still in their nightclothes, toward the hills of Miramar. We managed to survive.

"Admiral Sampson's bombardment lasted six hours, but the city, bobbing up and down in the distance, kept friskily cleaving the waves as in a game of tagalong. Sampson strode up and down the deck of the U.S.S. *Mississippi*, ordering more and more cannon fire, but no evidence of impact was perceived, no raging blazes were seen to fill the horizon with mournful curtains of smoke, no fiery orange tongues ate away at the lush greenery that peeked over the formidable battlements. Sampson was baffled. He didn't believe in magic and he couldn't figure out what was wrong. He had never visited San Juan; he didn't know there was a bay behind the city and that its waters were swallowing up all his fire and brimstone without a belch."

"Whoever insists that the Americans' arrival was not a military intervention is pissing outside the pot!" I burst out when I heard Juan's story. "The invasion of Puerto Rico by the Americans was like cooking beans. First you softened them by pounding and boiling them in water. Then you added the bloody tomato sauce and finally the bacon. A perfect recipe!"

34

Juan's family had a tobacco plantation in Cayey which went under. His relatives had been tobacco growers for generations, as his ancestors on his father's side were descendants of the Taino Indians. Every Taino head of family grew a tobacco plant in his backyard and smoked a handful of rolled-up leaves after each meal. After the Americans arrived on the island, American Cigar, General Cigar, and Consolidated Cigar all established huge warehouses in the central valleys and most of the local planters who had grown tobacco since Spanish times were wiped out. But Juan's family knew so much about tobacco, they managed to survive.

Tobacco was a very delicate crop, it was the spoiled brat of agriculture and required constant tending. They weeded it and pampered it, watered and stroked it like a baby. The seedlings had to be planted by hand, one by one, and it was a backbreaking job, but the Anduces did it as a family and didn't mind. The tender saplings needed to be protected under huge mosquito nets so the fleas wouldn't eat the leaves or the *pegas*—fat green worms—nibble the stems, and the Anduces did it with such love that their tobacco plants were always the lushest of all. At night their valley seemed to be peacefully asleep, spread out under the billowing folds of netting. But nothing could have been more deceptive.

A savage price war broke out in 1902 between the Anduces and the American corporations, and fire ravaged Don Aníbal Anduce's largest warehouse. Arson was suspected, but no proof was found. Don Aníbal still had three more warehouses full of tobacco leaves, and they were near his house. Every day he supervised the work himself, and he often sent his children, Juan and his two brothers, to scout around after dark. One night when Juan's brothers were scouting and Juan was home asleep, tragedy struck: the boys were knocked unconscious by a band of hooligans and left inside one of the palm-thatched barns, then it was doused in gasoline and set on fire. Juan woke up to the most terrifying howls he had heard in his life. Convinced a wild animal was devouring his family, he ran out of the house with a shotgun, only to find his father and mother on their knees, pounding the earth with their fists, the charred corpses of his two brothers still smoking at their feet.

Juan's father never recovered from the tragedy, but he refused to die until he had put his remaining son through school literally puffing on cigar smoke. It also helped that Don Aníbal had married Altagracia, the black woman from the mangrove swamp who was so strong, she could wash the laundry of an entire family in one afternoon and still have enough energy to iron it, fold it, and take it back to her clients on a tray balanced on her head. Thanks to his mother's efforts and his father's last tobacco warehouse, Juan bought a ticket and traveled by steamer to New York. He made his way on foot to Harlem and found a job as a dishwasher at a deli. The next day he registered at New York University.

He studied at the university for two years. Then his father

died and he had to return to the island, because his mother had to file for bankruptcy. But Juan was from hardy stock. He told Altagracia not to worry; he would take care of everything. He took her to live with his grandmother in the mangroves, and after tying his clothes in a bundle which he slung on his back, he boarded the *California*, an American steamship. He was contracted to work for the Tampa Tobacco Company and planned to work his way to Florida.

"When we neared the Cuban coast we stopped at Daiquirí," Juan told me, reminiscing about one of the saddest moments of his journey. "Around midnight, a fat American came aboard and picked out two hundred and fifty men who were traveling on deck because we had no money to pay for a cabin. From then on, each time we stopped at a coastal town, a blustering entrepreneur would board the ship late at night and pick out the strongest and healthiest among us to go to the tobacco fields, until only I and several other black men were left on board. At last we arrived in Florida. I managed to jump ship, aided by a kitchen hand who was putting a wicker basket full of dirty tablecloths to be washed on shore. The basket was hardly heavier than before I got in, I had lost so much weight.

"The ship's captain had informed us that in the U.S. it was illegal to bring workers in on contract, but I knew better. The rest of the men were contracted, but we were not allowed to go ashore because our skin was black. As I abandoned ship, I looked back and wondered what would happen to those poor men left on deck, most of whom were too weak to run away. And I remembered how those who had died during the journey were thrown overboard in sacks."

Juan finally arrived back in New York, and his knowledge of cigar manufacturing led him to look for a job as an overseer at a small tobacco factory on First Avenue and Thirtieth Street.

It was called El Morito. Like many tobacco workshops at the
time, it was a meeting place for immigrants, anarchists, and
revolutionaries. As the workers stripped the tobacco leaves,
chopped them up for cigarettes, or rolled them up for cigar
"tripe,"—the gut or inner lining—they sat at long tables at the
head of which an official read to them. The books chosen by
the *tabaqueros* for their distraction were often indirectly of a
political nature: Chekhov's *Uncle Vanya*, Dostoyevsky's *The Possessed* or *Notes from Underground*. No tobacco worker ever fell
asleep listening to them.

Juan felt unwelcome at first. He had arrived from the island
recently, while most of the men there had spent fifteen or
twenty years scuttling under the skyscrapers, struggling not to
perish in the freezing winds that wrapped their thin flannel
overcoats around their bodies like paper envelopes. Soon he
found them friendly enough, however. Puerto Ricans were as
close as ticks; they stuck together like dandruff, and left their
doors open to friends in need. Juan was strong, and he was always ready to help out—he carried furniture in and out of ten-
ements, pulled vegetable carts when the horses got sick, carried
the ill to the hospital in his arms when the ambulance didn't
arrive.

In Harlem, sometimes three families shared the same room,
together with rats and cockroaches. They survived thanks to *ron
pitorro*—a strong, amber rum distilled in bathtubs—and *la bolita*,
the illegal lottery everyone was always dreaming about. *La bolita*
gave people hope, and soon Juan became a *bolitero* and had a
profitable business going. When people dreamed about spiders,
scorpions, or beetles, they ran to Juan, who interpreted what
their dreams meant and sold them a number.

It was because of *la bolita* and its consequences that Juan
eventually returned to the island. Marta Gómez was a beautiful
tabaquera, and one day she went to hear Juan reading *Les Mis-*

érables. He had been named official reader because he was very tall and could be heard more clearly than his co-workers above the crowd. Juan had a university education and he loved novels; he would explain their meaning to the *tabaqueros*. Novels were very similar to dreams. In both, you escaped menaces unscathed and often found solutions to your problems.

Marta asked Juan to tell her the meaning of a dream she had had: A chicken was pecking away at a handful of corn in the yard of her old family house in Naranjito, near the mountains of Barranquitas, and she laid two eggs. A cat appeared out of nowhere and pounced on her. The chicken started cackling like mad, but couldn't get rid of the miniature tiger. Soon the chicken was too weak to run and collapsed under the paws of the cat, who then proceeded to suck the eggs dry.

Juan looked at Marta, who was chubby and rosy-cheeked, with pale white skin the color of jasmine in moonlight, and he fell in love with her. "There is a man stalking you; you must be careful and not go out alone. Meanwhile, play the double zero, since the chicken laid two eggs. If *la bolita* hits your number and you win, I'll help you protect the money and nobody will steal it." Marta did as Juan said, and when *la bolita* hit the double zero and she won ten thousand dollars, she immediately put it in the bank under Juan's name, without telling her parents or anyone else about it.

Marta's family came from the mountains and tried to pass for Spanish. If you were from Naranjito or Barranquitas, towns high in the *cordillera* which shone like hives of glowworms at night, your eyes might be blue and your hair honey-colored, and this made a huge difference when you were looking for a job in New York. But if you came from the coast, there was a good chance that you looked like Juan's mother, Altagracia, and it was more difficult to find work.

Juan didn't mind being called a spic, and he never denied his origins. But he believed that if he asked Marta to marry him, she would think he was doing it because of the ten thousand dollars she had put under his name in the bank. Months passed and he didn't dare confess his love. Finally, one day the owner of a *placita* in East Harlem that sold fresh vegetables and fruit went to see Marta's father and asked for her hand. The father was elated—Don Guzmán owned his own business and his daughter would lack for nothing, and he immediately said yes. But when Marta found out about it, she ran to where Juan was carefully ripping the veins out of a tobacco leaf and said, "If you don't marry me right now, I'll throw myself from the Brooklyn Bridge at dawn."

Juan was impressed, and they immediately went to see a judge on Second Avenue and Thirtieth Street, who married them in their tobacco workers' overalls. That evening, however, when they went to see Don Roberto, Marta's father, to tell him the good news, he went berserk. "But this man is tar black! Have you gone crazy? No one in our family has a drop of bad blood in them. Blacks are lazy, filthy descendants of sugar-cutting slaves. Our people are from the mountains; we're civilized, hard workers. Go to the judge this minute and have him annul the marriage."

But Marta was strong-willed, and she withstood the assault. Her father was in the kitchen serving himself a *ron palo viejo*, and she told him, her hands on her hips, "We're from New York now, Father; there are no mountains and no sugar coast here, and it's cold as hell. The color of our skin doesn't keep us any warmer than Juan's. I'm his wife now and that's that." Marta's father was peeling a lemon at that moment to put in his drink, and he began to hurl insults at her, calling her a whore, head-strong as a mule—didn't she understand she was throwing her life down the drain? Marta tried to calm him and Juan put his arms around her to protect her, but it was too late. Don Roberto suddenly turned around to face his daughter and plunged the knife deep into her ribs.

When Juan finished his story, there were tears in his eyes. Until the end of his days he cried whenever he spoke of Marta, and I respected the memory of his beloved.

Once back on the island, Juan established contact with his socialist friends, and it was then that he met Diamantino Márquez at one of their meetings. Diamantino was just a kid with a chip on his shoulder then. "I never would have guessed that one day he'd have the guts to defy Adolfo Bracale, the famous theater agent. But the kid was tough, and he stood up to Bracale. He wasn't just a reporter scribbling verses as his godfather had said." When he got back from the States he had published several articles in the press denouncing the producer's corrupt dealings, in which famous stars came to the island with hoodlums like Molinari escorting them to extort bigger payments from the theater owners. After the tragedy at Teatro Tapia, Bracale served several months in prison. He was finally set free by the sugar entrepreneurs who had put up the money for his business ventures in the first place.

Diamantino wanted to make his own place in the sun, not in the shadow of his famous father. That was why he defended political independence so fiercely. Everything he did, his poetry and his journalism—he always wrote about patriotic themes in the newspapers—even his violin playing—he often played *danzas* which he had arranged himself from the original piano versions—were ways of reaffirming his political ideals vis-à-vis Don Eduardo Márquez, who was always compromising.

Juan knew all this, and he agreed with me that that was why Diamantino became a friend of Los Tiznados, the suicide riders who hid in the hills. "Our island is so small it can hold no secrets, Masha," Juan told me, "and many people saw Diamantino ride with them, but they kept it from Don Eduardo. Los Tiznados remind me of my tobacco-worker friends at El Morito, the cigar factory in New York—only their faces are blackened with sugarcane soot rather than tobacco grime. They are willing to die for political independence, but I don't agree with them. What do they want political independence for? So hacendados like Don Pedro can exploit us all the more?

"The important thing is to be independent from poverty, Masha, to empower the working class! It's better to have 'La Internacional' as our national anthem instead of 'La Borinqueña,' Morel Campos's aristocratic *danza*. I can just see it—Don Pedro as president of the republic, whip in hand, making ninety percent of our population, black and white, plow his fields like oxen, after making sure that we remain illiterate. By that time, Diamantino and Los Tiznados will be mercilessly wiped out, because that's what happens to idealists in a republic.

"I'm a warrior—a strike to me is like a war," Juan said. "And in every war there are bound to be casualties. I know that Los Tiznados won't stop at anything, that they are willing to kill for what they believe, and I don't have a problem with that. But I don't believe in wasting bullets, and one should only shoot for the right reasons."

35 When Juan had read Dandré's ad in the paper for a shoemaker to repair the dancers' slippers, he had been curious about the company. He was a great admirer of Russia and knew quite a bit about it from the *tabaqueros'* readings at El Morito, so he went to the Hotel Malatrassi and answered the ad. Then Dandré left for the States and Diamantino Márquez joined Madame's troupe. Juan was full of enthusiasm; he knew who Diamantino was and admired the young man.

We met almost the same day Juan joined the troupe. He had never seen a woman who was as big as a man before, and there was a down-to-earth frankness about me that appealed to him. I always say what I think; I have no hair on my tongue. People may not like me, but they know what they're getting. Because of my awkwardness I was never given important roles onstage, but it never made me resentful. Like the proverbial goose girl, I went about solving everybody's problems, distributing clean towels, bringing trays with food or pitchers with juice or cold water to the other dancers, putting salve on the girls' bunions, or heating water for their aching feet. And I had one quality which surpassed all the others: my loyalty. I would have done anything for my mistress; I would have let myself be tied to a torture wheel and wouldn't have complained. Juan realized he needed someone like me by his side, someone who could be his faithful partner in business and in life.

After our performance at the Tapia, Juan heard about our impending trip to the interior of the island, and when Madame asked him if he would come (we would need our slippers repaired constantly, since we wouldn't be able to buy new ones on the road) he decided to join us. It would give us the opportunity to get to know each other better, he said, and the adventure was enticing. He agreed to close his shoe-repair shop temporarily and join our troupe.

When we left for Arecibo, we were still just good friends. Then the ordeal of seeing Madame fall in love with Diamantino during our stay at Dos Ríos pushed me into despair. Madame made me take charge of the rehearsals of the *Bacchanale* because she wanted time to be by herself—or so she said. I had to go into town every day from Dos Ríos to supervise the dancers. I was merciless with them: jousting, disciplining, ordering them into obedience, supposedly so that they would grow professionally, but really because I had to take out my frustrations on someone. I was very successful; when it was time for the performance, the company was dancing better than ever— but I was miserable.

Then Diamantino and Madame disappeared during the opening night at the Teatro Oliver, and I almost went out of my mind. For a whole week I hardly slept or ate. Juan, fortunately, was still with us. When Don Pedro put me on the train and I returned to San Juan with the rest of the dancers, he accompanied us. I stayed at the Malatrassi with the girls, where the other members of the company were expecting us.

I decided to renew my visits to La Nueva Suela. Talking with Juan made me feel better, and I wanted to discuss with him what we should do now. The girls were restless and I was worried about them.

But when I came into the shop, Juan didn't want to talk. He was sitting at his work stool in front of the lathe, and I remember he had a lady's shoe on the block and was nailing down a new leather sole on it. He flashed a wide smile, put his arms around my waist, and made me sit on his lap. "I missed you like fresh meat misses salt, my duck," he said. I laughed because I knew exactly what he meant. My adoptive father was poor and we didn't have an icebox, either. Salt was a luxury, but it was the only way we could keep meat from spoiling when we managed to have some. "And I missed you more than the onion loves the skillet," I answered.

Juan pulled me down and I felt a searing heat on the insides of my legs. Then he kissed me on the mouth, and my arms became two soft petals which curled about his neck of their own accord. Juan began to unbutton my blouse and soon had me naked on his lap. I straddled his body and everything became confused—the pain of pleasure and the pleasure of pain as he entered me. I was tumbling down a well which exited at the other end of the world, and never even looked back.

I didn't love him, but I couldn't live the rest of my life like dead coral, with brine washing in and out of my heart. To be the beloved, instead of the exhausted lover; to be the requited, instead of the forgiven—from then on, I lived in the shadow of my coming happiness, and looked forward to the day when I would no longer be alone.

My good luck didn't last long, however. A few days later, I went back to the shoe-repair store and was surprised to discover there was nobody there. The store was locked and all the windows were shut; the sign above the door—a laced boot that reminded me of my grandmother in Minsk, because she had a pair just like it—flapped forlornly in the wind. I sat on the sidewalk and waited for Juan all afternoon, but he didn't come. I went back to the Malatrassi alone when it was almost dark. A week later, Juan was still missing.

"In San Juan I'd heard rumors about Los Tiznados being very active in the countryside, but I couldn't be sure if they were true. However, when we arrived at Arecibo, the town was abuzz with news of the terrorists' activities. Wherever we went, people were whispering about them. At first I didn't pay much attention because I was too busy mending the dancers' shoes. Madame had loaded me down with work and I had very little time to myself. Nonetheless, there were miles of sugar-white sand beaches near to the town where I took Masha for long walks as often as I could. I didn't care about the 'marvelous beauties of the landscape,' as Masha kept saying. I kept scheming how to sweet-talk her into making love on the sand dunes, but I had no luck.

"After waiting for an anxious week to get the permits to the theater, the night when the company would perform the *Bacchanale* finally arrived. I was ordered by Madame to wait under the trapdoor with a straw rug to catch her as she fell. But someone made a mistake, and Diamantino fell through the trap also. Suddenly I found myself surrounded by masked men who elbowed me out of the way and took Madame and Diamantino prisoner. Then Los Tiznados forced me at gunpoint to go back to the theater and threatened that if I told on them, I would be dead. The whole thing was crazy, considering the island was occupied by military troops. But the rebels were mad to begin with. They were capable of assaulting a machine gun with a machete, so I did as I was told.

"I accompanied Masha and the rest of the girls back to San Juan on the train. I was glad to be there: they were so distressed, they probably would have lost their way and gotten off at the wrong station. Masha sobbed disconsolately the whole trip; it took all my patience to take her mind off her beloved Madame. I bought her freshly squeezed *guarapo, marrayo de coco, ajonjolí, pasta de batata*—all the humble delicacies of the country—which I knew Masha liked because she had a sweet tooth. But nothing worked—passionate tears still rolled down her cheeks like breakers. The girls slumped on their seats and didn't even look out the windows at the landscape. All they did was bad-mouth Madame and plan how they were going to get off the island. Several of them had met rich gentlemen in San Juan who had offered to be their mentors, and they were seriously considering them. The company would break up, but nobody cared.

"When we got to the Malatrassi I sent for Lyubovna and talked to her in the lobby. 'Please take care of Masha,' I said. 'She's suffering, but I'm sure her malady is curable. Fortunately, the heart is the only human organ that regenerates itself.'

"The next day Masha came to visit me at my shop. I was tired of being put off and couldn't wait any longer. I had made up my mind to take the Russian fortress by storm, and that same afternoon Masha, the unapproachable Russian amazon, fell into my arms.

"Things were going well with us, and Masha came to see

me every day at the shop; we were happier than a pair of footsies in comfortable brogues. Then something unexpected happened. Masha had just left for the Malatrassi after our rendezvous one evening. It was pouring, and I had given her my leather apron to protect herself on the way. I was about to put out the light and get into bed when I heard a knock at the door. I opened it and cringed with fear: Molinari was standing there, dressed in buzzard black and with a gun in his hand.

" 'Madame has sent for you' was his cryptic message. 'You're to go with me to the mountains.' I nodded silently and tiptoed around my room picking up a few things. At the last minute I took a pair of toe shoes I had just finished lining and put them into my duffel bag. I didn't say a word, afraid I'd whip up the storm even more.

"A pair of horses held by a masked man were waiting for us at the door. We got on them and set out immediately toward Arecibo, where we would turn left and begin our ascent of the mountains.

"Once we arrived at Otoao I was told I could go wherever I pleased, but that wasn't very far because of the remoteness of the place—the settlement was nothing more than a handful of shacks nestled between jagged peaks. My horse was taken away from me, so even though I was told I could go where I wanted, I was still a prisoner. I walked about reconnoitering the place and saw several groups of men with machetes at the waist playing dice on the dirt floor; a foursome was playing dominoes on top of an empty crate. Huge boulders with strange inscriptions on them stood everywhere, so that the place had a mysterious look about it. They protruded from the ground like dolmens, with animal shapes and human faces carved on them that looked strangely alive as they stared out of the wet mist.

"I went looking for Madame and Diamantino, and as I

didn't find them, I asked one of the men who was sharpening his machete on a flint stone. He pointed out a hut at the edge of camp, and at that moment I saw Madame coming out the door. She looked haggard, with deep circles under her eyes, but she was smiling. Diamantino came out after her. They were far away from where I stood, but I could see them embrace. Then Diamantino got on his horse and he joined Bienvenido down the road. A river could be heard in the distance and I wandered over toward it. It ran between blue boulders and looked inviting; I took off my clothes and dove in behind a bend in the river, hidden by some tropical fern. The water was wonderful, cold and clear.

"That afternoon there was a showdown between Diamantino and Bienvenido after they got back from their reconnaissance mission. The two young men had been reining in their animosity, but they couldn't control themselves any longer. They must have been arguing on the road about something, because as soon as they entered camp, they leapt off their horses and were at each other's throats in seconds. 'You've betrayed us miserably,' Bienvenido spit at Diamantino. 'You should have given us cover and you didn't fire a shot. You're still a Tiznado, whether you like it or not!' (Later I learned there had been a skirmish at *Cerro del Prieto*, a mountain nearby, and Diamantino had hung back.) Diamantino's answer was a punch in the gut. They kicked and twisted each other's arms, tried to strangle each other and poke each other's eyes out. The fight continued for what seemed like hours.

"Then, summoning the last of his strength, Diamantino yelled: 'You're just jealous! It's not my fault you're obsessed with Ronda. You're crazy not to put her out of your mind.'

"When Bienvenido heard this he lowered his head, his neck muscles bulging, and he tackled Diamantino full force. It was like seeing someone trying to fight in the middle of a trough of molasses. They rolled over each other on the ground in slower and slower motion until they were so exhausted, they were unable to lift a finger. Finally they passed out, lying on top of each other like lovers. Los Tiznados picked them up and carried them to a nearby clearing.

"The next morning, when Bienvenido woke up, Molinari was sitting on the ground in front of him, looking more than ever like a buzzard. No one had noticed us when we joined the group; Los Tiznados had accepted us as if we were two of them. Molinari leaned against an empty crate and his black wool suit was spattered with mud, but he still managed to project an air of confidence and energy. In fact, now that I think of it, I don't remember ever seeing Molinari look tired. There was something about him—perhaps his skin, which had a dark sheen to it, or his patent-leather hair, slick with brilliantine—that made him look indestructible.

"Molinari sat there flicking the flies away from his face with a malanga leaf as Bienvenido opened his eyes. 'It's about time you came to your senses, both literally and figuratively,' Molinari said, handing the young man a flask of rum. Bienvenido's head must have felt as big as a house; his whole body was probably sore, throbbing with pain, but he took the bottle and managed a swig. I crouched in the shadows, trying to pass unnoticed, next to the campfire's embers.

" 'What time is it?' the young man asked, shaking his head to clear his thoughts. His hair was disheveled and he had a crust of blood over his right eye. His upper lip had swollen and he dabbed rum on it with his handkerchief. He could hardly speak. A couple of Los Tiznados drew near and helped him get up from the ground. They had let him pass the night out in the open, lying on the ground, afraid that if they tried to help him to a bed before his fury was spent, he would lash out at them.

" 'It's nearly seven, by the way the sun's rays are slanting into the trees,' Molinari said.

"Bienvenido didn't seem surprised to see Molinari. Maybe he expected him to give testimony of how two men had taken justice into their own hands to prove which one was better. He walked toward the campfire, looking for some bitter coffee to shock himself awake. Molinari reached out with his foot and nudged Diamantino in the ribs. He was lying on the ground also, and let out a groan without opening his eyes.

" 'Go to hell!' Diamantino said to Molinari as he rolled away from him. After a few minutes, however, he slowly got to his feet holding on to a yagrumo tree. His head was reeling, but he managed to stumble off into the thickets to urinate."

37

" 'What are you waiting for?' Molinari asked Bienvenido when he came back. 'You've had your fun and haven't gained anything by it. The best thing you can do now is cut off an ear or a finger of your precious Diamantino and send it to Don Pedro to ask for his ransom.' But Bienvenido kept putting it off. 'We're waiting for help from Santo Domingo,' he said. 'A shipment of arms should be here at any moment; with it, we can launch our coup. We can ask for ransom later.'

"When Bienvenido wouldn't listen, Molinari stood up to face him. 'Has it ever occurred to you why your middle initial is "B"? Or why your skin is white when your father, Arnaldo Pérez, is a mulatto? Everyone in Arecibo knows you're Don Pedro Batistini's son. That's why Diamantino warned you about Ronda; there was no need for you to get so angry at him and provoke a fight.'

"Bienvenido didn't answer and hung his head.

" 'Don Pedro raped your mother and you need money for the coup,' Molinari added. 'It's as simple as that. Now, when you sack Dos Ríos, you won't have to feel guilty. Since Don Pedro's son committed suicide, you're entitled to his fortune.'

" 'Who asked for your opinion?' Bienvenido yelled at him. 'Shut up or I'll shut you up myself!' And he stalked off into the woods without answering Molinari.

"This information was all new to me, but I judged it wise to keep my own counsel. Soon Madame sent for me. I took my duffel bag and entered the tent that had been assigned to her. She was sitting on a stool in the middle of the airy canvas room, mending an exercise suit on her lap. 'At last, you're here!' she cried when she saw me. 'I have to dance *The Dying Swan* at a nearby town tonight, and my shoes are worn to a pulp.' No sooner had she said that than I brought out the new pair of toe shoes from my bag and laid them on the ground before her. 'You're an angel,' she said, kissing me on both cheeks. 'I know I can count on you when in need.'

"That was when I learned about Madame's solo performances around the island, during which she made good her promise to take ballet to the people. 'I'm finally exorcising my nightmares about the war, Juan, about the millions of people who are dying in Europe, especially in Russia! When I dance *The Dying Swan* for these people, I'm saying a prayer for peace,' she said. 'They must never know what a war is like.' When I heard this from Madame, I winced. What was she doing, talking about the war? About the people who were dying in Europe? Didn't she know there was a war going on around her? How could she be so blind? Frankly, I couldn't understand why Masha admired Madame so much. Either she had become completely estranged from reality because of her romantic involvement with Diamantino, or the high altitudes had unhinged her mind.

"Every morning Madame, a group of Los Tiznados, and I got on our horses and went on a trip to a different town. I enjoyed the mountains in spite of the danger we were in. It was cool, and they reminded me of my youth in Cayey on my father's tobacco farm. One felt safe, with many places to hide. The terrain was reassuringly familiar. Giant fern leaves blew like lungs of green lace in the breeze, yagrumo trees waved their silvery hands from the mountaintops, and my beloved *nicotianas* spread their wide, perfumed leaves over the valleys. As we mounted the steep hills, we crossed paths with several search parties, but they never found us. People always gave us shelter or told us where to hide. Los Tiznados had many friends. The farmers lied to the armed troops and pointed in the opposite direction from where we were going. After a couple of days we would return to Otoao, where Los Tiznados had their camp. There we rested and refurbished our provisions.

"*Otoao* is an Indian word; it means 'Rock Among the Clouds.' The terrain was so steep there it made you claustrophobic, and it was difficult to breathe. The mist traveled through the area in huge shreds of gauze, as if the mountains had wounds in them that needed to be bandaged. In Otoao the earth was a deep red, and when it rained it seemed to bleed from every jagged hillock and abrupt crag.

"Near the settlement a large, rectangular ball court had been discovered some time back, surrounded by giant boulders carved with Indian symbols and petroglyphs. This ball court, as well as the village beside it, was in the region of Las Brujas, one of the highest parts of the island. Bienvenido told us it was there that the last of the Taino Indians had entrenched themselves during the Spanish conquest, and now it gave refuge to Los Tiznados. Those bleeding mountains around camp made me fear our island would always remain cursed, that it would never heal.

"The trips seemed to be a kind of pilgrimage for Madame, a way to pay for her sins, for having enjoyed a privileged life.

She may have been estranged from her world, adrift in her own dreams, but she showed a great deal of grace under pressure. As we traveled by mule pack up the rocky paths, she was amazingly self-possessed. When we stepped over raging streams, her resiliency as a dancer was a great help to her in the dangerous leaps from boulder to boulder. Leeches, black and round like giant moles, stuck to our legs when we crossed the rivers and had to be removed with fire.

"In the small towns we stayed in third-class hotels and had to drink the turbid yellow water pouring from the faucets. Madame suffered from dysentery after the first few days. Some towns didn't even have a hotel, and we had to sleep in the plazas or on tables at the local restaurants once the customers had left. We rode the pack mules into the forest and wrapped plantain leaves dipped in water on our heads to keep cool. The further we went into the island the poorer the towns became, and yet the minute we entered a town Madame would ask if there was a theater or a movie house in which to dance *The Dying Swan*. In Barranquitas, Los Tiznados stole a Philips phonograph, the kind you cranked up, with a tin amplifier that looked like a trumpet, and a crateful of records of classical music from the local casino. They gave it to Madame, who was thrilled; now she could die to the music of Saint-Saëns.

"Even when it was raining and the roof leaked, Madame danced in the puddles. If the stage floor had holes in it, she asked for a canvas and spread it over the boards so her feet wouldn't get caught in them. Finally, when we arrived at Sabana Grande, a town between Mayagüez and Ponce, the movie house where she danced remained completely empty. She put two gas hurricane lamps on the stage floor and announced that the performance that night would be free, and people flocked to see her. In Ponce, where she danced at La Perla Theater, the rumor went around that Madame was giving her support to the terrorists, and no one bought tickets to the performance. But Madame ordered all the windows of the theater opened, and she danced for free to a crowd of onlookers who stood on the sidewalk. At other towns there were open stages and kiosks in the middle of the plaza, and she danced on them as well, using the headlights of the local automobiles for lighting.

"I pitied Madame: her tour wasn't just the whim of a prima donna Los Tiznados were catering to. They were using her, traveling by her side from one town to another, to gain support for their cause. And Madame let herself be used.

"After the fight, things between Bienvenido and Diamantino calmed down. They talked to each other like normal human beings and Diamantino suggested they visit Martina Arroyo, a sister of Bienvenido's mother, Aralia. Diamantino was convinced that if Bienvenido managed to overcome his passion for Ronda he would leave Los Tiznados' camp. 'To be a Tiznado is to be suicidal,' I heard him say to Madame one night. 'These men know they are going to die. If Bienvenido admits that Ronda is his sister, maybe he'll be able to put her out of his mind. Then, perhaps he'll let us go.'

"Martina Arroyo lived in Naranjito, a barrio near the town of Barranquitas. Since Aralia, Martina's sister, was dead, no one in Arecibo could confirm what Diamantino had told his friend, but Martina would know the secret.

"We traveled there and squatted in front of the palm-thatched hut drinking hot, bitter coffee out of *coquitos*—carved, rustic coconut cups. Martina was old and wizened, and her hand trembled as she fanned the embers of an open fire with a plantain leaf.

" 'The rich on this island are like the moon, they have two faces,' she said, stirring the embers with a stick of wood. 'The bright side is presented to the world. The dark is seldom made public, but the men are nonetheless proud of it. It's proof of their masculinity, being able to have children "in" more than one woman, like a *paso fino* stud.'

" 'Your father, Don Pedro, was like that. He was a bull of a man,' she told Bienvenido in a pebbly voice. 'Aralia became pregnant a few days before Doña Basilisa. I was midwife to both of them. Miss Ronda and you were born only hours apart.' This time Bienvenido couldn't retreat into denial; he was getting the information firsthand. His shoulders slumped and his face became ashen, so that his red hair stood out even brighter above his anguished face.

" 'Very well, it's true . . .' he said, then swallowed his bitter coffee in one gulp. 'But I love her just the same. I'll never give her up.' We were shocked, but there was nothing we could do.

"Why do we fall in love with one person and not with another? Love is a mystery no one can unravel. Ronda looked a lot like Bienvenido. They had the same square, chiseled chin, wide-set eyes, and high forehead. Maybe they fell in love because they resembled each other so much. Ronda understood the contradictions of Bienvenido's character. He loved good wines, was always impeccably dressed by the best tailor in Arecibo, and at the same time hated the *petrimetres* who were always lolling about the plaza, showing off their linen suits and reciting poems out loud. 'I love the whole of you, your sophisticated and your barbarian side,' Ronda would say.

"I respected Bienvenido. He was a born leader and he always rode ahead of Los Tiznados, but his desire for Ronda was like a sickness. He knew he could never have her. He was like Tantalus—the fruit was ripe and perfumed on the branch, but he knew that if he reached for it, it would shrivel in his mouth. He made me think of Absalom, King David's son. Absalom fell in love with his sister Tamar, who was exceedingly fair, and took her to his tent to force himself upon her. Still wrapped in the searing sheets of passion, Absalom regretted what he had done, and that very night galloped away on his horse to a far-away olive grove, where he hung himself from a tree. Bienvenido swore the same thing wouldn't happen to him. He was never going to lay a hand on Ronda, he swore, no matter what tortures life held in store."

38

"We were staying in a village near Loiza, on the north coast, when Madame saw a group of people dancing an atonal, rhythmic dance of African origin and she was curious. I know all about drums and so do many of our countrymen, so it didn't surprise me when she asked me to introduce the drums to her: 'This is Tumbador and this is Subidor,' I said solemnly. 'They are the high priests of Bomba. They were used by slaves to communicate with each other when a rebellion was afoot.' And I showed Madame the wooden casks covered with goat skin, which were tightened with rough-hewn wooden pegs at the sides. 'Drums can be as powerful as love—they push you toward the right or pull you toward the left. You have no choice but to follow,' my grandmother Zambia used to say. I thought of her when I placed Madame's hands over the drums so that she could feel the skins quiver.

"For years Madame had danced in pink tights and frothy tutus in deference to the formal etiquette of the czar's court, but now she burst out from all that as from a silk cocoon. She took off her toe shoes and concentrated on the rhythm of the drums. She danced wildly, whips of hair flailing around her. It was as if she were possessed by the spirits summoned by the drums. She choreographed a new ballet to them, which she said she would dance in the next town.

"A few days later we were sitting on the floor of a palm-thatched hut at Otoao when a messenger arrived from the coast. He brought depressing news. The cargo of arms Bienvenido was expecting had been captured soon after it had sailed out of the Mapeyé river, near San Pedro de Macoris, and its captain was now in a Santo Domingo jail. Without arms Los Tiznados would be annihilated. They desperately needed the money to obtain a second cargo.

"A new strategy was devised to garner funds. Los Tiznados began to hold up innocent travelers on the road from Arecibo to Otoao, which cut across the steepest mountains. Several victims died, among them a priest, a sick child, and his mother, who were going to the hospital in Arecibo when their coach was held up. The driver lost control of the horse and the coach hurtled down a ravine. When Madame heard this, her anguish knew no limits. The purpose of her art was to bring peace to the world, and now this crime would be on her conscience for the rest of her life. It didn't matter if Los Tiznados' cause was politically justified, no one had the right to take another person's life. Madame became physically ill. For two days she barely ate or drank.

"At Otoao's camp, every night after dinner, I sat with Madame and Diamantino in the dark and we would tell each other stories. Madame would stare into the darkness listening to the *coquís*, tiny frogs whose song streaked the night with silver.

"Finally, one evening Bienvenido came over to the hut where Madame and Diamantino were staying. He had impor-

tant news, he said as he pulled up a chair: Los Tiznados had decided to release her, but they wanted one last thing from her.
She had to write a note to Governor Yager asking for fifty
thousand dollars in ransom. If she refused, they would have to
kill her.

" 'I'll write it, if that's what you want,' Madame answered
quietly. 'But the American government will never pay that
much for a Russian ballerina, not even for a famous one. It
would be much wiser if you let me return to San Juan. Perhaps
I can get the money, and help you from there.'

"Bienvenido consulted with Los Tiznados, and surprisingly
they agreed to the plan. They didn't hold Madame in any special esteem. Instead, they ridiculed her, and whenever they saw
her dance *The Dying Swan*, they would guffaw and slap their
thighs in merriment, making obscene sounds or gobbling like
turkeys. When they saw she was head over heels in love with
Diamantino Márquez, they told him, laughing, 'May God bless
your balls. Madame may go in peace.' Then Los Tiznados told
her, 'If you disappear, you can be sure your boyfriend will pay
for it. Juan Anduce will go with you; if anything happens, he'll
know how to take care of you.' And they laughed uproariously
again, smacking Diamantino in the back.

"I looked at Diamantino, who sat on the floor next to
Madame, and I felt sorry for him. He'd been a prisoner now for
over two weeks, and except for the first day, they never tied
him down. Now his wrists were roped behind his back. He
didn't protest or try to defend himself, but stared defiantly at
Bienvenido. His eyeglasses had been cracked in the fight, but he
still wore them. People's characters shine through under stress,
and El Delfín was a gentleman's son, a true gentleman himself.
But he was also an anachronism.

"I didn't agree with Los Tiznados' cause and I certainly

didn't consider myself one of them. And yet, when I was ordered to accompany Madame to the capital and act as her guard dog, I did as I was told. Bienvenido trusted me even though we differed, and I decided to honor his trust. At the same time I'd do my best to protect Madame, who had won my admiration and sympathy. As soon as we were alone I approached her and whispered that she had nothing to fear. I'd take her to San Juan safely, and we'd work something out to get the money without violence.

"The next day, when Madame was about to leave for San Juan, we saw Molinari conferring with Los Tiznados. Madame was very nervous, and I began to suspect something was wrong. Was Molinari one of the guerillas? Or was he a member of the secret police, as his friendship with the commissioner had made me suspect? Was he going to San Juan in order to meet with the commissioner? He was like a moray eel, slithering here and there; it was impossible to tell where his den lay.

"Fortunately, when Madame saw me waiting for her under a mango tree to escort her to the coast, she immediately felt reassured. We rode down the mountain on horseback, and Madame, Molinari, and I boarded a sloop which set sail from Arecibo's port. We knew better than to ask Molinari any questions, as he would only add his blistering foul language to our ordeal. We arrived at the capital's wharf around four that same afternoon, with no mishaps and without anyone recognizing us. As soon as we got off the boat, Molinari disappeared."

39

I remember the day Juan brought Madame down from the mountains as if it were yesterday. He escorted her personally to the hotel and stayed only enough to give me a look I had no difficulty interpreting. But I couldn't concern myself with Juan Anduce at that moment. It was a day of joy because I was finally reunited with Madame.

When I saw her walk into the lobby of the Malatrassi, at least ten pounds thinner and with deep circles under her eyes, I couldn't keep the tears of happiness from running down my cheeks. I had come to check if there was a message from Dandré and saw her standing at the doorway, her slender figure cut against the blinding sunlight, looking as if she had come back from the dead. Everything was forgotten: Diamantino, the broken pledge, my own feelings of rejection. I took her in my arms and hugged her, then ordered the concierge to call Lyubovna, Smallens, Novikov, and the girls, to let them know Madame was back. They all ran down the stairs and there were hysterical embraces and kisses all around. We'd been deathly worried about her and at first we couldn't speak, so strong were the emotions caught at our throats. Then, when we saw Madame was all right, we began to talk at the same time. Her disappearance had been kept out of the news because the government wanted to suppress any publicity, but there were rumors that she had been kidnapped by Los Tiznados and that they were holding her for a huge ransom.

"Several search parties were sent out by the governor," I told her, "but they had no luck. In the meantime, there was nothing we could do."

"We wanted to search for you ourselves, but the police wouldn't tell us anything and we didn't know where to begin," Nadja complained.

"I managed to send Dandré a telegram," I said, "urging him to come back right away. He should be here any day now."

We sat around in the lobby and couldn't believe our ears when Madame denied having been in any danger.

"Why so much worry?" she said, clucking at us like a hen at her chicks and shaking her head just like one. She hadn't been kidnapped by Los Tiznados, she insisted. She had gone with Diamantino to the mountains of her own accord. "We must send a message to Governor Yager immediately," she told Novikov, "and inform him that I'm safe and sound so that he'll call off the search."

None of us believed her, but we pretended to. Novikov immediately did her bidding. Then Lyubovna brought Poppy, who began to lick Madame's face; Smallens and Custine brought her the cage with the nightingales, Madame began to whistle to them, and soon they began to sing. Best of all, Lyubovna brought the alligator case and showed her that her jewels were intact. A few minutes later the police arrived at the hotel, and they began to ask Madame questions. She repeated the same story to the commissioner.

The next day I invited Madame to have breakfast alone with me at La Bombonera, the cafeteria where the local artists met.

I was certain she wouldn't tell the commissioner what had really happened, and I wanted the truth directly from her lips; I knew her well enough to tell if she was lying. Lyubovna and the girls all went on different errands. Juan said he had to go back to his workshop and took leave of us. Madame and I walked under the shade of our umbrella to the restaurant, with a group of Swooning Swans trailing behind us like geese and clamoring for Madame's autograph.

Madame, as usual, graciously signed all their diaries and their newspaper clippings with her photograph before we finally ran into the restaurant to escape the mob. We found a booth at the back and sat down, relieved to get out of the crush. It must have been almost a hundred degrees outside; the street was like a skillet under your feet. I kept silent for a few minutes, letting our spirits simmer down. Once the waiter had brought us tall lemonades with ice, I took both her hands in mine. "What was the trip like? Is it true you weren't kidnapped? Why didn't you send a message that you were safe?" I asked softly.

"To tell the truth, Masha, I was getting tired of sleeping on wire cots and having Spartan meals of codfish boiled with green plantain in small-town *fondas*," she answered, as if excusing herself for her eccentric behavior. "It's wonderful to sleep in a bed again and eat in a real restaurant, with linen tablecloth and napkin." I could tell Madame was changing, reverting to her former self, that Diamantino's power over her was already waning. But I didn't want her to realize I was aware of it. I wanted her to talk and I listened attentively to what she had to say. That morning she had put in three hours of strenuous exercise at Teatro Tapia, and that was a good sign. She had begun to dance again; the rest would soon become chaff, falling away from her.

"At first it was all supposed to be a joke: galloping through the woods and dancing in the small towns—a heavy-handed joke, you must admit, like dropping an anvil on your foot!" Madame explained. "Diamantino sent his godfather a message the night we left Arecibo, telling him not to worry, that he wanted to give me a private tour of the island and that I would be treated like a queen before I was returned to Dos Ríos safe and sound. But Don Pedro never received the message. As you know, the old man was furious. He organized a police chase, and Diamantino had his hands full keeping his friends in the Home Guard, who accompanied us on the trip, from getting caught. But they were unarmed."

"And where is Diamantino now? What happened to him?" I finally managed to bring out the cursed name.

"He's all right. He's staying with some friends at a coffee plantation in the mountains for a few days. He'll be back in San Juan later on," Madame said.

I looked at her askance. "Are you sure you're telling me the truth? Would you swear by the Virgin of Vladimir that you weren't kidnapped?" But she wouldn't answer.

At that moment Lyubovna entered La Bombonera and we made space for her in the booth so she could join us. So many things had happened since Madame had left! Lyubovna told Niura about Novikov's new boyfriend, a young man who worked in the local circus as a trapeze artist. Nadja had discovered a trove of old musical scores in a bookstore in Calle San Justo, and when she noticed that they were by Felix Lafortune, the Creole composer from New Orleans who had toured the island many years earlier (so Don Pedro's story was true, I thought!), she was exuberant. She loved American music and these were unpublished scores; she could make a fortune from them when she returned to New York.

Lyubovna said she had discovered a convent in Old San Juan where the nuns did all sorts of embroidery, and they were wonderful company. She had moved out of the governor's palace and spent most of her time with them now, sitting on the convent's balcony overlooking the entrance to the bay, stitching away on sheets and tablecloths as she gossiped with the nuns. I, on the other hand, had kept to solitary confinement in my tiny room at the Malatrassi, waiting for Madame's return.

The azure sky, the clouds white as newborn lambs, the people—the friendliest we had met in our travels—the beauty of the city, gleaming like a gem on its medieval ramparts and yet with all the advantages of the modern age thanks to the Americans, with well-paved streets, houses with running water, sewer service, plentiful food—it all made our troupe want to remain on the island. It was as if a spell was woven around us, and we now looked upon Dandré's impending return as a threat. All except me, that is. I couldn't wait until he got back, so he would take Madame in hand.

40

Doña Basilisa and her daughter, Ronda, were waiting for us at the Malatrassi when Madame and I got back. They had come to San Juan because Ronda had been chosen to be the next queen of the Ponce de León Carnival, which would be held in San Juan in two weeks' time. Ronda was reluctant to accept, but being queen of the carnival gave the family a lot of prestige. "You know how I hate parties and balls, Father. And Diamantino is still missing, we haven't the faintest idea where he is! How can you think about the carnival now?" she said. Ronda was more worried about Bienvenido than about Diamantino, but she didn't admit it to her parents. She hadn't asked her father a single question about Bienvenido's mysterious disappearance, although she'd made plenty of inquiries in town, all of them fruitless. She knew Don Pedro didn't look happily on her friendship with the overseer's son, but she surmised that it was because Bienvenido's father, Arnaldo Pérez, was mulatto.

Don Pedro insisted that she accept the nomination to be queen of the carnival. "Diamantino has disappeared before," he said. "God knows what he's up to now—he's probably out hunting with his friends in the hills. One day he wants to be an artist, the next he'll want to be a mountain climber. We can't live our lives according to his whims. And anyway I'm sure Saint Anthony, the savior of lost souls, will keep him safe." And when Doña Basilisa herself came to Don Pedro grieving about Diamantino's disappearance and complaining that it wasn't a time for parties or celebrations, Don Pedro said, "*A mal tiempo buena cara*—one must keep one's chin up in adversity, my dear. Having Ronda preside over the carnival will be good for business. The governor will be there, and so will most of his cabinet members and many senators and representatives. Since we're the queen's parents, you and I will sit at the main table and be able to converse with all of them."

When Ronda still refused, claiming she'd look ridiculous in a ball gown—she'd never worn one and had dressed in pants at the farm ever since she was twelve—Don Pedro said he'd give her a special present if she accepted. "What, Papito?" Ronda asked, her curiosity piqued. "A *paso fino* horse you can ride in the carnival's races once the coronation is over," he answered, beaming. "It'll be first class; a son of last year's champion at the Hippodrome. I already picked it out for you." Ronda was ecstatic, and she accepted her father's offer.

Doña Basilisa was full of bubbly conversation, as usual, and soon Doña Victoria and Rogelio Tellez joined us in the lobby of the Malatrassi. We all sat around in a circle, talking animatedly. Rogelio told us how he had been ordered by the police not to publish the article he had written about Madame's disappearance in Arecibo. "You'd think this was a conspiracy of state!" he protested. "They said my story of Madame's kidnapping would make the shit hit the fan and that Puerto Rico would lose its tourism." Fortunately, he had heeded the official order and hadn't published the article, since Madame had turned up safe and sound after all.

Ronda took Madame's hand and led her to a quiet nook behind a potted palm in the hall of the hotel. She was solemn and looked worried. "I've heard rumors in Arecibo that Bienvenido and Diamantino are together in the hills, and I'm worried to death about them. Is it true? Did you see Bienvenido while you were there? I haven't heard from him since the night of the performance." Her lips were trembling and I was amazed at her sincerity. To admit to Madame that she was worried about Bienvenido Pérez, the overseer's son, was a daring thing to do.

Madame kept silent; she knew Diamantino's life hung in the balance. "I was with Diamantino on a tour of the island, and when I returned to the city he stayed behind at a coffee hacienda in the mountains. I haven't seen hide or hair of Bienvenido Pérez since the night of the performance at Teatro Oliver," she said. "I'm sorry, Ronda," she added, embracing her. "I know how you must feel, but I can't help you." Ronda nervously lit a cigarette; I could tell she didn't believe a word.

Ronda was to appear as Miss Liberty, and her gold-lamé dress—a draped copy of the Statue of Liberty's—was being made to order at that very moment by a fashion designer who had traveled to Bedloe's Island to sketch it. At this, Doña Victoria, whom I would have sworn hadn't heard a word of the conversation, sat up on the lobby's sofa and began to laugh. She had read Ronda's lips and understood every word. "The Statue of Liberty, Queen?" she tittered. "That's just perfect! A colony should always have Liberty as sovereign!"

Doña Victoria promised Ronda she'd be present at the coronation and bring all her friends with her in a *comparsa* of *jíbaros* that would accompany her to the throne.

"And who will be your king, dear?" Doña Victoria asked.

"It's too early. She hasn't got one yet," Doña Basilisa said.

"Why should I have one at all? I can very well reign by myself," Ronda answered smartly.

"Well, Miss Liberty, let me kiss your hand!" Rogelio teased, reaching for it.

Ronda frowned and pulled her hand away. She wanted to get away from Doña Victoria and her nephew as soon as possible; she couldn't stand either of them. "The carnival committee is dragging behind in a lot of things," Doña Basilisa explained, "but we're working on it." But Doña Victoria was scandalized. How was Ronda going to ride down the streets of Old San Juan in her carnival float alone? She had to find a young man from one of the best families right away or she'd have to settle for a nobody as king, she fussed.

"Don't worry about it. We'll get someone who's worth her while," Doña Basilisa said airily. She didn't like it when Doña Victoria implied her daughter was being spurned.

Doña Basilisa picked up her handbag, said they were under a lot of pressure, and got up from the sofa. They had been away at the farm for a month, she said, and she had just found out her daughter had been selected queen of the festivities. She had to see to thousands of details during the two weeks ahead— Ronda's gold-lamé dress, her mantle, a headpiece which would reproduce the Statue of Liberty's magnificent golden crown. They soon rose and left the hotel.

The next day Ronda invited me to go see Rayo at Don Cayetano Ramirez's horse farm, which stood just behind the Hippodrome. In San Juan Ronda didn't see me as Madame's maid anymore. After Madame's disappearance at Dos Ríos, Ronda had come to depend more and more on me. I accompanied her everywhere and we struck up a friendship which fortunately didn't fade when we met again in the city.

She picked me up at La Fortaleza in her father's Pierce-

Arrow, driven by a uniformed chauffeur. We went first to Miramar, to the Batistinis' mansion. It was just as magnificent as Juan had described it, with stained-glass decorations on all the windows and a wide balcony from which you could see the Atlantic glinting in the distance. Ronda took my hand and we explored the house together. We stepped into the living room, where Don Eduardo had passed away and the solemn silence of the Sacrament of Extreme Unction—administered in spite of Don Eduardo's protests—seemed to emanate from the wood-paneled walls. We visited Adalberto Batistini's room, where I thought I saw his ghost gazing out the window at the landscape he wanted to paint and of course we visited Diamantino's cell in the basement, to which Don Pedro had removed him when Don Eduardo had died. This was where El Delfín, who had created such havoc in our company, had lived for several years. In the two months we had spent on the island, these people had become more real to me than those of my beloved St. Petersburg.

We chatted and talked over tea, which Adelina brought out on the terrace—it *was* nice to be served rather than to serve, for a change—and then we rode out to the Hippodrome in the Pierce-Arrow. I could tell Ronda was still depressed; the fact that Bienvenido hadn't written her a single line since his disappearance was a bitter reminder that she had no assurance whatever of his love. Unless, of course, he were dead; and Ronda was certain he wasn't.

On our way to the Hippodrome, we stopped at La Casa de las Medias y los Botones, Madame's favorite store, to pick up an extra strand of rhinestones that had to be sewn by hand to Ronda's costume. We had to elbow our way in, there were so many people there. At carnival time La Casa de las Medias became even more popular than it usually was: people flocked to

it like flies to a jar of honey. Its jeweled buttons, luxurious brocades, feathers, fans, and masks, the elements that would create
the fanciful evening clothes *Sanjuaneros* loved, were all on display.

Ronda finally made her purchase and we fought our way
out of the store. Then we drove out to Don Cayetano's horse
farm. When we saw Rayo, with his curved neck, silky mane,
and delicate hooves plucking the ground, I was sure he would
help Ronda forget her impossible love. But I was wrong. "Isn't
he beautiful?" she asked the minute she saw him. "I'll ride him
with Bienvenido during the carnival's race. He's sure to be back
from the hills by then."

Doña Basilisa and Don Pedro were good friends of Governor
Yager, and the next day we heard that they had sent him a personal message informing him of Ronda's plight, asking for his
help in finding her a king. But the governor was so busy organizing search parties for Los Tiznados all over the island that
it slipped his mind. The letter lay on the governor's desk, unan-
swered, for several days, and Doña Basilisa didn't dare keep
looking for a suitable monarch because the governor might be
insulted if she took further steps to solve the problem.

One of the governor's aides dropped by the hotel the day
after Madame arrived. "Governor Yager would like you to be
his guest at La Fortaleza again, Madame," he informed her. "He
feels you'd be safer there until Mr. Dandré gets back. I'm supposed to drive you over to the mansion myself." Madame
thanked him and asked if I could go with her. Fortunately, the
aide said yes.

Half an hour later I was unpacking our valises and making
Madame comfortable in one of La Fortaleza's ample guest bed-

rooms. The butler showed us to our quarters. Madame's bed had a bronze canopy with gauze curtains falling down its sides and an absurd bronze crown sitting on top. It had been made for the diva Angelina Bertoli, queen of sopranos, when she had visited the island years before, the butler explained. I remembered Don Pedro's vivid story about the nightingale in the little red plush cart.

The room was beautiful, with a marble-topped console carved in dark, gleaming mahogany and a balcony that overlooked the bay and the Moorish gardens. The governor apparently wanted to make up for the discomforts Madame had suffered at the hands of the supposed "pranksters" of the Home Guard during her escapade in the mountains. He didn't believe her story for a minute and suspected Los Tiznados—he'd received several police reports that Madame had been seen riding through the towns of the interior with them—but concluded it was better not to stir things up by questioning her before Mr. Dandré got back.

This time I wasn't put away in a cell in the basement, like the last time we had stayed at the governor's palace. I had a small room to myself adjacent to Madame's, which opened to an inner patio. Since Lyubovna was staying at the convent and Dandré was away, I was considered Madame's official companion and everyone treated me with respect.

Madame said she wanted to rest for a few days before she danced again, and I was glad of the decision. No one in the troupe dared ask if she had been with Diamantino in the mountains, or if she planned to be reunited with him later, and I was reluctant to question her. We all wanted to believe she had changed her mind about abandoning the company. I was the only one she confided in, and that only by halves, always drawing a reticent veil over what had really happened.

Juan came every day to La Fortaleza as Madame's official shoemaker and told me confidentially that Diamantino aimed to rejoin Madame at some point, but that he didn't know exactly when. I pretended not to be aware of anything, and went on trying to make Madame's life as comfortable as possible. One afternoon we were sitting on the balcony that opened onto the bay, brushing each other's hair and doing our nails, when I heard a heavy step echo behind us. I turned around and saw Dandré's bearlike shape pause heavily in the doorway. "How are you, Niura, my little swan?" he said, his dark shadow looming over his suitcase. "The *Borinquen* just got into port this afternoon. I never had a chance to send you a telegram."

My heart did a triple cabriole, and I had to hold on to my chair so as not to fall off. Madame didn't move from her lounge chair. She kept on varnishing her nails with Revolutionary Rose as if Dandré had been away for only a moment. "You look thinner, darling," she finally said, looking up from her nails. "Have you been eating well? I've missed you." I didn't need to hear anything else. I sighed, picked up my hairbrush, and left the room.

The next days were agonizing. I was torn between feelings of relief at having Dandré back and my old jealousy, which sprang up in scarlet shoots around my heart. If it's true that absence makes the heart grow fonder, it was certainly true in Madame's case. Time had softened her image of Dandré, and his hoodlum ways now didn't seem so menacing. She had missed his pampering and his attention to detail, which were very different from the undependable embraces of her firebrand lover. Dandré seemed to guess this and was very tender with Madame, so that soon her old dependence on him began to resurface. He went back to his coddling: "Don't you think you should do this, darling? Why do you want to do that, dear?"— the you-know-it's-not-good-for-you kind of advice. To make matters worse, at night Dandré and Madame slept in the bronze canopied bed, which took to jingling and jangling like a two-penny orchestra. Meanwhile, I lay in the next room stifling my hot shame under the sheets or gazing out of the window and counting the cold stars nailed to the sky.

Dandré had recovered Madame for us, but I feared it was only temporary. I was tempted to tell him what I knew, but I chose to be compassionate. They had spent too many years to-gether, had braved many storms arm in arm. They were like two trees whose trunks had grown into each other and it was pitiful to separate them. Better to wait and see if things would resolve themselves.

The girls, on the other hand, were happy to see Dandré and no longer minded when he patted their cheeks and pinched their behinds. They followed him everywhere, chattering and laughing, and when he gave them their new passports, they were exuberant, kissing him on the tip of his nose or on his bald pate. Dandré, for his part, had apparently talked to Moli-nari, because a few days after his arrival, he had more infor-mation about Diamantino Márquez and about Madame's carryings-on with the young man than I ever would have dared reveal. His reaction was totally different from what I expected. He wasn't jealous, he bantered in front of Madame; he was too old for that. But didn't Madame feel guilty robbing the cradle? And wasn't the corn just a little green behind the ears? From now on, every time he made love to her he was going to take a milk bath first, so Madame wouldn't be able to tell the differ-ence in how her two lovers tasted. When I heard him talk like that and heard Madame's peals of laughter shaking the bed's ridiculous bronze crown at night, my fears of Madame's aban-doning us or of a crime of passion being committed in the bedroom next to mine were scattered to the wind.

At other times, however, I wondered how Madame really

felt. At times she looked sad; she reminded me of the Swan of Tuonela, gliding silently on the icy Gulf of Finland in search of its lost reflection. Maybe Dandré wasn't smart enough to realize that something was wrong, that perhaps Madame wasn't sincere in her loving behavior. I desperately wanted her to stay with him and to forget Diamantino, so that our lives would return to normal, but she looked like she was waiting for something. She would sit out on the balcony staring out to sea for hours or watching the cargo ships sail in and out of the harbor. Even with Dandré constantly urging her to get up and practice, to round up her dancers and begin rehearsals again, Madame said she just didn't have the energy—until the day I saw Juan coming up La Fortaleza's stairs with a new pair of toe shoes tucked under his arm, asking to see her.

I was going to take the package from him, but Juan refused to hand it over. "I'm supposed to give them personally to Madame, my duck," he said quietly. I thought it was odd and immediately suspected something. I went to Madame's room and silently mouthed the words behind Dandré's back: "Juan Anduce is asking for you. He has something to deliver personally."

Quick as lightning, Madame went downstairs to meet Juan. When she came back, she was beaming, holding the new shoes tightly against her chest. "Diamantino is finally coming back," she whispered breathlessly, and she made me swear I'd keep the secret.

41

A few days earlier Daniel Dearborn had flown into San Juan from the island of St. Thomas. Danny Dear, as he was known, was the all-American hero of the moment. He had thousands of fans across the nation, and the president conferred on him the Congressional Medal of Honor. When he smiled, he looked like a wholesome American farm boy, and if he frowned he reminded you of a Viking god. Sitting on his frail wicker chair inside the *Silver Hawk*'s cabin, he appeared on the front page of every newspaper in the world.

Dearborn was independently wealthy, and had set himself the task of becoming his country's first Ambassador of the Air. He had devised to fly nonstop from Washington, D.C., to Mexico City in a twenty-seven-hour flight, financing the trip himself. From Mexico he flew to Venezuela and from there set across the Caribbean, hopping from island to island on a fourteen-country pan-American "goodwill tour." That was when he visited Puerto Rico, on his way to Santo Domingo and Cuba.

Unmarried, blond, and blue-eyed, Dearborn chose to fly his monoplane alone, without weaker souls to distract him. He had already crossed the Atlantic in a radarless flight from New-foundland all the way to Paris, which first propelled him to in-ternational fame. During that heroic voyage, nights were dark as a wolf's maw, and he had had only the stars to guide him. He had had to battle sleep, ice needles forming inside the plane's unpressurized cabin, disorienting fog, islands appearing before the cockpit which turned out to be mirages, and even a whole array of ghosts who supposedly sat on the tail of his plane, laughing at him for his audacity. But he expected none of this to occur on his trip to the sunny Caribbean.

I didn't share the public's overwhelming admiration for "the Viking." Dearborn was the son of a Swede; his real last name was Mansson, and his father had changed it to Dearborn when he emigrated to the United States. In my eyes, he was just an-other phlegmatic Scandinavian, the same kind that for centuries had tried to invade Russia from the Baltic. The American gov-ernment, bent on fostering his image as a demigod come to impart the blessings of civilization to the inhabitants of the is-lands, took advantage of Dearborn's altruism and launched a huge publicity campaign. His airplane was like the moon—it pulled a human tidal wave behind it, and mobs would spill over airport fences and into landing fields every time the *Silver Hawk* was about to touch down.

Danny's visit was proof that Americans were able to pilot the destinies of the sleepy-eyed, lazy people of the tropics. "The young colonel's mission," a mainland journal proclaimed, "is to make men of alien races forget their differences in the common admiration of bravery." But I knew what was going on. I wasn't ignorant like the other dancers, who never read a newspaper or leafed through a magazine.

I knew that the Caribbean was besieged by American war-ships. The American president had recently sent the marines to occupy Haiti. In Nicaragua and Honduras, United Fruit was king, and the marines were there to make sure it stayed that way. Mexico had been invaded by U.S. troops fifty years earlier, but the wound of that brazen act was still fresh in people's minds. And now along came Danny, winging his way in like a dove of peace and claiming he wasn't interested in politics, only in the "adventure of flying" and in bringing the modern world to Latin America. Masha, the peasant girl from Minsk, knew better than that. Dearborn's trip was just another example of big white brother setting the example for little brown brother in the South to follow. Or else.

Danny was in very good shape as he approached the island. St. Thomas was only a short hop away, and the flight from Charlotte Amalie to Puerto Rico was a piece of cake. He followed the coast from Fajardo all the way up to San Juan, often swooping down as low as he could and sticking his head out the window to identify the landmarks. San Juan's streets and rooftops were crammed with people waving American flags and scanning the empty horizon when suddenly, out of the blue, a silver sliver began to dance merrily in the sky.

The *Silver Hawk* appeared in all its glory and, under the blazing hot sun, a display of fireworks burst forth. One long, uninterrupted cheer went up and down the length of Ponce de León Avenue, and radio commentators began to yell out the news. Donkey-paced, sleepy Puerto Rico, *el Jibarito*'s territory for more than three centuries of backward Spanish rule, had finally winged into the modern age. Dearborn had joined it to the future of mankind.

Madame and I negotiated our way around the street vendors who were selling all sorts of Dearborn souvenirs. There were models of the *Silver Hawk* crocheted in silver thread by little old ladies; there were Dearborn busts cast in bronze or in silver-plated alloys, done in plaster, or carved in bone and soap; there were Dearborn ashtrays, toothpick holders, and beer mugs; stickpins of his monoplane were sold at every corner (in New York, J. P. Morgan had one with the *Silver Hawk* cut from a single diamond); a company in Massachusetts produced the Lucky Dearborn shoe for women, which featured the silhouette of the *Silver Hawk* sewn in patent leather, with a propeller on the toe and a photograph of Danny inserted in a leather horseshoe sewn on the side, and some had made their way to the island (Juan, who liked fine shoes, was furious when he saw them; he considered them an example of the horrendous taste Americans would impose on Puerto Rico). And for each product Dearborn endorsed, he was paid a generous sum. Madame bought a Dearborn tie and put it in her handbag to give to Dandré as a present.

A few minutes later, Dearborn circled the capitol's dome several times, waving to the cheering crowds below; then he did three Immelmann turns and soared almost straight up and over until he was flying upside down. Finally, he landed at the city's *canódromo*, the dog-racing course, where Governor Yager was waiting for him in his classic white linen suit and immaculate white suede shoes. The official caravan whisked Dearborn away in a black Packard limousine and brought him straight to La Fortaleza, where Danny would spend the night in the bedroom next to Madame's.

The following day, over breakfast, the governor congratulated Dearborn: "Your trip is a monumental step in the development of mankind; we need more peacemaking missions like yours," he said. Then he confided that the island was going through a dangerous period of unrest, and that there were rabble-rousers everywhere. He told Dearborn all about Los Tiznados, and how, after kidnapping the famous Russian ballet star who was staying next door to him—she had turned up in San Juan drugged and with a scarf tied over her eyes a few days earlier—they still remained out of reach in their redoubt in the mountains. "We need your help, Colonel. Your motto, 'Airplanes give the eyes of birds to the minds of men,' could be of great value to us. Would you take a turn or two around the island in the *Silver Hawk* in order to see if you can discern any sign of them? I hear that, from an airplane, one can discover places that are very difficult to reach by land. The truth is, we have no idea of Los Tiznados' whereabouts."

Dearborn didn't think he could be of help, but he asked for a map of the island to humor the governor. He would gladly fly over the hilly forests a few times—the island was very small, after all—only thirty-five miles wide by one hundred miles long and shaped like a crumpled lozenge—to see if he could discover some clue to the desperadoes' whereabouts. While he was at it, however, he wondered if the governor wouldn't mind telling him if there were any Indian ruins around, because he was an amateur archeologist and there was nothing in the world he loved to do more than discover archeological sites from the air. He had done it in Mexico, where he had taken the first air photographs of Chichén Itzá, the famous Mayan metropolis, and he had then proceeded to discover half a dozen Mayan cities in Quintana Roo.

Governor Yager agreed to his request, gave him a map, and pointed out the general area of the ancient Taino baseball park of Otoao, which had never been reconnoitered from the air. The following day, Dearborn flew southwest toward the jagged peaks that rose like a spine the length of the island. After twenty minutes of scanning and swinging in and out of the clouds, he saw a large, rectangular clearing with rows of huge stones standing on edge. He swooped down to get a better look and suddenly found himself being fired at by what looked like a band of scraggly, bearded men with straw hats on their heads. Their camp was practically an arsenal, and there were rifles and ammo boxes everywhere. No doubt they were Los Tiznados.

Dearborn turned his plane around and twenty minutes later he was back in San Juan, landing at the dog-racing course. In less than an hour he had traveled to and from Otoao, a distance which usually took a week to reach, scaling steep gorges and mountain paths, and a week to return. As soon as Governor Yager was informed of the location of the Indian site, a police detachment was sent to the spot and most of Los Tiznados were wiped out or captured. The news was published in all the papers. Bienvenido and Diamantino, who barely managed to escape, read about it at El Carite, a *cafetín* near Arecibo where they had taken refuge. They swore they would make Colonel Dearborn pay.

42 That afternoon I was ironing Madame's clothes when I heard a knock at the door. It was Estrella Aljama and Diana Yager, who had come to visit Madame. They were dressed in muslin, one in pink and the other one in white. They came in laughing and embraced Madame affectionately. They were surprised to find Dandré in the room and immediately stopped chattering, but I introduced him and told them who he was and that he had just arrived from the States. Dandré bowed graciously and left the room after paying his compliments. The girls went on jabbering excitedly. They told Madame all about Dearborn's arrival; he was as good-looking as it was rumored, six feet tall, lithe, with a golden cowlick on his forehead. To top it off he was a bachelor, the dream man of every single young woman on the island. Madame definitely had to meet him.

The girls wanted Madame to hear the plans for the Ponce de León Carnival, which was to be held the following night. Preparations for the celebrations were almost ready. The ball was to be named the Democracy Ball, and everyone was to attend masked. Ronda's ladies-in-waiting would be Diana and

Estrella, dressed respectively as Fraternity and Equality. In fact, a marvelous idea had occurred to them: since Ronda Batistini, the carnival queen, still hadn't been able to find a king, if Dearborn could be persuaded to stay on the island one extra night and postpone his flight to Santo Domingo, he could take the king's place and it would make the event an even greater social success. Ronda had suggested it to her father, who told Governor Yager. The governor thought the idea brilliant—he had just read Don Pedro's letter, which he had finally stumbled on under a pile of backlogged correspondence—and immediately sent a message to the committee in charge of organizing the festivities. They wouldn't have to pick a king for the Democracy Ball after all, he said. He promised to take Dearborn to them in person, and the famous aviator would escort the queen to her throne that evening.

The ball would be held at Teatro Tapia, and they were charging ten dollars per person; the money was going to the war-relief fund overseas. Many people would go just to see Dearborn and they could raise quite a bit of money that way. "We'd love it if you also took part in the celebrations, Madame," they begged. "We thought you could dance *The Dying Swan* one last time before you left the island." I looked away from Madame, not wanting to influence her one way or the other. I thought the whole thing was ridiculous, but Dandré, who had come back into the room, was very accommodating. "Of course she will, my dears," he said, humoring them and plucking at his mustache. "It'll be a good opportunity for Niura to get back to her dancing." "All right, I'll dance," Madame agreed softly. "But not *The Dying Swan*."

"The word 'carnival' comes from the Latin *carne vale*, which literally means 'good-bye to the flesh.' Before doing penance for the death of Christ one can kick up one's heels for the last time," Juan explained, pinching my ass and trying to grab one of my breasts. I skipped away, laughing, just in time. Although I had promised to marry him, I didn't see any use in hurrying. *Matrimonio y mortaja del cielo baja*—wedding and winding sheet both fall from heaven, as the popular Spanish saying goes. I still didn't know if Madame would let Juan travel with us abroad, as a member of the troupe, as I hoped.

Meanwhile, all we could do was wait. I knew Dandré had everything ready for our departure, our new passports checked by the police commissioner and our expenses at the Hotel Malatrassi taken care of with money he had taken out of the company's account in New York. But there were no ships sailing for Panama in the next few weeks, and we would have to wait in San Juan for the arrival of one large enough to accommodate us all. I didn't mind the waiting, I was well entertained. After Madame went to bed, I discreetly went out of La Fortaleza through a secret door in the wall that faced the sea and sat with Juan at the water's edge, kissing and caressing till all hours of the night.

Since Spanish times, the carnival had been the most important social event of the year on the island. People saw it as a way to forget their painful day-to-day existence. Poverty, hunger, and sickness were all too common on the island then, Juan said. Epidemics were frequent: typhus, tuberculosis, even the bubonic plague ravaged Puerto Rico from time to time because of ship's rats. Thousands died—poor and rich alike. The carnival was a way to exorcise all that. It took place just before Lent, but it was very much a pagan celebration, during which people burned the candle at both ends.

"All of society attends it," Juan went on. "There's dancing in the casino, at the wharves before the customhouse, and in the narrow cobblestone streets, as several orchestras play simultaneously in different locations. Horse races are also an important part of the celebrations, as men and women here are very good riders, and they gallop wildly across the city in every direction, competing in speed and dexterity into the wee hours. Lit up at every corner, with bonfires of perfumed cedar and sandalwood blazing well into the night, our city resembles a magical coral reef, spilling fireworks from every rooftop and church belfry. It's a marvelous spectacle, Masha! I swear, I'll make it worth your while!"

Juan's eyes shone like embers and his breath made my skin tingle with excitement. I knew he wanted me to stay on the island, but nothing could have made me give up Madame.

Governor Yager was well-intentioned, but, being an American and a Presbyterian, he didn't have the faintest idea of what the Juan Ponce de León Carnival was all about. In the era of Spanish rule the king was paid homage during the celebrations, and then El Rey Momo took the king's place. Momo was dressed like a grotesque *monigote*—a giant puppet in flowing, brightly colored satin robes. He was the king of partying, the monarch of drink and good food. He was also the butt of all the dirty jokes and pranks the population could devise. When the carnival began, El Rey Momo was taken for a ride around the city and everyone would pelt him with garbage, jeer at him good-naturedly, or throw cow bladders full of water at his head. It was a harmless way to exorcise frustrations.

On his way to the carnival ball, however, Momo paraded down the streets on a white stallion decorated with golden ribbons and bows, throwing silver coins to the crowd while everyone cried "*Qué viva el rey!*" "Long live the king!" Once at the Tapia, Momo would stand next to the queen as she was crowned. Thanks to Momo, political authority—be it Spanish or American—could be safely ridiculed, and no one had to worry about having his head chopped off.

Governor Yager was completely unaware of this custom when he agreed to take Dearborn to the Tapia Theater and have him occupy the king's place as Ronda Batistini was crowned queen. It never occurred to him to ask the young man if he liked the idea. Dearborn was twenty-five, and all young chaps his age loved balls and pretty girls.

By nine o'clock the following evening, Madame and I were putting on our costumes and our black silk masks. Madame had decided to dance the *Bacchanale*; I suppose she chose it for sentimental reasons—it was the piece she had danced with Diamantino in Arecibo. She had had enough of frothy tutus and swan feathers, she said. Glazunov's *Bacchanale* was about the liberation of the body. It was the only ballet she wanted to dance that night at the carnival.

Madame would perform the role of Ariadne, Novikov would perform that of Dionysus, and the girls and I would dance the maenads, as usual. We were getting ready to go out when we heard two men arguing loudly in English. Surprised, we stopped in our tracks to listen: it was Governor Yager and Dearborn in the room next to Madame's.

I had seen the governor, wearing his tuxedo, enter Dearborn's room a few moments earlier. Apparently Governor Yager had just conveyed Diana's request to Dearborn, and was totally unprepared for the pilot's irate reaction. "Impossible! I couldn't exhibit myself in public that embarrassing way. Carnival king? That's absurd!" Dearborn exclaimed. Governor Yager's voice was lower, but we could still hear him. "You must do it, my friend. I've already said you would," he said anxiously. "If you don't, you'll cause a diplomatic incident, and the people will never forgive you. You have no idea how important the carnival is for them. An insult such as this would be terrible for the image of the United States." Their voices carried clearly because of the echo produced by the vaulted ceilings in the ancient building.

Madame was darning her toe shoes while I put the last touches to the red chiffon skirt she would wear that evening when she danced the role of Ariadne, and we stared at each other in wonder. The silence that ensued let us guess that Dearborn had agreed to go, although unwillingly. From the way he slammed the door behind him when he went out, we could tell that the young colonel was scalding mad.

I finished clasping Madame's diamond necklace around her neck—she had insisted on putting it on, as well as her diamond earrings and bracelets, for that night's performance. Dandré had already left for the theater with Molinari, who came to pick him up, and there was nothing I could do to prevent her from wearing the jewels. We ran down the stairs to the first floor, where one of the governor's official chauffeurs was to take us to the ball.

Within a block of Teatro Tapia, we had to get out of the car because of the crush of people milling around at the door. We could see the governor's black limousine parked in front of the entrance; a cordon of policemen and secret service agents were holding the mob back. We half pushed, half squirmed our way over between the merrymakers, and finally stood just behind a police agent. The queen, wearing Liberty's Greek robe and golden sandals instead of shoes, had just gotten down from her blossom-decked float. She stood in front of the main entrance, a bronzed papier-mâché torch in her hand and her gold-lamé cloak spread behind her, and she was in tears. Don Pedro and Doña Basilisa tried to calm her. We could hear the Tapia's orchestra already playing Verdi's Triumphal March from *Aïda*, to which the queen traditionally made her entrance. Dearborn, dressed in his formal colonel's uniform, with golden braid shining on his shoulders and his cap tucked under his arm, stood next to the governor, explaining why he couldn't possibly escort her inside the theater.

"I've come this far to congratulate you on your having been elected queen, mademoiselle, but I can't go any further. Please accept my regrets," he said, bending politely at the waist. He took the queen's hand and was about to kiss it when there was a mad rush: one of the cavalcades hastened down the street, led by masked revelers dressed in satin robes with large three-cornered hats on their heads, and they pushed us from behind. Dearborn, the governor, the queen, and all those standing near the entrance, including Madame and myself, were propelled by the mob into the Tapia.

All the chairs of the theater had been removed, the floor had been cranked up, and a giant ballroom had been made of the stage and orchestra. As we half walked, half slid into the ballroom, borne by the tide of the crowd, I could see Dearborn's blond hair bobbing over the sea of heads in front of us. He had finally taken the queen's arm, apparently resigned to perform the duty that had been imposed on him. Don Pedro, as the queen's father, took her other arm, and a few seconds later they were mounting the stairs to the throne together. Verdi's march filled the air with martial grandiosity as the French horns and trumpets swept the ballroom. Ronda Batistini raised her head and smiled at the deliriously applauding audience; I wondered if Bienvenido wasn't in the crowd and she had recognized him. In fact, she looked very much like the Statue of Liberty as she stood on her throne, a faux-marble platform supported by Greek columns. Dearborn reluctantly took his place beside her on the stage, and Don Pedro walked proudly down the steps to rejoin Doña Basilisa in the ballroom.

People seemed both elated and vexed to see the famous pilot take the place of their beloved Rey Momo: half of them cheered, the other half booed and began to throw paper cups and napkins at him. Dearborn was Dearborn and they admired him enormously, but he was also a usurper. He had no right to be there. His presence threw a wet blanket on the whole purpose of the carnival, which was to make fun of authority. The orchestra began to play a waltz, but people didn't want to dance; instead they pounded the floor in anger. I looked around nervously for Madame and saw with relief that she was standing close by, though her hand gripped her throat in anxiety. I put my hand on her shoulder to reassure her and advised her to stay near me. I could tell there was going to be trouble.

"Have you seen Dandré?" Madame asked, looking around in a daze. I had to laugh! I knew it was Diamantino she was really looking for. She was on pins and needles because she had no idea of El Delfín's whereabouts, or whether he would try to reach her.

Novikov and the girls were already positioned at the foot of the raised dais, ready to start the *Bacchanale* as soon as the preliminary ceremonies were over. Out of the corner of my eye I saw Dandré standing guard near the ballroom's side exit, where he had taken his lookout post after I warned him that Diamantino Márquez was coming back. The Tapia's president walked over to the stage to introduce the governor and Colonel Dearborn, his honored guest. Then he announced the first act of the program: the debutantes would dance the pavane. A dozen young girls dressed in glittering white gowns began to float like magnolias over the dance floor, sinking in graceful reverence before the queen and then gliding on. They danced for several minutes, fluttering their fans to the rhythm of the music. Then several politicians, bankers, writers, and other well-known public figures got up and read the pompous verses they had composed in praise of Her Majesty. Finally, Estrella Aljama and Diana Yager ascended the stairs carrying Liberty's golden crown on a silk cushion and pinned it to Ronda's hair. When the ceremony ended, the orchestra finally started to play Glazunov's score, and the overture of the *Bacchanale* began.

But we never got to dance it.

What happened next was a shock to everyone. Suddenly I heard a murmur to my left, and the crowd parted to let a masked group disguised as *jíbaros* file through. They wore black pants and white shirts with red kerchiefs around the neck, and the women were dressed in long flowered skirts with flounced petticoats underneath. They had come into the Tapia thanks to Doña Victoria, who said they were her guests at the door. She was right there leading them, in spite of her deafness. She had on a *rumbera*'s muumuu which was so large, it made her look like a swaying tepee. The men's faces were blackened with burnt cork and they carried short machetes tucked in at the waist. Under their leader's direction, they began hauling in several cases of liquor and two large drums, which they set down on the floor next to Madame. Then they passed around jiggers of rum to everyone on the dance floor. Liquor was still strictly forbidden, but the crowd immediately began to drink.

Then someone blew a whistle and a stream of blue uniforms poured into the ballroom. Law-enforcement troops were never far away at carnival time because of the frequent brawls, and now they encircled the revelers. I immediately guessed who they were after, but the *jíbaros* rapidly mixed with the crowd and soon it was impossible to identify them. Everyone on the dance floor was in costume, and the *jíbaro* dress was par-

ticularly well liked by the social set, while the middle class preferred to dress up as kings and queens. The band of *jíbaros* with
blackened faces and machetes at the waist was just another *comparsa* of partygoers. They began jumping, whirling, and noisily
scattering a storm of confetti and serpentine over the heads of
the merrymakers.

Madame and I watched from the sidelines when one of the
jíbaros approached the orchestra and ordered it to stop playing.
The brawniest of the group, a hatless man with a shock of red
hair, walked up to the dais, picked up one of the drums, straddled it, and began to play. Suddenly, as if energized by the beat,
Madame walked determinedly toward the center of the dance
floor, and the girls followed her. I looked on in bewilder-
ment—this definitely wasn't on the program. The drumbeats—
hand to hand and skin to skin—penetrated to the bone, and we
swayed to the rhythm as if in a trance. The women lifted their
skirts and petticoats to the waist, fanning themselves with them,
as if directing the fumes of their genitals toward the crowd.
Madame, in her red chiffon skirt and golden bra, stepped into
the middle of the dance floor. She transformed herself into a
flame, writhing and burning before us.

I couldn't say for sure when the drums ceased and the
mutiny began, but suddenly the whole ballroom broke into
chaos. The revelers were divided between those who were anxious to see Dearborn up close and wanted him to be carnival
king and those who were furious because the tradition of El
Rey Momo had been violated and wanted the colonel to step
down from the throne. Dearborn, dressed in his white gala uniform, stood next to the queen, and everybody had to curtsy.
This couldn't be tolerated.

More police marched in, but people began to laugh and
taunt them, knowing that they couldn't fire on the crowd. The

dancers fought each other for the jiggers of rum; women bashed their neighbors over the head with their handbags. Others blew their toy horns and threw handfuls of confetti and colored streamers into each other's faces. Many found themselves robbed of their jewelry by the fierce, unruly, machete-wielding *jíbaros*. A second police battalion came in, brandishing heavy sticks, and it formed a circle around Colonel Dearborn. They urged him to come down from the stage and began to escort him cautiously toward the door.

Then several shots were fired, and I saw Don Pedro running up the stairs of the throne, trying to pull Ronda away to safety. Ronda wrenched free of him and fled to where the *jíbaros* were beating the drums. Don Pedro followed her and, recognizing Bienvenido by his red hair, immediately ordered the security agents to surround the young man. Don Pedro carried a gun and aimed it at Bienvenido, but Ronda got in front of him and shielded her half brother. "Go ahead, shoot!" she cried. "I'm not afraid of death." Don Pedro paled and lowered his gun. Bienvenido managed to escape in the turmoil, and a few minutes later I saw him run out the door. A group of horsemen was waiting for him there, and they galloped away down San Juan's narrow streets.

Madame stopped dancing, and one of the masked *jíbaros* took advantage of the confusion to propel her toward the exit. He caught her by the wrists and held her fast, using her as a shield to push his way through the crowd. The diamonds around her neck shimmered as the spotlights hit her, and she held her head up defiantly. Dandré tried to make his way toward them, but unfortunately, he was too far away; it was Diamantino who stepped in and blocked the man's way. "Let her go, Molinari!" he cried. "This is as far as you'll get." Molinari aimed his gun at Diamantino and ordered him to move to one side, but, surprisingly, the young man stood his ground. At that moment, Dandré approached them from behind, spun Molinari around, lifted his bear paw Russian-style, and slapped the gun away from him as if it were a toy. Then he punched Molinari in the jaw. Madame was just turning toward Diamantino when a shot rang out and the young man crumpled to the floor. Madame let out a wrenching howl as she bent over him, trying to revive him, but it was no use. Her cry tore the air.

"This is your fault, Masha," she wailed. "You told them Diamantino was coming!"

I tried to reach out to her with my hand to calm her, but she pushed me away violently. "Don't you dare come near me," she shrieked. "Ever again!" And she fell sobbing into Dandré's arms.

The following week was a nightmare. This time there was no way to keep the press from scattering shit to the winds. The news of the carnival's debacle was spread all over the front page. There were photographs of the governor hiding behind his aides-de-camp, trying to get away from flying chairs; of Queen Liberty running down the stairs, dragged by Don Pedro, her crown askew, brandishing her torch to keep Los Tiznados away; of Madame in provocative poses which made her look more like a vulgar Folies Bergère *vedette* than an imperial ballerina from the Maryinsky, which made me horribly ashamed.

After Diamantino's death, Los Tiznados disappeared, mingling with the crowd. The police rounded everybody up and we ended up in the commissioner's office, where we were interrogated. We all spent the night in jail with the exception of Madame, who was picked up by the governor himself as soon as we arrived and taken to La Fortaleza in his limousine. The next day Madame appeared at the police station. She was dressed all in black and she looked terrible. She had wiped away all her makeup, and it was as if she had erased her face and grief had been left in its place. She smiled at us behind a mask of ice and handed the commissioner a note from the governor, ordering him to release Dandré. When he was brought out, she led him out by the arm as if he were an old man.

A week later the dancers boarded the S.S. *Courbelo*, bound for Panama. The whole company sailed with Madame and Dandré—without me. I stayed behind on the island. I knew what it was like to be like a feather in the wind, or, as Madame once put it, "like flotsam at the mercy of the waves." I decided to put down roots here. And yet I must admit that wasn't the only reason. I stayed because Madame ordered me to. I was obeying her for the last time.

Dancing has to do with feet, of course, with the way you move in the world. Perhaps that's why I fell in love with Juan. Although "fell in love" is perhaps not the most accurate description. "Blazed in love" would be more precise. We always kept a cheerful bonfire going between us.

Our relationship had one immediate effect, however. The minute Juan touched me, I became pregnant. Fortunately, we both loved children, and we ended up with six of them—the joy of our life.

Juan spent many years making shoes, giving people a solid foundation on which to stand, so they could make their own way. He was a wonderful man. He insisted that life, like the pounding of the heart, was never predetermined. "It's the beat that makes the blood flow through the body," he used to say, "not the other way around. Freedom has to do with the way you dare to live your life." That's why, when I think of Juan, I can't be sad.

Before Madame's troupe left the island, Juan asked Dandré and me to meet him in Old San Juan, and we sat forlornly at La

Bombonera in one of the red plastic booths at the back. We all ordered coffee and *mallorcas*, and while we dipped the perfumed buns in our cups, we replayed the events of Diamantino's passing. Neither the murder weapon nor the assassin of the young man was ever found; they were swallowed up by the mob that night. But in the days that followed, Diamantino was hailed as a hero. It was pointed out in the press that he had rallied the Home Guard around him and had saved the carnival queen's life, as well as Daniel Dearborn's. His picture was in all the papers and everyone remembered that he was Don Eduardo Márquez's son, the heir without a kingdom, El Delfín without a crown. Molinari was accused of attempted kidnapping. In the preliminary hearing held just before they left, Madame and Dandré both testified against him, and managed to convince the judge that Molinari was a member of the Mafia through his connection with Bracale. The impresario had once been convicted in New York for racketeering, and Dandré presented enough evidence to help land him in jail.

Several months later it was revealed in court that Bracale was losing money on Madame's tour, and that he had had her followed by Molinari—whom Juan and I had mistakenly taken for a police agent. Bracale felt, therefore, he had a right to the jewels, and if Madame refused to hand them over, he would simply take them by force. But then the governor had invited Madame and me to stay at La Fortaleza while Dandré was away in New York, and the jewels were out of his reach. Molinari had to do something to lure her away. He used Diamantino as bait, and he was very successful. The young man was at the end of his tether; everyone knew he was a revolutionary and that he couldn't find a decent job. Molinari offered him a payoff and sent him to the Tapia Theater to play his violin for Madame. Then the unexpected happened. When the group left for Arecibo, Lyubovna had stayed behind at La Fortaleza, and kept with her Madame's coveted alligator case. But Molinari didn't know this until the night Juan and I caught him snooping around in Madame's room at Dos Ríos.

Molinari's efforts to kidnap Madame at the carnival—this time wearing her jewels—was his last chance, and Bracale sent Los Tiznados—a band of hoodlums disguised as revolutionaries—after him to make sure he did the job. Before Madame sailed she left a written statement as evidence of what she had gone through, and I read it out loud for her during the trial. Juan had informed her of everything except Diamantino's last-minute refusal to cooperate with Los Tiznados.

Juan thought it better not to tell Madame the truth about him. She believed Diamantino had died a hero's death, persecuted by the police for being a revolutionary, and it was better to leave things the way they were. At Juan's urging, Dandré and I withheld the story—to protect Madame.

Once the madness of the carnival was over, San Juan's bonfires were put out and its many churches were shrouded in purple. Madame returned to her previous dependence on Dandré, as I had known she would. The embers of their affection were still alive under the mantle of ashes, and they patched things up as much as possible.

There had been, however, one more tragic event on the night of the ball. Ronda Batistini, upon hearing that Bienvenido had fled from the Tapia with the police in hot pursuit, had run to the back of the theater and got on Rayo, the *paso fino* that was waiting for her there because she planned to ride him in the carnival after the ball. She was still wearing her billowing Statue of Liberty robe and golden crown when, during her maddening race down the streets of San Juan searching for

Bienvenido, she lost control of the steed on Calle Cristo. Both horse and rider plunged headlong over the ancient city walls and landed on the rocks below. The next day the news broke on the front pages of all the local newspapers: "Queen Liberty Falls Headlong into Abyss." Madame was deeply saddened by the news and went to the scene of the accident with Doña Basilisa, who was devastated, to light a candle to the Virgin of Vladimir and pray for Ronda's soul.

Not long after these events Governor Yager was ordered to return to the States because of the loss of prestige his administration had suffered. The United States had to reverse its fundraising policy on the island and could no longer force people to donate the shirts off their backs to buy Liberty Bonds; nor could the Americans go on making the natives grow food for the troops in their own backyards when the people themselves were perishing from hunger. Years later, thanks to President Roosevelt, the Puerto Rican Recovery Act was passed in Washington, and economic aid finally began to flow to the island.

The day Madame left, Juan went to say good-bye to her at the wharf. They stood on the deck of the S.S. *Courbelo*, taking in the windy blue of San Juan Bay, which sparkled in sharp-edged waves around them. Dandré went around giving orders right and left, carrying a barking Poppy in his arms, and Smallens held the cage with the nightingales. Everybody was sad: Lyubovna because she was leaving her friends at the convent, Novikov because he was saying good-bye to the trapeze artist, Nadja because she wouldn't find any more wonderful old musical scores in San Juan. There were reporters everywhere taking "flashlight" photos.

Juan finally approached Madame. "I know you're suffering

because of Diamantino's tragic accident," Juan whispered softly when the reporters had left and they were finally by themselves. "Is there anything I can do to ease your sadness?"

Madame's eyes glistened suspiciously, but she didn't answer. She just stood there gazing at the walled city she would never see again. She never once asked about me, and Juan had to keep the apology I had entrusted him with to himself. Embarrassed, Juan looked away and was about to head down the gangway to the dock when he mustered up his courage, turned around, and said: "We know how much you loved him, Madame. And he was very young. Maybe donating something to the island would make you feel better—Diamantino would have liked that." Although Madame promised she would, Juan doubted his words would accomplish anything. Now she was under Dandré's thumb again and would have to beg and wheedle for every penny she spent.

At the last minute Madame asked Juan to wait. She went down to her berth and, a moment later, brought up a pair of worn-out toe shoes which she gave to him. She wanted them to be a memento of her visit to the island, she said. Juan couldn't help feeling disappointed. He had expected some donation to charity, no matter how modest. Instead, Madame presented him with the toe shoes, and he couldn't return them to her without seeming impolite.

Juan kept the shoes for months, and after we got married we hung them from a bedpost in our bedroom. To Juan, they were worthless, but, as they were a relic of Madame, I refused to throw them out.

Then one day I decided to try them on. I sat on the floor, tied the silk ribbons around my ankles, and stood up.

"There's something inside them!" I cried, clumsily losing my balance and stumbling to the floor. Juan ran in and helped me untie the slippers. He took them from me and examined them closely. The darning on the toes, which Madame had done herself, camouflaged a slit at each end. He cut them open with his shoemaker's *chaveta*, and out tumbled Madame's diamonds.

Today, Madame's memory is revered on the island. With her money, several gymnasiums were built for schoolchildren, as well as ballet academies; our Russian Dance Academy is one of them. Most important, she gave many young women the opportunity to become professionals, so they could fly on their own.

44

I thought I'd never see Madame again, but I was wrong. One day, a few years after she sailed on to South America, I traveled to New York with my husband. We had to go there periodically to replenish our academy with materials for the students' yearly productions, and this time I had decided to accompany him. Following the tradition of the Imperial Ballet School, we were staging *La Sylphide* on the first of June as a graduation ballet. We needed yards and yards of white tulle for the nymphs' costumes and two dozen diamanté wings delicately wired so they would tremble at the slightest movement. I knew Madame was in New York; I had seen her picture in *The New York Times*, standing at the top of the marble stairs in the lobby at the Waldorf-Astoria, looking as gaunt as a heron and holding on to Mr. Dandré's arm. She was back from her tour of Argentina, where she had danced for the president of the republic at Teatro Colón; the company had made thousands of dollars, just as Dandré had envisioned. Madame had managed to postpone her return to Europe once again, and had decided to start out on a third tour of the United States. From New Orleans to San Francisco, she would dance in the grandest theaters for fabulous sums of money. Dandré would push her bourreés just a little farther, make her soar in the air just a little higher when she did her grands jetés, until she folded her wings for good many years later in Amsterdam.

When I arrived in New York, I heard Madame was going to dance *The Dying Swan* at the Metropolitan Opera House, and I went alone to the matinee performance.

Her dance hadn't lost any of its magic. The feather-light jumps, the inflection of the delicate wrists, the tremulous lifting of the arms had all remained the same. At the end of the performance I was so moved, I couldn't go backstage as I had planned.

Juan and I were spending the week at a friend's apartment on the West Side. The next day, while my husband took a taxi down to Sixth Avenue to shop for some special material he couldn't find close to where we were staying—luminescent paint and a generous amount of silk tulle for *La Sylphide's* costumes—I went for a walk in Central Park. It was a brisk fall morning and I wanted to take my mind off melancholy recollections. I was walking toward the duck pond just north of the Plaza, on Central Park South, when I saw a forlorn figure sitting alone on a bench. She had her back to me and I couldn't see her face, but the way she tilted her head sideways on her long, slender neck and pulled her shawl more closely about her reminded me of Madame. I walked over gingerly, hardly daring to breathe, and sat down unobtrusively at the other end of the bench. She gazed at the pond in front of her and didn't turn around to look at me, so for a few moments I could examine her at leisure. It was Madame.

She must have felt my eyes, because she slowly turned her head, a look of wonder on her face. "Is that you, Masha?" she said softly, her lips drawn in an incredulous smile.

I was pregnant with my second child and had grown matronly, so her hesitation wasn't surprising. "Yes, Madame, it's me," I whispered as I lowered my head. I must have paled, because Madame rose and came to sit beside me. "Are you all right, my dear?" she asked. I couldn't bear it, and I burst into tears.

Madame took my hand in hers and patted it; then she brought out a handkerchief from her handbag and handed it to me. "Why cry, Masha, darling? You have a baby and I have my art. What a wonderful thing is love! The world is irreversibly transformed by it."

I was going to tell her how much I'd missed her, how sorry I was for what I'd done. That now I understood perfectly why she'd been willing to go with Diamantino to the ends of the earth, because I, too, had fallen in love, with Juan. But I would have been lying. I had never loved anyone as Madame had loved Diamantino. Except her; I had loved *her* much more. But before I could say another word, Madame rose and walked away.